ZOO

JAMES PATTERSON is one of the best-known and biggest-selling writers of all time. He is the author of some of the most popular series of the past decade – the Alex Cross, Women's Murder Club and Detective Michael Bennett novels – and he has written many other number one bestsellers including romance novels and stand-alone thrillers. He lives in Florida with his wife and son.

James is passionate about encouraging children to read. Inspired by his own son who was a reluctant reader, he also writes a range of books specifically for young readers. James is very supportive of the National Literacy Trust, an independent, UK-based charity that changes lives through literacy. In 2010, he was voted Author of the Year at the Children's Choice Book Awards in New York.

Also by James Patterson

STAND-ALONE THRILLERS

A list of more titles by James Patterson is printed at
the back of this book

JAMES PATTERSON
& MICHAEL LEDWIDGE
ZOO

arrow books

Published by Arrow Books in 2013

5 7 9 10 8 6 4

Copyright © James Patterson, 2012

James Patterson has asserted his right under the Copyright, Designs and Patents Act, 1988 to be identified as the author of this work

This novel is a work of fiction. Names and characters are the product of the author's imagination and any resemblance to actual persons, living or dead, is entirely coincidental

First published in Great Britain in 2012 by Century

Arrow Books
Random House, 20 Vauxhall Bridge Road,
London SW1V 2SA

www.randomhouse.co.uk

Addresses for companies within The Random House Group Limited can be found at:
www.randomhouse.co.uk/offices.htm

The Random House Group Limited Reg. No. 954009

A CIP catalogue record for this book
is available from the British Library

Typeset in Berkeley (12/16 pt) by SX Composing DTP, Rayleigh, Essex, SS6 7XF

Penguin Random House is committed to a sustainable future for our business, our readers and our planet. This book is made from Forest Stewardship Council® certified paper.

MIX
Paper from
responsible sources
FSC® C018179

Printed and bound in Great Britain by Clays Ltd, St Ives plc

To the Archackis—M.L.

PROLOGUE

IT'S ALL HAPPENING AT THE ZOO

One

LOCATED IN GRIFFITH Park, a four-thousand-acre stretch of land featuring two eighteen-hole golf courses, the Autry National Center, and the HOLLYWOOD sign, the Los Angeles Zoo and Botanical Gardens is more of a run-down tourist attraction than a wildlife conservation facility.

Funded by fickle city budgets, the zoo resembles nothing more than a tired state fair. Garbage cans along its bleached concrete promenade spill over. It is not uncommon to catch the stench of heaped dung wafting from cages where ragged animals lie blank-eyed, fly-speckled, and motionless beneath the relentless California sun.

To the northeast of the entrance gate, the lion enclosure is ringed by a slime-coated concrete moat. Once—if you squinted, hard—it might have resembled a small scrap of the Serengeti. But these days, undermaintained, underfunded, and understaffed, it looks only like what it is: a concrete pen filled with packed dirt and bracketed by fake grass and plastic trees.

By 8:05 in the morning it is already hot in the seemingly empty enclosure. The only sound is a slight rustling as something dark and snakelike sways slowly back and forth through a tuft of the tall fake grass. The sound and motion stop. Then, fifty feet to the south, something big streaks out from behind a plywood boulder.

Head steady, pale yellow eyes gleaming, Mosa, the Los Angeles Zoo's female lion, crosses the enclosure toward the movement in the grass with breathtaking speed. But instead of leaping into the grass, at the last fraction of a moment she flies into a tumble. Dust rises as she barrel-rolls around on her back and then up onto her paws.

Lying deep in the grass is Dominick, Mosa's mate and the dominant male of the zoo's two Transvaal lions, from southeast Africa. Older than Mosa, he shakes his regal reddish mane and gives her a cold stare. As has been the case more and more over the last few weeks, he is tense, watchful, in no mood for games. He blinks once, briefly, and goes back to flicking his tail through the high blades of grass.

Mosa glances at him, then toward the rear fence, at the big rubber exercise ball she was recently given by one of the keepers. Finally, ignoring the ball, she slowly leans forward to nuzzle Dominick's mane, giving him an apologetic, deferential social lick as she passes.

Mosa cleans the dusty pads of her huge paws as the large cats lie together under the blaring-blue California sky. If there is an indication this morning of something being amiss, it is not in what the lions are doing, but in what they aren't.

For lions as for other social mammals, vocalizations play a major role in communication. Lions make sounds to engage in sexual competition, to compete in territorial disputes, and to coordinate defense against predators.

Mosa and Dominick have become less and less vocal over the past two weeks. Now they are all but silent.

Both lions smell the keeper well before they hear him jingle the chain-link fence a hundred and fifty feet to their rear. As the human scent strikes their nostrils, the lions react in a way they never have before. They both stand. Their tails stiffen. Their ears cock forward as their fur bristles noticeably along their backs.

Like wolves, lions hunt and ambush in coordinated groups. The behavior the two display now shows their readiness for taking down prey.

Dominick moves out of the grass and into the clearing. Even for a male lion, he's enormous—five hundred pounds, nearly nine feet long, and four and a half feet tall at the shoulder. The king of the jungle sniffs at the air and, catching the human scent again, moves toward it.

Two

TERRENCE LARSON, THE assistant big-cat zoo-keeper, opens the outer chain-link door of the lion enclosure, swings its hook into a waiting eye to keep it open, and drags the red plastic feed bucket inside. The sinewy, middle-aged city worker swats at flies as he lugs in the lions' breakfast, twenty-five pounds of shank bones and bloody cubes of beef.

A dozen steps in, at the end of the chest-high wire mesh keeper fence, Larson, a former studio lighting tech at Paramount, dumps the meat over the fence and retreats a few steps. The meat plops onto the dirt in a tumble of wet slaps. Beside the open outer fence, he flips the bucket over and sits on it. He knows he's supposed to stand behind the tightly locked outer fence to watch the lions feed, but it's July Fourth weekend and all the bosses are on vacation, so what's the fuss?

Sitting in the enclosure with the lions in the morning before the zoo opens is the best part of Larson's day. Tommy Rector, the young head of the big-cat department, likes the smaller, sprier, more affectionate cats, the jaguars and lynx, but Larson, ever since a life-altering trip to a Ringling Brothers circus at the age of seven, is a passionate lion man. There's a reason this animal is a symbol of might, danger, and mystery, he thinks; a reason that all the famous strongmen—Samson, Hercules—had to wrestle these guys. Their power, their physical grace, and their otherworldly beauty still amaze him, even after fifteen years of working around them. Just as he did when he was working on films, Larson often tells friends he can't believe he's actually getting paid to do his job.

He takes a pack of Parliaments from the breast pocket of his regulation khaki shirt, and as he slips one between his lips and lights it, the Motorola radio clipped to the pocket of his cargo shorts gives off a sharp distress-call beep. He reaches for it, trying to guess what the problem could be, when the reedy voice of Al Ronkowski from maintenance comes squawking through the static; he's bitching about how someone's parked in his spot.

Larson half laughs, half snorts, turns down the radio's volume, and exhales smoke through his nose in twin gray streams as he scans the grass at the other end of the hundred-by-two-hundred-foot enclosure. He wonders where in the hell the two lions could be. Mosa is usually waiting for him when he opens the gate, like a house cat who comes running at the sound of an electric can opener.

When he hears the splash, Larson flings away the cigarette and stands up. Panic.

What? *No! The moat?*

There is a raised berm and a protective platform to prevent the lions from falling into the water, but it actually didn't stop one of them from falling in once before. It took the staff two hours to direct a terrified, soaked Mosa back to dry land.

That's all he needs, with the bosses gone and the crew at half-staff. Play lifeguard to four hundred pounds of pissed-off, sopping-wet lion.

Going into a cage without backup: definitely a no-no policywise, but in the reality of a workday it's done all the time. Quickly, he throws open the keeper's gate and runs to the edge of the raised berm above the water.

He lets out a breath of relief when he spots one

of the green Swedish exercise balls bobbing in the moat. He forgot about the stupid things. That's all it is. Mosa somehow knocked the ball over the platform. Whatever. Whew.

Turning back around from the edge of the berm, Larson stops. He stands by the edge of the moat, blinking. Directly between him and the open gate in the keeper fence is Dominick, the male lion: still, tail swishing methodically, golden amber eyes riveted to Larson's face. His breakfast lies untouched beside him. He sits there, huge, silent, staring at Larson with those flat, flame-colored eyes.

Larson feels his saliva dry up as the immense cat leans forward, then back, like a boxer feinting.

He's posturing, Larson reasons to himself as calmly as he can, trying to keep his body perfectly still. Of course, the old tomcat's simply surprised by his presence out here in the middle of his territory. Larson knows that in the wild, this grumpy twenty-year-old would have long ago been killed by a younger challenger who wanted the females in his pride.

Larson figures he's in a spot of bother here. He thinks about the radio, decides against it. At least not yet. He's been in the cage with Dominick before. The old man's just throwing his weight around. He'll get bored with this little game of chicken and start eating any moment. Dominick has known Larson for years. He knows his scent, knows he isn't a threat.

Besides, if worse comes to worst, Larson has the moat behind him. Three steps and he'll be over the side and safe. Wet and humiliated and maybe with a broken ankle, but by the time the other keepers arrive, his skin will still be covering his bones and his guts will still be on the inside of him, where he likes to keep them.

"There, there, buddy," Larson says—in a whisper, a *shhh,* baby-go-to-sleep voice. "I like your Mosa just fine, but she's not my type."

Larson senses more than sees the movement at his left. He turns in time to see something burst from the grass, massive, tawny, throwing a column of dust into the air as it rockets at him, growing bigger, picking up speed.

The keeper isn't able to take one step before Mosa springs. Her head slams into his chest like a wrecking ball. All the wind is knocked out of him as he goes airborne and then down on his back ten feet away.

Larson lies on his back, dazed. His heart is beating so fast and hard, he wonders if he's having a heart attack. The thought goes away as Mosa's low, compressed growl reverberates beside his ear.

He reaches for the radio as Mosa puts her paws on his shoulder and bites into his face. Her great upper canines puncture his eyes at the same moment the cat's lower incisors slide with ease into the underside of his jaw.

Larson is as helpless as a rag doll as Mosa shakes him back and forth by his head. When his neck breaks, with a crack remarkably similar to a pencil snapping, the sound is the very last thing his brain registers before he dies.

Three

MOSA GRUNTS AND releases the dead keeper. She uses the thumb-like dewclaw of her right front paw as a toothpick to dislodge a sliver of meat from her teeth. What's left of Larson's wristwatch falls to the dirt as she licks blood from her mouth.

Dominick, having already fed, is starting to jog for the open gate. At the end of the fenced corridor, the two pass the tiny crush cage the keepers shove them into when they need medical attention. They aren't going to miss that.

They quickly cover the length of the big-cat service yard. At the far end, by the hoses, is a low gate and the zoo's bright white concrete path on the other side. Both Mosa and Dominick clear the gate in a leap easy as a breath, and soon are racing down the zoo's empty promenade. The two lions spring over the turnstiles and skirt the parking lot for the nearest cluster of Griffith Park's oak and walnut trees.

They trot up a scrubby brush-dotted hill and down its other side. They catch a human's scent again on a hot breeze. They spot its source a moment later on one of the golf course fairways. He's a handsome young black man in a red shirt and black pants. Getting nine holes in before work. He looks surprised to see lions on the golf course.

Dominick charges, knocking the man sideways, out of his shoes. His death bite takes away most of the golfer's neck in a flowering burst of blood.

Dominick releases the dead man and rears back slowly as a police car glides down alongside the fairway from the north. He can smell that there are more humans inside this shrieking, shining box. He wants to stay and attack, but he knows that this box full of humans is of the same cold, difficult material as his cage.

The two lions run for the cover of the trees. At the top of the ridge, Dominick stops for a moment, gazing down at the city. Los Angeles spreads out beneath him, a brown field of humanity, woozily shaking in the smoke and the gathering morning heat, dissolving into fuzz at the edges.

That smell is stronger now, coming from everywhere. From the buildings and houses, from roadways, from the tiny cars snaking along the highways. The air is saturated with it. But instead of running away from it, Dominick and Mosa run toward it, their paws digging for purchase, mouths wanting blood.

BOOK ONE

THE BEGINNING OF THE END

Chapter 1

I WOKE UP shaking.

I panicked at first, thinking I was having a stroke or something. Then I opened my eyes, relieved, as I remembered it wasn't me that was shaking. It was my apartment.

Outside the wall of dusty industrial-style windows beside my bed came what sounded like a regiment of giants rhythmically striking concrete with their rifle butts in a parade drill. But it wasn't the jolly green marines. I knew it was the elevated number 1 Broadway local, rattling to shake the dead back to life next to my new fifth-floor Harlem loft apartment. Hadn't gotten used to that train yet.

I winced, covered my head with a pillow. Useless. Only in New York did one have to actually pay for the privilege of sleeping beside an overpass.

But I was so broke I couldn't even afford to complain. I sat up. I couldn't even really afford to sleep. I couldn't even afford to think about money. I'd spent it all and then some; my credit was in the sewer. By that point I was in tunnel-vision mode, focusing my entire life on one desperate need: to figure things out before it was too late.

Things hadn't always been so dire. Only two years before, not only had I lived in a nonvibrating apartment, I was actually on the PhD fast track at Columbia University. I was the golden boy in the ecology, evolution, and environmental biology department, so close to the brass ring I could practically smell the book contracts, the cocktail parties, the cushy university appointments.

But then I came into contact with the event— what others called the mistake—that changed my life.

I noticed something. Something that wasn't quite right. Something I couldn't let go.

That's the way it happens sometimes. Life is flowing along like a fairy tale, and then you see something that you just can't categorize. Something that starts filling your every thought, your every dream, your every waking moment.

Zoo

At least, that's the way it happened with me. One minute I was about to realize my goal of academic greatness, and the next I was wrestling with something I couldn't stop thinking about, something I couldn't shake, even as my world crashed around my ears.

I know how nuts it sounds. Intellectual promise plus obsession plus throwing away conventional success usually ends pretty badly. It certainly did for Ted Kaczynski, the Unabomber, and Chris McCandless, the *Into the Wild* guy, who died on that bus.

But I wasn't some malcontent or mystic trying to form a deep intrinsic connection to an ultimate reality. I was more like Chicken Little, an evolutionary biologist Chicken Little who had detected that the sky actually was falling. Except it wasn't the sky that was falling, it was worse. Biological life was falling. Animal life itself. Something very, very weird and very, very bad was happening, and I was the only voice shouting in the wilderness about it.

Before I get ahead of myself, my name's Oz. My first name is Jackson, but with a last name like mine, no one uses it. Unfortunately, my father is also known as Oz, as are my mother, my three sisters,

21

my uncles, and all my paternal cousins. Which gets confusing at family reunions, but that's neither here nor there.

What is here and there—everywhere—is the problem I was monitoring, the global problem I'd by that point pretty much devoted my life to trying to figure out.

It sounds grandiose, I know, but I feared that if I were right—and for the first time in my life I truly hoped I was wrong—a planetary paradigm shift was underway that was going to make global warming feel like a Sunday stroll through an organic community garden.

Chapter 2

I HOPPED OUT of bed wearing a pair of wrinkled gray pajama bottoms that Air France had gifted me with on a recent flight to Paris. Shaved, showered, teeth brushed, I got back into the fancy French pajamas. Working from home has its perks. Okay, "working" implies I was making money. This was another kind of work. Anyway. They were really comfortable pajamas.

Coming out of my bedroom, I retrieved another prized possession from the doorknob—my fire-engine-red woolen hat, which I'd acquired on a recent trip to Alaska. With my thinking cap firmly on the bottle, I got down and pumped out my daily hundred push-ups, a habit I'd picked up on yet another jaunt, a four-year stint in the US Army before college.

PE complete, I headed into my shop. I flipped the surge-protector switches, turning on the TV sets that I'd lined across a metal workbench in the center of the industrial-style room. There were eight of them in all. Some were nice new flat-screens, but most were junkers I'd picked up diving Dumpsters after the digital signal changeover. Behind them, a Gordian knot of wires connected them to cable boxes and satellite receivers and a set of laptops and computer servers that I'd modified with the help of some electronic buddies of mine into the world's biggest, baddest DVR.

As I waited for everything to boot up, I popped my first Red Bull of the day. Another number 1 train kicked up my heart rate along with a cloud of dust off the windowsills. Call me crazy—go ahead, you wouldn't be the first—but after the initial shock, I kind of liked my apartment's MTA-provided sound track. I don't know why, but from the time I was a little kid up until I received my Rhodes Scholarship, my ADD-addled brain tended to fire on all cylinders when it was surrounded by headbanging noise. Old-school AC/DC, that was my bag. Metallica, Motörhead, with all the knobs cranked to eleven.

I frowned at the lightening screens, remembering my father, a lieutenant in the FDNY, watching the evening news. After a Bronx four-alarmer, he would come home, drop in front of the tube, and at the first commercial, after a Miller High Life or two, he would say, "Oz, boy, sometimes I think this world of ours is nothing but a goddamn zoo."

In front of me, animals began to fill the screens. Lots of them. All of them behaving very badly.

Fathers really do know best, I guess, because that's exactly what was happening. The world was becoming a zoo, without cages.

Chapter 3

SETTLING BACK INTO my tag-sale leather rolling chair, I lifted a new legal tablet from the fresh stack on the table to my right, clicked a pen, wrote the date.

I turned up the volume on set number four.

"A missing seventy-two-year-old hunter and his fifty-one-year-old son were found dead yesterday," said a correspondent from WPTZ in Plattsburgh, in upstate New York, a good-looking brunette in a red coat. She held the microphone as though it were a glass of wine. "The men were apparently killed by black bears while illegally hunting outside of Lake Placid."

The camera cut to a shot of a young state trooper at a press conference. Buzz cut, lanky. Country boy, uncomfortable in front of cameras.

"No, there was no way they could have been saved," the trooper said. He blew his *p*'s and *b*'s straight into the mike. "Both men were long dead and partially eaten. What's still puzzling to us is how it happened. Both of the men's weapons were still loaded."

He ended the report with the claim that the father and son were known poachers, fond of using an illegal hunting method known as deer dogging—using dogs to chase out and ambush deer.

"Back to you, Brett," the brunette said.

"Not good, Brett," I said as I muted set four and cranked up set eight. Blip, blip, blip went the green bars on the screen.

On it, a news program from NDTV, a sort of English-speaking Indian version of CNN, was starting.

"A Keralan mahout was killed yesterday while he was training elephants," the middle-aged anchorman said. He had a mustache and a Bollywood swipe of hair; there was something of Clark Gable about him. "Please be advised: the footage we are about to show you is graphic in nature."

He wasn't kidding. I watched as an elephant, tied to a stake in a village square, stomped a little guy in front of her into the ground. Then she wrapped her trunk around the guy's leg and tossed him up in the air.

The anchorman explained that the attack had occurred while the mother elephant was being separated from its baby during a training ritual known as *phajaan*.

I'd heard of it. Also known as torture training, *phajaan* is the preferred way of elephant training in rural parts of India. A baby elephant is separated from its mother and put in a cage so villagers can whack it with hot irons and sticks that have nails on the ends. The brutal beating continues to the point where either the baby elephant allows itself to be ridden or dies.

"Guess Ma wasn't down with the program, dude," I said to the dying elephant trainer on the screen.

But the pièce de résistance was the breaking news I pulled off Fox News on set two. The Barbie doll on TV informed me that two lions from the L.A. zoo had not only killed their keeper and escaped, they'd also killed some guy on a nearby golf course. On the screen, half a dozen LAPD with M16s cordoned off a block lined with palm trees, people from animal control milling around behind them in white jumpsuits. "The lions were last spotted in the La Brea neighborhood, near Beverly Hills," chirped Megyn Kelly, her vacant eyes nailed to the teleprompter.

I threw down my pen. I was pissed, pissed, pissed. Skin itching, heart going like a hammer. Was everyone asleep? Under hypnosis? High? *Was everybody frigging stoned?*

I grabbed the pen again and scribbled three letters on the pad, hard enough to tear the paper.

H A C !!!!!!!!

Then I threw the pad of paper across the room.

"When will you people *listen?*" I yelled at my wall of media.

It was time for more caffeine.

Chapter 4

I SAT BENT over in my chair for a few minutes of therapeutic seething. I listened to an uptown train blasting by my window, then a downtown one. Then I crossed the room, picked up the pad again, and went back to work.

HAC: Human-Animal Conflict. This was the theory I was working on.

Basically, it was my belief that all throughout the world, animal behavior was changing. Not for the better, either. Not even a little. On every continent, species after species was suddenly displaying hyperaggressive behavior toward one particular animal.

The enemy was us. You and me. People. *Man*, man.

Zoo

The facts were undeniable. From Romania to Colombia, from the Pyrenees to the Rockies, from St. Louis to Sri Lanka, there'd been an exponential increase in animal attacks on humans—by wild leopards, bears, wolves, boar, all kinds of different animals, you name it. In fact, the worldwide rate of wild animal attacks in the last four years was double the average of the previous fifty. For emphasis, I repeat: double.

It wasn't just wild animals, either. In Australia, injuries from cats and dogs had swelled by 20 percent. In Beijing, it was 34 percent. In Britain, nearly four thousand people had needed hospital treatment for dog bites in the previous year.

For some reason I hadn't pinned down yet, some kind of concerted transspecies evolutionary backlash against Homo sapiens was underway. Or, to put it in other terms, something was driving animals to go haywire, and the time to do something about it was running out quicker than the plastic wand supply at a Harry Potter convention.

I know how it sounds—wing-nut city. Different species of nonhuman animals working in some sort of collusion against humans. It's absurd. Insane, impossible. I used to think it was a big, strange coincidence, too. Just lots and lots of totally unrelated, isolated incidents. Initially, it was just a goof among my colleagues that I'd started to track the phenomenon on my tongue-in-cheek blog, *Man Against Nature*.

I stopped laughing when I started looking at the evidence more closely. Nature, actually, was at war with man. And our side wasn't even noticing.

The expression "between the devil and the deep blue sea" is a nautical one. The devil is what old sailors used to call the seam between two hard-to-reach planks on a ship. In order to caulk it, one had to be suspended from a plank held over the water. If you fell into the ocean, it was certain death. If you didn't caulk the plank, the ship might sink. Either way was dangerous. Either way, you were screwed.

That's exactly where I was now, out on a line, suspended between bad and worse. I felt like I was out there caulking the devil, hanging above the deep blue sea.

If I was wrong, I was crazy. If I was right, the world was doomed.

I'd been doing my best to get the word out, but was getting nowhere. I'd maxed out all my credit cards and those of several sympathetic relatives, speaking to anyone who would listen. My trip to Paris was for the purpose of attending an animal rights conference that I'd fibbed my way into in order to get some speaking time. I only got about halfway through before I was laughed off the stage.

No, people weren't getting on board in the slightest. You'd be shocked and dismayed at the amount of intellectual intolerance directed at people who favor red lumberjack hats and wrinkled pajamas.

The L.A. zoo thing I'd just seen was the topper. The report had said that the cats had been born in captivity. Why would a pair of zoo lions one day just decide to start killing people and rampage through a city? Because there are two hundred channels and nothing is on? It didn't make sense. Zoo lions don't just go out berserking. There's simply no reason for them to. Until now.

I speed-dialed my press agent to try to get on Fox. As usual, I got kicked immediately into voice mail. Even she thought I was nuts, and I *paid* her. Not a good sign.

After I recorded my latest plea to her, I decided to do the only thing I could think of. I plugged myself into my iPod and blasted some Motörhead to get some much-needed mental juices flowing. Help me, Lemmy. I slurped more Red Bull and tried to think while watching some more of the world's unfunniest videos.

I sat up when Attila yanked my earbuds out.

"Yo, Attila," I said. My roommate held out his hand for a low five. I gave it to him. "Look at this craziness. Every time I think things are going to calm down, the activity doubles. Sarah won't call me back. Boy Who Cried Wolf, I feel your pain, you know?"

"*Heeaagh! Heeaagh! Heeaagh!*" said Attila.

Then he made a few panting hoots and scrambled into my lap and gave me a sloppy kiss and hairy-armed hug.

Attila, by the way, is a chimpanzee.

Chapter 5

I KNEW THE TVs bothered him, so I took Attila by his hand—it was leathery and surprisingly soft, like a glove—and led him into the kitchen. Attila: five years, four feet, and a hundred pounds of chimpanzee.

For breakfast I gave him a mango, a stack of Fig Newtons (which he went ape over), and half a leftover turkey club. Today's featured dessert was applesauce mixed with crushed-up vitamins and Zoloft.

That's right, Zoloft.

Even apes need happy pills in our crazy world. Or maybe just the ones who live in New York City.

I brushed Attila's teeth and brought him back to his room. Scattered across the newspaper-covered floor were Attila's playthings: a sandbox, a toy chest filled with balls and dolls, an air hockey table, and an old pop-a-shot basketball machine. Actually, those last two were more my toys than his. But the Wii was definitely Attila's. He could kick my ass at bowling.

I stood in the doorway and watched him play a little while. I'd fixed up the doorway to his room with a sturdy grate of steel wire, though he was getting older and I knew it wouldn't be long before he found a way around it. I'd have to find another home for him soon. Attila's favorite toy these days was an American Girl doll I'd recently bought him. She had braids and a gingham dress, very *Little House on the Prairie*. Attila rocked the big blond-haired doll back and forth and kissed her. Then he brought her over to me and held her up so I could kiss her, too. Attila panted, content, and took the doll back over to the beanbag chair in the corner and began to pretend to feed her.

The people who say their dogs are like children to them never lived with a chimp, believe you me. I shook my head and smiled at my little buddy. It was nice to see him quiet, calm, having fun. That certainly hadn't been the case when we first met.

I found Attila two years before at the Willis

Institute, a South Jersey bio-med shop where I'd been hired as a lab temp. I was cleaning up late on my second day when I opened a door, and there he was. The cutest damn three-year-old ape you ever saw, lying there with his pink face pressed against the cold bars of his tiny cage.

He was staring at me miserably, his eyes red-rimmed, his nose running to beat the band. Most biomedical research with chimps works like this: they infect the chimp with some disease before giving it the new cure they wanted to test out. If the cure doesn't work, then whatever; the chimp dies. Or they look for side effects and so on. Flipping through the paperwork attached to the cage, I saw that some intrepid human had been doing some type of weird olfactory research on him. Testing perfumes or something.

When this little ape—he wasn't Attila yet; back then he was number 579—looked at me so searchingly, so sadly, with his big brown eyes, my sucker's heart came up with a plan. A week after the job ended, I found myself heading south down I-95 again with the DO NOT COPY lab key I'd very absentmindedly forgotten to return. When I pulled out of the lab's parking lot after midnight, Attila was lying down in the back of my beat-up Hyundai

Sonata, covered in Papa John's pizza boxes.

The first few weeks in my apartment he'd been wary, hypervigilant, hardly getting any sleep as he waited fearfully to see if I would hurt him. A vet friend of mine diagnosed him with post-traumatic stress disorder and wrote out a scrip for the Zoloft, which worked like a charm.

I know what you're thinking. I'm either a left-wing animal rights loon or I watched one too many episodes of *B.J. and the Bear* as a kid. Or insane. Or an idiot. I usually don't tell other scientists I have a chimp in my apartment. I never planned on being the twenty-first-century Man with the Yellow Hat. It just kind of happened. My original thought was to drop Attila off at an animal sanctuary in rural Louisiana that takes in retired research monkeys. And that is still my eventual plan. But for the time being, Attila lives with me.

Attila put the doll down and walked to the door of the terrace off his room, tapping on it to be let out onto the fenced-in outdoor space, where I'd set up a tire swing.

"Think fast, Attila! Pit attack!" I said, digging in for tickles.

"Oo-oo-oo-oo ah-ah-ah *heeaagh heeaagh hyeeeaaaaaghhhh!*"

Zoo

I watched him knuckle-run over to the swing and jump on it with a scream of joy before I turned, shut the gate, and headed back to work.

Chapter 6

LYING FACEDOWN IN the tire swing, Attila waves his long, powerful arms to swing himself back and forth. The tips of his long, knotty fingers graze the ground. Strong, lean arms, built for climbing trees. Like most chimps, Attila likes to play. He likes wrestling, laughing, being tickled.

And, like humans, he is sharply status-conscious and capable of deception.

He is more like people than any other living creature. When Attila spies the man down the hallway, he makes a high, curt cry, indicating his agitation, his anxiety. Getting no response, Attila crashes back into the tire swing and hurtles himself back and forth, the chain creaking loudly under the strain.

Everything is so strange. The moving, boxlike

shapes below. The small thunder overhead some-times. Sometimes, everything suddenly has the smell. The Smell. The scary smell, the Bad Smell, the one that used to fill his cage in the big bright room, the smell that makes Attila's stomach hurt and the fur on his back stand straight up. The smell is getting stronger. Always stronger. Even outside. More and more each day.

Bored, angry, afraid, Attila turns away from the window and searches around his play area until he finds the mirror. He holds it up in front of his face and looks at himself. Like all chimps, he recognizes himself. He's now five, and his face is losing its pinkish tinge and getting darker. His tuft of wiry white chin hair is almost gone.

Tiring of the mirror, he puts it aside and runs back and forth, shaking the fence, shrieking down at the strange walls and moving things. After a while, he begins to amuse himself by tossing around the stuff on the terrace. The plastic chair. The Thomas the Tank Engine big wheel. Then his gaze falls on a stuffed bunny. He picks it up and brings it over to the corner.

He cuddles it, delicately petting its soft fur with his fingers, when a breeze wafts in over the terrace, and the Bad Smell hits his nose like a punch.

Attila rips the bunny in half with his hands. A chimp's grip is as powerful as a pit bull's jaws. He makes a low howling sound as he tears it to fluff and tatters. Then he stuffs the pieces of bunny through the holes in the fence, hooting as they flutter like snow, like ash, down to the rear alley of the building.

This makes Attila feel better.

After a minute, Attila flops himself back into the tire swing again, and wheels himself in circles with his long arms.

Chapter 7

FOR THE NEXT hour or so, I sent out feelers to all my contacts about the lion attack in L.A. to get their reaction. I made an effort to get in touch with a man named Abraham Bindix, a safari guide living in Botswana, whom I'd met in Paris. Guy knew a hell of a lot about lions, and he was actually one of the few people I'd met who didn't think my HAC theory was total loony tunes.

I was still waiting to hear back from people and putting in my second call to my press agent when I got a text.

HAC 911! WHERE R U?

"Shit," I said. I knew I'd forgotten something.

On my way, I text-lied back. Then I called down to my super's apartment. Five painfully long minutes later, an elderly woman arrived, faded floral-print dress dangling from her little bones, arms full of needlepoint and Spanish crossword-puzzle books. It was the super's mother, Attila's occasional babysitter. She didn't have to do anything except call me in case of an emergency.

Attila was looking in the mirror I'd bought him when I arrived at the terrace door.

"Hey, good-lookin'. Mrs. Abreu is here to watch you, buddy, so be good, okay? I have to check something out, but when I get back, we'll play some soccer. I promise."

Attila dropped his head, his lips protruding in a pout. Until I opened my arms. He almost knocked me over as he leaped into them. He let loose with a series of whooping howls. It was his signature pant-hoot, which chimps use to identify themselves.

Attila was visibly pleased as I copied his pant-hoot back at him, whoop for whoop.

Farewells over, I threw my Cannondale road bike onto my shoulder, carried it down the five flights of stairs, and started to ride north up traffic-clogged Broadway. Head down, I put it into overdrive, sailing past gypsy cabs, C-Towns, flower shops. My thighs began to throb around the 140s as Broadway started its long ascent into Washington Heights.

Cutting off a garbage truck at 159th Street, I made a left onto Fort Washington Avenue and followed it as it looped around to the north. A few minutes later I took a right onto narrow 181st Street and squealed to a sweaty stop in front of a once-grand prewar building. There was a 99 cents store beside the building's entrance, and after I U-locked my bike, I went in and made a purchase that made the stone-faced Chinese lady behind the counter break into a leering grin.

I dripped sweat in the building's dingy vestibule as I thumbed the buzzer for the apartment of "N. Shaw" and received an immediate buzzing-in. N. Shaw met me in the sixth-floor hallway just outside the elevator, her sneakered foot below her blue-green scrubs tapping agitatedly against the faded tile floor. This really was one HAC emergency, it seemed.

"I can't believe you. You know how little time I have between class and my shift," said Natalie, as she shoved me down the hallway and into her apartment.

Natalie was statuesque in scrubs. Bottle-green eyes, red hair—and I mean red, red, Irish girl's red hair—creamy skin, so many freckles on her it was like a pastry chef had been at her with a cinnamon shaker.

"You promised you'd be here waiting. 'With bells on,' I believe was the term you used," she said, green eyes glowing like kryptonite as she yanked at my shirt in her foyer. Now her hands were on my belt. "Let's see some bells, Ozzy."

Natalie was an explosion of sex, a queen-size libido in hospital turquoise. She was also a brilliant Columbia med student on track to becoming a neurologist. It was a nice combination, though sometimes I wondered if she wanted me more for my body than my mind. Guess I'd have to live with it.

"No bells, but I did manage to pick you up a little something," I said as I took my 99-cent purchase out of my back pocket.

Dangling from my finger was a pair of the slightest, rudest thong panties Thailand had ever produced, candy-apple red and transparent as cellophane.

"Who says I don't know the value of a dollar?" I said. Natalie planted her hands on her hips.

"Let me get this straight. First you're late for the only chance we've had to have sex in three days," Natalie said, cocking her head, eyes in slits. "Then you show up wanting me to slip into some slutty trash a streetwalker would be embarrassed to wear?"

"Pretty much," I said.

"You didn't kiss that monkey before you came over here, did you? If you did, then turn the hell around."

"Nope," I lied with perfect conviction.

"In that case," she said. She grabbed the panties from my hand. They stretched, snapped like a rubber band off my finger.

"I really hate you, Oz," she shouted over her shoulder on her way to the bedroom.

"I hate you too, honey."

"Get on the couch," she ordered from behind her open bedroom door. I could just see her shimmying the panties up her legs in the bedroom mirror. "Take off your shirt, leave the pants. I want to undo the belt with my teeth."

Chapter 8

"THAT . . . WAS . . . ," NATALIE started to say. She was out of breath, biting a knuckle, her slippery body sprawled like a broken marionette on the floor of her bedroom, where we'd ended up half an hour later.

"Jungle love?" I asked, untying the 99-cent purchase, which had somehow become tangled over my left shoulder. I brushed back some broken glass from a picture frame that had fallen off the wall. It was a photo of her dad, a Connecticut equities trader. Girl had some blue blood in her. I turned it over and scooted it under the bed.

"Equatorial rain forest love," Natalie said, rolling on top of me. She licked my earlobe. "I mean, doing it standing on a couch?"

"Well, if you recall, I was the only one standing," I said. In the corner of my eye, the winking red light of my iPhone let me know I had a message.

"How could I forget?" she said, thumbing sweat out of her eyes. "That wasn't biology. That was geology. You know, seismology, tectonics."

"It's like Archimedes and I always say," I said. "Give me a place to stand, and I can move the world."

I waited until Nat headed for the shower before I retrieved my phone. My message was a text from Abraham Bindix, my lion man.

Oz, unbelievable. It's not just L.A. It's happening here, 2!

I called him immediately.

"Oz, you are not so crazy after all," Abe said in his Afrikaans accent, with his slightly rolled *r*'s and chopping-block consonants. "You were right. Lion behavior is wrong, absolutely wrong. Wrong, wrong, wrong.

"I just got back from a curtailed hunt, up north, near Zimbabwe. We came upon a village—an entire village—emptied out. From one end to the other was lion spoor and blood. I've never seen or even heard of such a thing."

There was a note of panic in Abe's voice. Which

was odd, coming from this burly Afrikaner who looked like a retired strongman from the circus.

"In fact, I'm here dealing with the military, so I cannot exactly talk about it. But when I saw on the news about the lion attack at the L.A. zoo, I knew I had to call you. You have to come here to Botswana, man. And bring cameras. You and the rest of the world have to see this to believe it."

"Say no more," I said. My iPhone pinched under my jaw, I snatched up a pen and looked around Nat's bedroom for something to write on. "I'm packing a bag and catching the next flight. Where can you meet me? At the airport in Maun, is it?"

"Right, man. Maun. Let me know which flight you'll be on as soon as you can. This is incredible, terrible, incredible."

"I'll call you when the first flight changes over," I said as Nat came in, wearing a towel.

"Right, man," said Abe, and hung up.

"Um, flight? You're going somewhere?" she said. I was scribbling notes on the receipt for the panties.

"On a, uh . . . a trip," I said.

"I gathered that much. Where?"

"Botswana," I cough-said.

"What?"

"Botswana."

"Botswana. Africa?! Are you nuts?" She flicked her wet hair over her shoulder. "No, of course you are. Silly question. But you can't do that. People can't do that. You can't get a phone call, and then, like, call a taxi out to JFK and go to Botswana! Especially if you're unemployed!"

"You're right," I said. "What the hell do I do with Attila? Can you watch him for me?"

Chapter 9

"SO NOW I have to babysit a monkey?"

"An ape," I said.

Nat was beginning to get actually pissed at me now, not just play-pissed.

"The answer's no, Oz. You know how creeped out I get. Besides, I have class."

"Relax. My super's mother has it mostly covered. You just have to check in on him once a day and give him his meds. Please. You could polish up your bedside manner."

"On a monkey?" she shrieked.

"An ape!" I said. "Besides, this trip is the breakthrough I've been waiting for. If I get some tape of abnormal lion behavior in Africa and couple it with the L.A. zoo breakout, people might listen, and we can start trying to figure this thing out for real. Humanity is in jeopardy. We can—"

"Please," she said. "Don't give me the HAC spiel again. Just don't. I really can't believe you, Oz. First, you drop out of the PhD when you're practically ABD—"

"I was bored."

"Then for over a year—I don't know, for a hobby?—you decide to randomly disrupt classes at New York's finest institutions of higher learning. You were lucky NYU didn't press charges for the chemistry thing."

"I was trying to get people to use their goddamn heads."

"I like you, Oz," Natalie said. "I know you're brilliant, but this HAC thing is really starting to get between us. With my class schedule, there's barely enough time for us to even see each other. I mean, I can't even remember the last time you took me out to a real restaurant. Now you're leaving for Africa."

I looked at my girlfriend, perched on the edge of the bed. She was gorgeous. And she liked beer and Chris Farley movies. She played Modern Warfare 2 with me—and was good at it. We watched basketball together. She was a Celtics fan, but that was one of her only flaws.

That's when I shocked her—and myself.

"How about this?" I said. "I go to Africa. If it's another dud, I pack up my End-Is-Nigh sandwich boards, hand in my white–Harlem Globetrotter ID card, and get a job where I have to wear pants. Agreed?"

"If you come back."

"Don't be ridiculous. Is it a deal?"

She rolled her bottle-green eyes.

"Fine, Tarzan. I'll watch King Kong while you go into the jungle, even if it means for the last time. But concerning Attila, don't think this is some sort of mommy tryout. I told you I don't want kids. Not with you. Not with Leonardo DiCaprio. No one."

"I know, I know," I said. "Relax. I just have a chimp who needs to eat. Have you seen my boxers anywhere?"

She finally smiled.

"Try the couch cushions in the living room."

Chapter 10

I LEFT NATALIE'S apartment, a little uncertain of what I'd just gotten myself into. What if Botswana was a bust? Sometimes I wish I could put my mouth in a cage. It's always pushing me into corners. I'd rather picture myself in a coffin than in a cubicle.

But by the time I unlocked my bike, I decided that I actually needed my own ultimatum. This was it. It really was time for me to put up or shut up concerning HAC. If a pride of maniacal lions didn't open the world's eyes to what was coming down the pike, then nothing would.

Back at the apartment, after I relieved and paid Mrs. Abreu, I took out Attila's folding cage from the closet and assembled it. Attila whimpered when he saw me putting it together, knowing what it meant when I had to bust the thing out. I hated to delegate the poor guy to six-by-four-foot solitary for the time I'd be away, but there wasn't much else I could do. I wrote a quick note for Nat to double his Zoloft and increase his vitamin D supplements, since he wouldn't be able to exercise out on the terrace.

After I got the cage put together, I let Attila in from the terrace and set him up in his beanbag chair for a special treat. I gave him his lunch as I played his favorite Beatrix Potter DVD, *The Tale of the Flopsy Bunnies and Mrs. Tittlemouse*.

As he sat contentedly watching, I ran downstairs to get my bags from the storage bin. When I came back less than five minutes later, I couldn't believe what was going on.

Attila wasn't in front of his DVD player anymore; he was in the shop. He'd already hurled two of my TVs into the wall and was standing on the table, banging a laptop against the corner.

"Attila!" I shouted. "Stop it! Get down this instant! What the hell are you doing?"

Attila turned, screeching.

For a moment—just a brief, brief moment—I saw something in his eyes, a coldness, a meanness, that I'd never seen before. I actually thought he would swing the laptop at me.

Then the moment passed. Attila dropped the computer and leaped off the table and into the corner with his head down.

"March, mister," I said, grabbing his hand and taking him to his cage. He tried to pick up the American Girl doll as we passed his room.

"No," I said, snatching it away.

"Bad Attila. Bad boy," I said, shutting the gate and locking it.

After I swept up the broken glass and cleaned the chimp crap off the DVD player, I got on the Internet to book a flight to Botswana. The best I could do was a flight that left the next morning, with a stopover in Johannesburg, for three thousand bucks. My parents wouldn't be happy, but I'd have to dip into the principal of the small trust Grandpa Oz had left me.

I packed. Passport, clothes, gear. I had a 35-millimeter Nikon with a superzoom lens, but my pride and joy was my professional-grade Sony DSR-400L camcorder. I took it out of its padded bag and tested its lights and charged up its lithium batteries before I stuffed it all away again.

I was hustling, bringing everything into the hallway, when I heard the whimpering.

It was Attila. He was sobbing after receiving his scolding.

I went into his room and opened the cage.

"Are you sorry, Attila? Are you really sorry?"

A high yelp assured me that he was, and we hugged it out for a while.

I let him romp around while I kept getting things ready. I was almost all packed when Attila tugged my shirt and clicked his teeth repeatedly. I knew what he wanted. We finally kissed and made up. Natalie would have puked.

"I have to go away for a few days now," I said after I put him back into his cage. "It won't be easy, but you're going to be fine. Mrs. Abreu will look in on you early tomorrow, and so will Natalie. You remember Natalie. You be good to her, hear me? I know you understand me."

Attila made a couple of whoops of complaint.

"I know, I know. It can't be helped. I'm going to miss you, too."

Chapter 11

IT WAS EARLY summer. The morning light illuminated the crushed Marlboro boxes and Happy Meal cups in the roadside weeds.

Terrific. I'd just started my amazing journey, and I was already lost in the wilds. Of Queens.

Staring out from the back of my sticky JFK-bound taxi, I cursed as we slowed to a dead stop. Again.

We lurched forward a bit, and then stopped again. The cabbie bashed the horn and spat out a string of curses, went back to talking to somebody on his headset. Sounded like he was talking business. He was very dark and matchstick-skinny, a lot of red in his eyes.

Above the dash I could see that the LIE had

become a frozen, curving conveyor belt of red brake lights. It was so bad even the jackasses on the shoulder trying to cut people off were jammed to a halt.

Surrounded by my bulky camera case, laptop, and carry-on, I checked the time on my iPhone for the five hundredth time. It was looking like making my 9:05 a.m. flight to Africa was going to need divine intervention in order to happen. I also noticed an e-mail from Natalie and made the mistake of opening it.

You don't have to do this.

I sighed. Maybe my girlfriend was right. Maybe this was nuts. Wouldn't it make more sense to head out to the Hamptons with her instead? Get some sand in my shoes. Eat some oysters. I could certainly use a Long Island iced tea or ten, not to mention a tan. Couldn't this trip wait?

No. I knew full well it couldn't. I was committed to this thing, far past the point of no return. Hamptons or no Hamptons, HAC was happening. Right here. Right now. Right frigging everywhere. I could feel it in my pores.

I went through my travel kit again. I sorted through my passport, my insurance, my federally mandated less-than-three-ounce travel toiletries, my skivvies, T-shirts and shorts, my red wool hat. Then I scooped up my antimalarial doxycycline pills that had spilled over my folded-up poncho until everything was wired tight.

To hell with the naysayers. I was good to go. Botswana or bust. The last thing to do was print out my e-ticket when I got to the airport, if I ever got there.

When we finally started moving, I took out a map of Africa. I was a forty–sixty mix of nervous–excited. Just the sheer size of Africa. Three times as big as Europe. I had learned so much about the continent during my first trip, when I was still in grad school, but this was different. This was no field trip.

The cabbie quit nattering into his Bluetooth and turned to me.

"Which terminal, sir?" The airport was finally beginning to crawl into sight.

"I'm not sure," I said. "My flight's on South African Airways."

"You are going to Africa? South Africa?" asked the cabbie. I'd been preoccupied—now I noticed the guy looked and sounded African himself. His voice had that melodic lilt of African English. Nigerian, maybe.

"Botswana," I said.

"You go from New York *to* Botswana? No! For real?" the cabbie said, his red eyes wide in the rearview.

He seemed even more skeptical than my girlfriend. I was getting nothing but unbridled support and good omens from all corners tonight.

"That's the idea," I said as we pulled up in front of a bustling terminal.

"Well, I hope is a busy-ness trip," he said as he printed my receipt from the meter. "You make damn sure is a busy-ness trip, mon, you know what I mean."

I did know what he meant, unfortunately. He was referring to Botswana's AIDS epidemic, the second worst in the world. One out of every four adults in the country was supposed to have the dreaded sexually transmitted disease.

I wasn't too worried about it. Between my long trip and dealing head-on with a frightening global epidemic, I didn't think I'd have much time to squeeze in any hot, wild, condomless third-world sex. Besides, I had a girlfriend.

"Don't worry," I told the cabbie as I opened the door. "I won't have any fun at all."

Chapter 12

ABOUT FOUR HOURS later I woke up thirty thousand feet above the Atlantic.

Blinking in the low, lonely roar of the 747's cabin, I raised my seat and looked out the window beside me. Through spaces in the milky floor of dim clouds I could see the silver squiggles of the surf on the ocean far below. I definitely wasn't in Kansas anymore—or Queens, thank God.

I yawned, unlocked and lowered my seat-back tray, and worried my laptop out of my carry-on bag. I was going to write some e-mails, but instead I found myself clicking open the file for the HAC PowerPoint presentation I'd shown in Paris.

It began with a photograph of a primitive painting from the famous Lascaux caves in France that clearly showed a guy being killed by a bison. Next was Rubens's *Chained Prometheus*. In the painting, the torment in the upside-down Titan's face is pretty damn visceral as an eagle tears into his, well, viscera. The Rubens was followed quickly by Nicolas Poussin's haunting Renaissance painting *The Plague at Ashdod,* depicting a scene in which God has sent a plague of disease and mice onto the Philistines for disobeying him.

Next came stranger, darker, lesser-known images.

I felt my pulse skip a little when an ancient sculpture of a reclining jaguar appeared. It was found in an Aztec temple along with an apocalyptic prophecy of animals devouring all humanity.

The jaguar was followed by an eerie illustration from the Toggenburg Bible. It shows a man and a woman dying of bubonic plague. There's something about its bright, static flatness—a characteristic of medieval art—that makes it particularly disturbing. The naked figures lie stiffly in bed like paper dolls, their pale bodies polka-dotted with protruding buboes. The Black Death, which killed 40 percent of the known world's population, had been started by marmots and carried throughout Europe by rats.

I looked out the window again. As I stared out

at the clouds thousands of feet below me, and the ocean below that, I had a strange sensation. It was a sinking, chilling feeling. For a moment, hurtling six hundred miles an hour toward Africa, I felt suddenly very tiny and very alone. I wasn't religious, but as I sat there, I started wondering about the inexplicable nature of these things.

It was as though I could actually feel the apocalyptic shift that was occurring. I thought of horses, birds, snakes. I thought of the curse God puts on the snake in Genesis: he will crush your head, and you will strike his heel . . .

The wrath of God?

Or maybe it was just my jet lag, I thought, rubbing the gunk out of my eyes. There was no doubt that I'd become obsessed with HAC. I thought about all the sleepless nights; the quitting school. And now I was actually on a plane to Africa. Maybe I would finally find the answers I was looking for. Or maybe I was delusional. I was beginning to doubt my own sanity.

I glanced down at my laptop and saw that I had another e-mail from Natalie. This one was a real picker-upper.

Oz, I know this is probably a bad time to say this . . .

Oh, boy. I knew what was coming. I almost quit

reading then and there. The same way I looked at my bank statements in those days. Just flick my eyes over it, knowing I don't want to see it. Anyway. I read the rest quickly:

. . . but I've been thinking about everything, and I guess, bottom line, I just can't do all this anymore. At least not now. I just got back my immunology midterm. I flunked it. I'll be lucky if I get a C now. It's not just that. I'm distracted, and I have to concentrate on school and my career. I know I shouldn't e-mail all this. We'll talk when you get back. And you need to get someone else to check on Attila. I'm too swamped.

Okay, then, I thought. Whoopee. I'm back on the market.

I considered replying to her e-mail, but then decided to just ignore it, leave things alone. I couldn't turn back now. Natalie knew that, and I knew Natalie's priority was to become a doctor. She'd always been clear about that. Maybe we did need a break.

I'd just have to call the other woman in my life. I left a message for Mrs. Abreu on her machine, begging her to feed Attila for me until I came back. She wouldn't let me down.

I closed my laptop and stretched. I had twelve hours to go before I reached Johannesburg for my stopover. I reached into my laptop bag for my iPod, put in my earbuds, cranked some Black Sabbath, and headed down the aisle of the speeding plane in search of the stewardess and some Red Bull.

BOOK TWO

INTO AFRICA

Chapter 13

MY FIRST GLIMPSE of Africa, twelve hours later, was actually sort of a letdown. Johannesburg, beyond the massive windows of the airport, was just a bunch of nondescript buildings; it could have been Cleveland.

An hour later, when we took off northbound for Botswana, my mood lifted considerably. The green-and-tan expanse of seemingly endless landscape looked the way the little kid in me wanted Africa to look. Hot, wild, secluded.

As we were beginning our final descent into Maun, I saw there were some modern buildings, but most of the structures were cinder-block and tin. Coming down the steps onto the tarmac, I saw that, beyond the flimsy chain-link fence along the airport's perimeter, there were donkeys everywhere. There were also rondavels, the traditional African thatch-roofed round huts built of stone and cow dung. The feel of the place—the heat, the sweetish smell of manure and diesel, even the sharp, blinding yellow light—was pleasantly strange.

After I made it through customs, Abraham Bindix took off his tattered straw hat and greeted me with a bear hug inside the run-down terminal. Abraham was a boiler tank of a man. Broad-shouldered and blocky, the fiftyish, weatherbeaten man reminded me of a Sun Belt college football coach. His face was as hard and creased as an old work glove, with a mustache fading into the scruff on his cheeks. A shag carpet of chest hair burst from the unbuttoned neck of his sweat-dampened linen shirt. Some faded blue tattoos on the furry wine barrels he called his arms were reminders of his navy days. It was good to see his loopy, gap-toothed smile. The last time I'd seen him was in Paris. We'd sat at the hotel bar and gotten drunk as swine after I'd been booed off the convention stage.

He seemed heavier than I remembered him in Paris. He also seemed noticeably older, and a little slower on his feet. I wondered if he was ill.

"Thank you for coming, my friend, but I have

bad news," he said as I scooped up my bags from the pile of luggage beside the plane. I liked Abraham, but took him with a grain of salt. Like a lot of Afrikaners, he was crude as oil and casually racist in a way that can make a white American dude a touch uncomfortable. Still, there was something almost grandfatherly about him, something Papa Bear.

"Unfortunately, a problem has arisen," he said. "A family thing. Is it possible for you to wait a day before I can take you up to the village near Zimbabwe?"

"Of course. What's up, Abe? Can I help?" I said.

"No, no. It is a family thing," he said. Abe had a warm, brassy honk of a voice, like a muted trumpet. "My little brother, Phillip, the pacifist, is the manager at a game-spotting lodge over in the bush near the Namibian border. I take rich American tourists out to kill animals, but he takes them out just to look at them, take pictures. Lions, actually—two huge prides of them that eat the Cape buffalo up there in the Okavango Delta."

"What's the problem?"

"Don't know, man. His lodge has been out of radio contact for over twenty-four hours, and me mum is worried. It is probably nothing, but with all the craziness going on I need to make sure the wanker is okay."

"So let's head out," I said. "You said the lodge has lions, right? Lions are what I just came eight thousand miles to see."

My enthusiasm seemed to brighten Abe's spirit.

"Right, man," he said, slapping my shoulder. It hurt a little. "I knew you were a friend, Oz. I tried to get my trackers to come with me, but the superstitious boogies are still completely spooked by the slaughtered village we came across. The pagan bastards said they wanted nothing to do with lions until, quote, the spirits are calmer, unquote."

Uncalm spirits; lions. I thought about my sinking feeling on the plane, the feeling of God's wrath in the air. Then I dismissed it. I wadded up my uneasiness and tossed it over my shoulder.

"Which way to Okavango?" I said, hefting my camera case.

Chapter 14

INSTEAD OF HEADING out of the airport, Abe and I walked south, inside the terminal, and made a right into a narrow, dingy corridor.

"What are we doing? I thought we were going to your brother's lodge," I said.

"Right, man, we are. In the northern delta, there are no roads, only airstrips," Abe explained. Walking, he dug a tin of chewing tobacco out of one of the pockets of his khaki utility vest, scooped some of it into his fingers, and put a wad under his lip. "We need to rent a plane."

"Rent a plane?" I said. "I hope you know how to fly one, because I only know how to jump out of them."

"That skill might come in handy," Abe said. His

jaw was working, moistening the chaw. He winked. "I have a license, but I have not flown in some time."

We went through a door and walked right back out onto the tarmac beside the plane I'd just exited. I noticed they were a little more lax with security here on the Dark Continent. No one even asked me to take off my shoes.

We turned a corner into a hangar. A half-black, half-Asian man in a greasy fedora sat behind a desk eating some kind of barbecued meat with his fingers. Another African, who looked like a soldier or policeman, judging by his soiled gray uniform and gray beret, sat next to him and wore a flat black AK-47 over his shoulder. They both had their feet up and were watching a movie on a portable DVD player. I peeked over the policeman's shoulder: it was *Happy Gilmore,* the Adam Sandler movie. They weren't laughing. Granted, it wasn't very funny, but they didn't seem to get that it was a comedy.

Abe spent about ten minutes bellowing like a bull at the two of them in a language I soon learned was Setswana. In the end, Abraham, his face sweaty, red, and puffy with heat, fished around in the pouches of his utility vest and handed the guy at the desk a folded wad of bills. The man thumbed through them with hands that were still sticky from the meat he'd been eating, seemed satisfied, and directed us outside with a Mafia tough's chin jerk that he'd probably learned from American movies.

We walked outside and down a lane between two rows of small bush planes. Abe threw open the door of a rust-flaked red-and-white Piper Super Cub that had cartoonishly oversize tundra tires and squeezed my bags behind the seats.

"Wait here, man," he said. "I'll be right back."

Abe went back into the hangar. When he returned a moment later, he was coming from the other end of the airport, riding in a battered Range Rover. Two dogs, sleek red-brown Rhodesian ridgebacks, tumbled out when he opened his door. They hopped into the plane as though they'd done so plenty of times before. Then Abe heaved two large gun cases from the truck and packed them into the plane as well.

He caught me looking at the guns.

"Better to have and not need than need and not have, right, man?" he said, giving my cheek an avuncular pinch.

Soon my ears were nestled in squishy radio headphones and we were taxiing onto the runway. On the other side of the airport's dusty service road,

I spotted a fenced field that had stones and strange striped tents in it.

"What's that, Abe?" I shouted over the gathering roar of propeller chop, pointing.

"That's a graveyard," Abe shouted back. He opened the plane's throttle and we began bouncing down the tarmac.

"So many dead from AIDS around here, they cannot dig fast enough. So they pile the coffins under tents. What's the American joke about cemeteries?"

"People are dying to get in?" I offered.

"Right, man. That's the one." Abe gave me a sardonic smile. His teeth were jumbly-crooked and tobacco-stained. He pulled back the throttle and our tiny plane left terra firma. "Welcome to Africa, man."

Chapter 15

EVEN WITH MY jet lag, the claustrophobic confinement of the plane, and a dog panting fragrantly in each ear, that thirty-minute plane ride was the most exhilarating of my life.

Flying over the Okavango Delta was like going back in time. I half expected to see dinosaurs walking around below us. There wasn't a single building, not a house or even a rondavel, on the endless brown plain rippling along beneath us. I watched the shadow of the aircraft glide over white islands dotted between clear blue ribbons of water. On them were palm trees and giant lumps of earth that Abe told me were termite mounds.

Now that it was July—one of the winter months, Abe explained—the delta dried up and swelled to three times its normal size, attracting one of the greatest concentrations of wildlife on the planet. We flew over hippos, hyenas, a herd of massive Cape buffalo, horned and black, which Abe told me were considered by some professional hunters to be more dangerous than lions. There were river birds, seemingly in the millions, scattering from the dry marshes at the sound of our plane. The first humans we saw were a couple of African fishermen in a hand-cut dugout. Who needs the Discovery Channel? I thought.

"This is it," Abe said a few minutes later, his voice crackling over my headphones. We lowered our speed and altitude as we banked down toward some thatched roofs beside the faint white scar of an airstrip. I was expecting the landing to be as bumpy as the takeoff, so I was surprised when Abe laid the Piper down as smooth as silk. I pulled off my headphones, and in the wake of the noise, the silence was almost ghostly. My ears rang a bit.

"That is funny," Abe said as we climbed out of the plane and into the heat. "Not funny ha-ha."

"What?" I said.

"The staff—when they see a plane landing, they are usually waiting here, clapping, singing their silly folk songs and holding a stiff drink and a hot towel.

I do not see or hear anything. Do you? Not even any animals."

He was right. The only sound was the thrumming drone of insects under the glaring sky. The thatch-roofed buildings in the distance, which we could see at the end of a dusty path lined with brittle brown reeds and papyrus, all seemed empty, deserted. A silvery band of light shimmered on the horizon, vague, shaking with heat.

Abe whistled and the two sleek red dogs broke into a trot, scouting ahead, heads scanning, their sense of smell going into overdrive. The camp we followed them into was as bustling as a graveyard. We searched all six platform tents, along with the dining area. We found clothes, luggage, safari gear, tourist stuff—pith helmets and khaki utility vests—open portmanteaus spewing socks and underwear onto unmade beds. But no tourists and no staff.

There was what looked like a shipping container —a giant red box of corrugated metal—behind the kitchen. Alongside it we found a Land Rover with two extra rows of raised seats to accommodate wildlife watchers.

Abe half coughed and half cursed in a language I didn't recognize. He spat a jet of shit-brown tobacco juice into the grass and wiped his mouth with his shirt.

"Two of the trucks are missing. Besides the guides, there are another half dozen maids and cooks. This is very strange, Oz. Where the devil is everyone? Where's my little brother? I have a bad feeling."

Abe put his fingers to his lips and pierced the air with a whistle, and the dogs came running. He hopped into the Rover, found the keys, and started the engine. After we drove back to the plane and retrieved his rifles, we drove north from the camp over a badly rutted car path. Pebbles popped and crunched under the tires, and the car rattled and shuddered over the washboard-like waves in the road. When the car path petered out, we hit an even bumpier field of tall dry grass. Around a stand of ebony trees, some baby hyenas were wading in the shallow river water, fat gloves of reeking mud on their paws. I couldn't help but gawk as though I were on safari, but if Abe noticed them or the family of giraffes drinking in the shallows a hundred feet south of them downriver, he didn't say anything.

We were steering around a stand of fig trees when we finally saw people. A group of Africans stood milling around by a dock at the river's edge.

It was two men and a pudgy boy, all in chef's whites, and they were preparing to get into some dugouts. Abe pulled hard on the wheel, piloted the Rover over to the men, and brought it to a jerky stop. He shouted something quick at them in Setswana. The men yelled something back. They seemed to be arguing. The conversation took a few minutes. At the end of it, the three kitchen workers reluctantly got out of the canoe and climbed into the back of the car. I turned around and looked at them. Their faces were stolid and blank, hard to read. They didn't acknowledge me.

"What's the story?" I said to Abe as we pulled away. Abe tucked another pinch of tobacco into his cheek.

"It's worse than I thought, man. Two groups went out day before yesterday—twenty people, including my brother. Haven't heard from them since. Not only that, they said lions were actually in the camp last night. Roaming around like stray kittens, picking at scraps. These bozos back there hid themselves in the shipping container. When they woke up, the radio transmitter had been broken, smashed somehow. Just now, they were going to try to go downstream to get help."

"Why were you arguing?"

Abe took off his straw hat and wiped sweat off his sunburned brow. Abe perspired like a leaky faucet.

"I told them to come with us to help find the tourists and guides, but, like my trackers, they're terrified. They said something is wrong with the lions. The same superstitious boogie shit. The gods are angry. There's black magic about. Ooga booga booga!"

Behind us, the cooks started singing some sort of chant.

"Ah, here they go," said Abe, jerking a thumb over his shoulder at them. "Ooh, ee, ooh ah ah, ting, tang, walla walla bing-bang!"

Abe stomped the brake and brought the Rover to a sudden stop. He hopped out, went into his bag in the back, and took out one of the hunting rifles. It was a Winchester Model 70 bored for a massive .458 cartridge. He loaded a magazine with the huge brass shells and slapped it home with a clack. He climbed up into the back, maneuvering around the men, bags, and dogs, and strapped it into the truck's gun rack.

"You bozos want black magic? I'll show you some black magic," he called back at them as he revved the engine and threw the truck into gear.

Chapter 16

A LITTLE LESS than a mile northeast of the safari camp's river dock, two massive male lions lounge on the highest rocks in their pride area. They lie on their stomachs, still as golden rugs, panting, catching the breeze. Their impassive amber eyes lazily scan the horizon.

Like dogs, but unlike humans, lions are unable to sweat through their skin. Their only effective means of thermoregulation is panting. The heavy breathing they are doing now, though, isn't from the heat, or even from exertion.

It is from eating.

Beneath them, scattered throughout the thorny scrub of the forest glen, swarms of fat, shiny flies hover above the meat that lies rotting under the sun's steady blaze. They tickle across the bones, collectively making a wavy droning noise like a cello holding a note in sustained vibrato. Human bodies—or, rather, human body parts—are strewn in the bloody grass. Rib cages and hip bones shine white as aspirin under the blinding sun.

The rest of the pride is arranged in a large, loose circle around the bones. Vultures hop around in the mess, their wings like shrugging shoulders, their necks like little worms, yanking rubber-snap strings of meat off the skeletons with their beaks. The lionesses and the cubs have eaten their fill, and are happily active now, tumbling around in the grass.

The two males are massive as golden hills. They are brothers, twins, almost identical, except now the older one is missing an eye, recently lost while taking over the pride. The brothers, having killed two of the former alpha males and driven off the third, have further established their dominance by devouring all their rivals' cubs, four young females.

But the swell of power and dominance they felt when they took over was a feeble feeling compared to the killing of the two human groups.

A new feeling has overtaken the lions, a new understanding. One that changed their perception of humans from fellow predators—irritating, inconsequential animals to be ignored, mostly—into prey.

They saw them coming. Two of the smaller, swifter lionesses had climbed into a sausage tree above the tire trail and lain in wait. When the cars passed, the lionesses dropped in from above on the open metal boxes full of the pathetically weak mammals. Once those big naked monkeys were on their slow, idiotic feet, it had been a quick rout.

It wasn't because the lions were particularly hungry. The humans had been nothing compared to the eighteen-hundred-pound Cape buffalo, the pride's more typical prey. The cars had been like boxes full of snacks.

The two males slip off the rock, first one, then the other. They amble through the pride, heads held high, ears perked up, mouths closed, tails swishing from side to side. After a moment, the females begin to follow, heads held low.

As the two lions approach, a vulture standing on a woman's face shrugs its shoulders and takes flight, flapping, awkward and sloppy as a big pigeon. The one-eyed lion nudges the meat with his paw. He holds it down and takes a bite, his jaw making a popping sound as his carnassial teeth efficiently peel meat off the bone.

After a moment's chewing, he looks up and turns his remaining eye to the east. His ears swivel, his nostrils dilate. His sense of hearing is only slightly above average, but the sebaceous glands around his chin, lips, cheeks, and whiskers give him a powerful sense of smell.

He smells something. He glances at his brother, who is looking in the same direction now.

Humans, the two convey to each other with a glance, a growl. More humans.

The two males turn to the pride, changing their expressions and postures. They go through a repertoire of vocalizations, varying intensity and pitch, telling everyone what to do.

Chapter 17

A CHATTERING FLOCK of storks burst from a treetop as we drove through a field some three miles or so north of the camp. They were marabou storks, distinguished by their wiry white hair, featherless pink necks, and tuxedo plumage—carrion eaters often found with vultures around carcasses. Undertaker birds, they're called. Abe grimaced up at them. He was projecting a cool facade, but I could tell he was worried, which made me worried.

Actually, I had already been worried.

Since we'd landed at the deserted camp, I'd found myself thinking about my first trip to Africa. It was a grad-school field trip to the famous rock beds of the Karoo desert region in South Africa, which showed one of the world's clearest geological snapshots of the history of life.

What I kept thinking about was a layer of sediment from two hundred and fifty million years ago that was completely empty of fossils. The lack of fossils in the rock was evidence of the Permian–Triassic extinction event—P–Tr, in geology shorthand. P–Tr, or the Great Dying, was the biggest and baddest of Earth's major extinction events. Ninety percent of all species on the planet rapidly perished. It took many millions of years for the earth's biodiversity to recover. There have been five such major extinction events; statistically, we're about due for one.

The K–T event, the one that killed the dinosaurs, was almost certainly caused by an asteroid impact. But we're still not sure about P–Tr. Some theorize that the P–Tr extinction was caused by volcanic activity. Or maybe an asteroid, or cosmic radiation. But no one really knows exactly why almost all the animals, vegetation, and insects in the world suddenly died.

It was the mysterious nature of that ancient total global ecosystem collapse that made the present HAC activity so unsettling. An animal's behavior is the result of millions of years of evolution, thousands upon thousands of generations of adaptation. This evolution happens in response to changes in the environment. The environment changes, and some animals adapt to it, some don't. To suddenly observe such anomalous behavior in wildly different species of animals all over the world wasn't just alarming, it was unprecedented.

I opened my camera case and began to ready my video camera. I clipped in the battery, polished the lens, strapped on the shoulder mount.

As we rolled deeper into the Okavango Delta in search of the missing tourists, I was suspecting more strongly that some kind of macro-level environmental disturbance was underway.

I'd clacked in a new mini DV tape and was switching on my pricey-ass Sony image stabilizer when there was a commotion behind me. Abe's two Rhodesian ridgebacks started barking like hell. Then, in an instant, my camera was no longer in my hands and something hard and cold was pressed against my throat and collarbone.

One of the men in the back was holding something against my neck, which I guessed was a machete, as that was what the other man had against Abe's neck.

Abe brought the truck to a careful stop and

began speaking in Setswana to the man holding the machete to his throat. Abe's negotiation skills seemed to be all that stood between me and a severed jugular. My heart was going like a jackhammer. I could feel every hair on my arms standing straight up. The man holding the machete to Abe's throat kept shaking his head and gesturing back in the direction behind us. Abe kept talking. The man shook his head.

"No-no-no-no-no-no-no," he said. "No, mon."

The man lowered the machete in order to hop out of the car. He held the machete pointed at Abe, but was only half paying attention as he worked with the other hand to liberate the Winchester from the gun rack. Abe reached into the inner lining of his utility jacket and his hand came out holding a nasty little snub-nosed .38 Special. Abe put the pistol barrel between the man's eyes: they crossed just as Curly's do when Moe pokes him in the nose. The man took his hands off the rifle and lowered the machete.

Then the guy behind me removed the machete from my neck. The men and the teenager exchanged glances, shrugged as though they'd just lost a bet fair and square, and hopped out of the truck. Without another word to us, they started walking away, back in the direction we'd come from. The dogs growled and barked after them, but Abe whistled them silent. Abe was red-faced and shaking. At first I thought it was from fear, and then I realized it was mostly anger.

"Cowards!" Abe yelled back at them between his cupped hands. "Boogie shite-asses! Scoundrels!"

He spat brown juice out the window, wiped his face on his sleeve, cursed under his breath, and released the clutch.

"Superstitious traitorous idiot boogie sons of bitches," he muttered, half to me and half to himself, maybe half to the dogs. "It's just us now, gents."

I leaned back in my seat and wiped sweat off my face as I closed my eyes. My pulse was still hammering when I turned and lifted the camera off the seat behind me.

Maybe Natalie had been right about my coming here to Africa, I thought. A cubicle in an air-conditioned office building wasn't looking quite so terrible to me right about now.

Chapter 18

A COUPLE OF miles farther north, we came upon some salt flats forked by a river delta. The scenery beyond them was breathtaking. An endless patchwork of more grassland and salt flats ran as far as the eye could see. I could understand why rich European and American tourists came to the Okavango Delta for safaris. The landscape was spectacular.

The trail we'd been following passed through a ford in one of the river deltas.

"Jesus, are you sure—" was all I could get out before Abe impassively stomped the accelerator and plowed us headlong into swirling water the color of chocolate milk. The water came up to the truck's door handles. I was expecting the motor to quit at any moment. I mentally prepared myself to go swimming. We got wet.

"You New Yorkers," Abe said, pushing us through the flood with his hand on the clutch and his foot on the gas, getting us through it with a mix of horsepower and will. He jerked his hat brim at the snorkel on the side of the truck. "Got it handled, man. Leave it to Beaver."

We slogged through to the other side and up the steep, muddy bank onto a plain of tall, light green grass, maybe about three or four acres wide. A path of tire tracks cut straight across it toward a lagoon that sparkled like silver, where a herd of seventy or so Cape buffalo were shouldering each other in a shallows.

"Look sharp," Abe said, pointing to the herd. "We're getting close now. Those are the buffalo the lions hunt."

I almost dropped the video camera when Abe stomped the brake and brought us to an abrupt stop halfway to the lagoon. At the other end of the tall glade of faded grass, an open Land Rover exactly like ours, with the name of the safari company on the side, was parked by a sausage tree.

Abe took a pair of binoculars from one of his kit bags and stood up on his seat. He slowly swept the glasses over the grassy plain. Then he lowered the binoculars, draped the strap over his neck, sat back down, and drove cautiously across the clearing toward the empty truck.

We stopped beside the vehicle and got out. Something shiny caught Abe's eye. He bent down to the ground and lifted something from the grass. I zoomed in on it with the camera.

It was a woman's gold Cartier tank watch. It looked as out of place here in the African veldt as a shrunken head would have on a plate at the Four Seasons. The alligator strap was encrusted with blood.

We got back in the truck and kept bucking and rocking over the grass. We weren't talking. There were clothes littering the ground around the empty truck and the trunk of the sausage tree, scattered among the grass and dwarf savanna shrubs. Blood-stiffened scraps of shirts, pants, a woman's sneaker, a fanny pack. Bits of fabric blew across the fields. There was a piece of what looked like a Hawaiian shirt stuck in the tree, fluttering on a branch like a flag.

Abe looked up into the canopy of trees and then over at the Land Rover.

"Look, man," he said, pointing. "See the rifle? It's

not even out of the rack. The safari guides who go out with the guests, they're no superstitious pussies like our dear kooky friends back there. They're professionals. This all must have happened in seconds. Too fast for them to get their guns."

"Male lions will protect their pride from humans, but this looks like some sort of ambush," I offered, trying to be helpful.

"And what did they do with the bodies?" Abe said. "Lions usually feed where they kill. I've never seen anything like this."

Chapter 19

STRETCHED FLAT IN the tall grass, the dominant one-eyed male lion crouches, waiting. Since hearing the distant grumble of the engine, he has been lying on the edge of the clearing about eighty feet to the east, just within charging range.

His powerful chest rises and falls under his almost strawberry blond mane. His dusky amber eyes narrow, focused on the distance. He opens his mouth slightly, whiskers tingling as he scents the dry wind.

Having hunted this pride area almost from birth, the ten-year-old male knows every inch of the terrain. At first, he'd lain in wait to the west, but moved when the wind shifted. A keen predator, he takes up a position downwind, so his scent won't be detected by his prey.

Zoo

He is waiting patiently for his prey to put its head down or face the other way, the optimum position for attack. Just a moment or two of distraction will give him enough time to charge. He will finish the stalk as he always does, by quickly knocking his prey off its feet and clamping his jaws on its throat.

He would have already attacked, except he is wary of people, unused to hunting them. He has been shot at several times before by hunters and game preserve rangers during his days of wandering, before he had joined his pride.

Without taking his eyes off the prey, the lion makes a low vocalization. It is answered by a soft growl, almost a purr, in the grass to his right, and then by another string of moans in the grass to his left.

In response to his call for a stalking attack, the two dozen lions at his back split into two groups, one to flank and herd, the other to wait in ambush.

The flanking lions begin skulking quickly, silently through the grass, using every scrap of cover. Their yellow and brown fur makes them all but invisible, tawny masses of grass-colored animals in the vegetation. They string themselves into a loose net around both the sausage tree and the prey, cutting off any chance of escape.

Chapter 20

ABE COCKED HIS head and whistled, and the dogs leaped from the truck and into the tall grass.

"Listen, man," Abe said as he sighted through his rifle's telescope. "If it comes up, the best way to kill a lion is a head shot, right between the eyes."

"Thanks for the tip," I said, continuing to film.

I lowered the camera a moment later when two sharp, loud dog whines rose in the air at the clearing's edge. One right after the other.

Abe whistled for the dogs. Nothing happened.

He put his fingers to his lips, whistled louder. Silence. "That's not good," he said.

Abe raised the Remington to his shoulder and pressed an eye to its sight. I swung my camera in the same direction and held my breath.

Zoo

A lion appeared in the grass twenty yards to our east.

I had never seen a lion in the wild before. It is a beautiful and terrifying sight. The sheer bigness of the animal. It truly makes something spin in your soul, deep below the ribs.

I was still in a state of unprofessional awe when Abe pulled the trigger. The blast of the rifle so close to me was like a kick in the head. It left a mosquito whine in my left ear. In the place where the lion had been standing a moment before, there was nothing. It was as if he had disappeared.

Abe climbed back up into the Land Rover.

"Get your ass up here if you feel like staying alive, man." That sounded like a good idea to me. I slammed the door, and then there was motion from the other end of the clearing. A second male lion broke cover and stood up in the tall grass, stock-still, tail swishing. Watching us. There was something otherworldly and bleak about his implacable, amber-eyed gaze.

The lion roared and began moving toward us. Slowly at first. Then something triggered in him, and he tumbled into a charge, coming at us at breakneck speed. Abe pulled the trigger just as he began his leap. Another jolting crack of firepower in the air. I saw a fistful of brain fly out of the back of his head. He died in the air and slammed onto the ground in a tumble, rolling into the driver's side of the truck, rocking it as though it were a cradle in the grass.

I kept filming as Abe kicked out the bullet casing. It pinged off the edge of the windshield with a sound like a wind chime. On the ground below, I noticed that the lion was still breathing.

Not for long. There was another whamming thud as Abe shot it right above the buttocks through the spine.

Abe replaced the three spent cartridges in the rifle's magazine. When he was done, he lifted off his hat and swiped his brow as he looked around the clearing. Silence. No insects, no birds. The shadow of a high white cloud raced over us. I took my eye from the viewfinder for a moment and glanced at Abe beside me. He looked sick.

I panned the camera, following his gaze.

In the grass about thirty feet away, surrounding the truck, was a circle of tawny heads.

All the lions had manes. They were males. Two dozen male lions.

Abe was blinking, a finger to his open lips. He was so puzzled that confusion got the better of terror.

"Impossible," he whispered. "All males?"

It didn't make sense. Male lions just don't do that. A pride of lions consists of a dozen or so related female lions and one, sometimes two, at most three or four males, if it's an unusually large group. Adult male lions who aren't part of a pride will hunt alone. Never—absolutely never—in the wild do male lions congregate in large numbers. It just doesn't happen.

Except it was happening.

I kept rolling with the camera as the male lions began moving. They moved forward for a few steps, then stopped to allow the lion behind them to go forward. They seemed like trained soldiers, coordinated, choreographed, synchronized.

I expected Abe to stomp on the gas and get us the hell out of there. Instead, his mouth pinched into a hard set. Almost in a single fluid motion he raised the rifle to his shoulder, sighted, and fired. Off to the left, the head of the lion closest to the truck blew open and the animal slumped into the grass.

Abe was swinging his rifle around for the next one when the grass in front of the truck opened up and a golden blur streaked in front of the camera.

A paw caught Abraham in the face, and there was a cracking sound as he flipped out over the driver's-side door.

Chapter 21

FOR A LONG—much too long—moment, all I could do was sit there in the passenger seat of the truck as if my ass had been nailed to it.

I was visited with the same sudden, gut-squeezing spike of fear I'd experienced when I first jumped out of a Black Hawk as an Army Ranger medic in the Battle of Fallujah. I'd stood there at the door like a dunce with his dick in his hand, unable to move. *Okay, here we go. Here we go. Okay, now.* Paralysis. *Here we go.* I even did the same thing I'd done that day as bullets sang past my confused, cotton-filled head.

Act, jackass! I mentally screamed at myself. *Do something!*

Abe's gun was lying cockeyed across the driver's

seat next to me. I snatched it up and anchored the barrel on the driver's-side door. The lion had Abe in his mouth, and was dragging him backward through the grass by the collar of his shirt.

The rifle kicked hard against my shoulder as I shot the lion in the head. I jumped out of the truck and ran the fifteen feet or so across the grass to where the dead lion lay and where Abe, his head pouring blood, was shakily climbing to his feet. My only goal at this point was to get us the hell out of there, get Abe to a doctor.

I draped his arm around me and we hobbled back to the truck. Abe was bigger than me and much heavier. It was slow going.

There was so much blood bursting from Abe's head I couldn't tell where the wounds were. I got him into the backseat of the truck, and I was trying to MacGyver a bandage out of his shirt when the truck rocked like a boat and almost tipped over. A lion had leaped onto the hood like a cat scrambling onto an armchair. He peered curiously through the windshield. His eyes were warm amber stones. They glowed like heat, blood, and honey.

I decided—if you want to call it that—the best place to be was under the steering wheel. I crawled into the front of the truck, toward the lion instead of away from it, a bit like a boxer leaning into a punch. I dropped under the steering wheel and squeezed myself in until I was crouching against the floorboard and clutching the gun. As I was waiting for my life to end, I reflected on the fact that the Rover was still running. I slammed my palm down on the gas pedal.

The engine roared in place, and nothing happened.

It wasn't in gear.

I pounded the clutch with my elbow and reached up and toggled the stick shift back and forth until I heard something catch. I let out the clutch and gave it some more gas with my other hand.

The truck lurched backward. I'd managed to put it in reverse, which was fine with me. We were moving. I pressed the accelerator onto the muddy floorboard with my palm and held it there, and I felt the driverless truck rocking and fishtailing at random across the grass. My head whacked against the steering wheel and the metal door frame as the Rover went bumping backward over the field. On the hood above me, I could hear the lion snarling; his claws clicked and shrieked against the glass.

With the car still in motion, I unwound a little from the fetal position to see his front paws and his massive shaggy head peeking over the top of the windshield—he looked like one of those old "Kilroy was here" drawings—and I reached up and cut the wheel hard to the left. The lion roared as he slid, scrabbling for purchase, off the windshield and fell beside the car, yelping as the Rover thumped against him.

And then we were flying. The Rover went airborne, backward off the steep riverbank, and for a moment, we were in the air. While bracing for impact, I had a good long two seconds of quiet time to reflect on the situation my life was in, and in those seconds, I decided that I really couldn't blame Natalie for dumping my ass. Then we hit the ground.

Chapter 22

ABE AND I both went sailing out of the Rover as it smashed backward into the riverbank a good ten feet below the sandy ridge. My body whumped into the muddy shore and the truck beside me tipped onto its side with a groan and a decisive crunch of metal, plastic, and glass.

I staggered to my feet, slapped mud from my face, and checked myself for injuries. I could feel bruises galore blooming all over my body, but nothing worse. The truck was still running, its engine panting, its back end submerged in muddy water. One sideways back wheel spun uselessly in the silt, stirring the muddy water.

Abe was in bad shape—as in probably dead. One of his legs was pinned beneath the sideways Rover, and his head was all wrong, almost perpendicular to his body. It looked like his neck had broken in the crash. He wasn't breathing.

I checked his pulse and wasn't surprised to find that he had none. Then I glanced up at the edge of the riverbank shelf we'd just been flung from. The heads of lions peered over it. A moment later they were spilling over its edge.

I backpedaled into the shallows of the river. There was one lion in particular—huge, bigger than the others, with a reddish mane and one eye. This one had it in for me. He came right for me.

I turned and dove deep into the river. Kicking as hard as I could, I swam as far out into the slow-moving muddy current as possible. This was a river in a time of drought—the water wasn't cold and it wasn't deep. It was warm, shallow, and dirty. I stood on my tiptoes in the middle of the river, and the water line was just below my head. I shook my hair, blinked water out of my eyes, spat, watched the shore. Abe's body was surrounded by six or seven lions, their manes rustling against each other. They pawed and picked at him as less majestic animals would do. But the other one, the big lion, strode past the sideways Rover and dove into the water after me, panting like mad as he paddled in my direction.

I'd thought I was safe. But no.

Lions hate water. They're not good swimmers—their dense, muscular bodies aren't built for it. They'll swim if necessary, to ford a river during the rainy season, for instance, but for a lion to chase prey into water is pretty much unheard-of.

I turned again and headed toward a sandy spit of land in the middle of the river.

Ten paces from the shore of the islet I saw a long black box bobbing in the water, drifting like a chunk of wood in the lazy current. Flotsam from the overturned Rover upstream. I splashed toward it, thinking I could maybe use it as a makeshift life preserver.

It was a life preserver, in fact: one of the gun cases Abe had brought. I snatched it from the water and slogged for the shore.

Stumbling, hurt, tired, with the gun case under my arm, I fought my way toward the reedy islet and felt the embankment rise under my heavy feet. I had no plan. I was beyond thinking. Ashore, I fell to my knees in the sucking reedy mud like a sinner in church, popped the clasps, *thwack-thwack,* and retrieved a flat-black bolt-action Mauser 98, a truly badass piece of machinery that had a barrel gauge like a plumbing pipe.

What had Abraham said? I thought as I slung the bandolier over my shoulder and filled the magazine to its limit. *Better to have it and not need it.*

Walking slowly backward onto the islet, I took aim at the giant cat that was paddling toward me in the river like a dog. He was mere feet away, emerging from the river, shaking off, flinging a thousand twinkling beads of water from his mane. I squared up the rifle, aimed between his eyes, and squeezed the trigger. The gun butt rocketed against my shoulder and the lion went down before me like a sack of potatoes, tumbling in a sopping heap into the river mud. PETA, forgive me. It was a beautiful creature, but it was also a very big, beautiful creature that was trying to kill me.

I turned my eyes back to the riverbank. I watched in disbelief as the lions loosed Abe's corpse from underneath the truck and hauled him back up the steep, sandy embankment.

Chapter 23

I SAT FOR a long time on the shore of the river island, staring at the spot on the opposite riverbank where the lions had carried off Abe's body. I didn't think they would come back for me, but I kept the rifle in my lap with the safety off as I sat on the muddy islet, reflected on what had just happened, caught my breath, and collected my wits.

Beside me, the lion I'd just killed lay on his side, sinking into the loose mud, his back legs in the river, tail floating, blood darkening the grass and eddying in the brown water.

Time to assess the situation. Okay, Oz, here's the 411: you're lost and alone in the African bush without any supplies. This is a situation that needs to be addressed, quickly. But every time I tried to start figuring out what to do next, my mind would wander. I couldn't stop thinking about what had just happened.

The more I thought about it, the less sense it made.

Lions are textbook examples of social mammals. Their pride structure, especially when it comes to group hunting, is one of the best-known and most well-documented social organizations in zoology. Lions live in prides, and female lions do the hunting. Nomad male lions will hunt alone, but male lions never hunt together in groups.

Except now, all that was out the window. I'd never even heard of mass male group hunting in lions before, let alone witnessed it. Also: why were these lions carrying off their kills? And why no females? Female lions are better at hunting, anyway. That's one reason why they do most of it for the pride—their lighter, more agile bodies are better built for it. Where the hell were the girls? I hadn't seen a lioness all day.

Such bizarre behavior in these lions wasn't just curious, it was mind-blowing. These lions were doing things that lions just did not do. What I'd just seen contradicted everything I knew about the behavior of this apex predator. Why?

This is to say nothing of the fact that lions are almost never actually harmful to humans. What's the point in hunting a human? We don't have a lot of meat on us. The way those lions had come after us, it was as if it were personal.

I knelt and cupped some river water in my palm, splashed my face. I would have to save my confusion for a time when I was in a more comfortable position. For now, I had to snap out of it. Ponder later. I needed to do something to fix my current predicament, stat.

Shifting the rifle in my lap, I patted a rectangular lump in the pocket of my wet khakis. It was my iPhone, which I'd jailbroken the day before so it would work in Africa. Ha-ha.

I shook it off: bubbles wobbled under the screen and water dribbled from the battery compartment. So much for calling for help. In any case I wouldn't have gotten coverage out in the remote African bush. Sure as hell not with AT&T.

I chucked the now-useless chunk of sleek Apple design over my shoulder and saw two huge, gray lumps the size of oil tanks float past me in the river. I stilled as two river hippos swam past.

Hippos are herbivores, of course—but they're enormous and aggressively territorial animals.

They'll kill without hesitation when they feel their territory is being invaded. They're actually some of the most dangerous animals you could encounter around here. I held my breath until the two malevolent tugboats disappeared around the bend in the channel.

Chapter 24

I HELD THE rifle and the bullets high in one hand to keep them dry and waded back into the river.

I emerged beside the sideways Land Rover with my eyes on the rim of the riverbank where I'd last seen the lions. All I had to call a plan was this: get back to the safari camp where Abe and I had landed, figure something out from there. Brilliant, wasn't it?

I searched the crashed truck for my things: I'd left my bigger bag back at the camp and taken a small canvas backpack with me. There it was, one strap stuck on the busted gearshift. I disentangled it and shouldered the pack. As I gave the truck another once-over, I spotted something curious. In the backseat, on the ground, was a little pinpoint of glowing red light.

Zoo

I knelt in the silt and retrieved my Sony camcorder. I'd forgotten about it. I mean, I'd had a lot on my plate for the last hour or so. The thing was splattered with mud and the lens was scratched half to hell, but not only was it still working, it was still on.

I stopped the recording, rewound it, and watched the footage on the view screen. After the crash, the camera had lain on its side in the mud and had accidentally filmed the rest of the attack. No, it hadn't been a nightmare. The lions filled the screen, manes flaring and eyes burning as they swarmed the Rover. It was a mess of snouts and teeth and paws.

Thing was—adversity aside, Abe's death aside—I had actually done it. I'd gotten what I'd come to Africa for.

Here was video evidence of inexplicable, hyperaggressive, aberrant animal behavior.

The footage was incendiary. This footage had the power to change the conversation. This was a cute story to tell at a Molotov cocktail party. The scientific community wouldn't be able to wrap their minds around this footage. Or be able to explain it.

It wouldn't be just the scientists, either, I thought. My gears were turning in double time now. The world would have to listen—they would have to start to realize that some sort of widespread environmental disaster was already underway.

Your first job now, Oz: survive long enough to get this thing back to civilization. That means not getting eaten. That means getting the hell out of here, now-ish.

I powered off the camera and zipped it up in the backpack. I checked the clip in the Mauser. Four rounds left. Bad news.

It didn't matter. I'd have to figure it out. This was bigger than me. I needed to make it out of here with this tape so the world would know what was happening. Ten-hut, Oz. Let's rock.

I glanced up at the sky: vultures were dropping to earth from their gyres. Back on the river islet where the dead lion lay, a peppering of flies already tickled the carcass, the sound of their wings reverberating in the air. A couple of marabou storks pranced daintily around the lion, piercing its flesh with their beaks now and then. They jostled for real estate with a smattering of African white-backed vultures. Speckles of blood flew as their rosy wrinkled heads bobbed up and down to beat the band, their beaks ripping delicate threads of tissue from the body and catching them in their throats.

Ah, the circle of life. The rivers flow into the

sea and yet the sea is never full and all that. Death becomes a meal ticket. Death was the modus operandi out here in the African bush.

Now if I could only avoid becoming part of this regularly scheduled programming: I had to get back to humanity with an important message.

Chapter 25

BACK UP ON the tall grass clearing where we'd been attacked, I hunched down and watched the other Land Rover, parked beneath the sausage tree, for a time.

I listened carefully. Nothing. The wind hushed the grass in rippling waves. Birds reeled in circles high overhead in a punishingly empty blue sky. I guessed it to be late afternoon. I debated going back to see if the truck was still working. Had the keys still been in it? I couldn't remember. What with all those lions leaping for my throat, I'd forgotten to check. Though it was a nice day, I definitely would have preferred to drive. A wide expanse of grassland the length of a football field stretched flat between me and the parked truck, which seemed deserted.

Zoo

But it was almost too quiet.

At last I decided against it. It was too risky. It would be foolish to go toward the lions. Though they were nowhere to be seen, that didn't mean anything. This was their neighborhood, and besides, there was no way to predict their unstable behavior. They could be on their way back right now. I knew I had to go in the other direction, on foot, back toward the camp.

I kept as low as I could as I skirted the glade. I found the rutted tire trail we'd driven in on and began following it back to the safari camp. Glumly I glanced up at the sun, which was starting to descend toward the salt flats on the horizon. It would be dark in a few hours. I wasn't looking forward to that.

I picked up my pace. The camp was only about five miles away, but I was looking at five miles through a zoo without cages, where some of the animals seemed to have gone schizoid.

The sun dried my clothes to a crust and then I got soaked again as I waded back through the river ford. I was hot and exhausted and starting to get thirsty, but decided not to drink the water for fear of parasites.

I walked for an hour or so before I spotted the

river dock where we'd picked up the Botswanans at the other end of a grassy field. They and their canoe were gone. After almost getting eaten, I didn't blame them for pissing off. They'd known how wrong things were in the environment. How important it was to get out while there still was a chance.

I headed toward the dock to see if there might be another boat. That's when I noticed a sudden movement in the trees off to my right. Though there was no breeze, the trees seemed to be waving—undulating—ever so slightly. They also seemed to glisten, as if they were slathered in oil.

I felt something crawl up my ankle.

It was an ant. And not just any ant. It was a *Dorylus*: an African driver ant. By its badass mandibles, I knew it was a soldier. Some indigenous tribes actually use the driver-ant soldiers themselves as makeshift sutures: their bite is so strong that putting one of them on each side of a gash will hold it together.

That's what was covering everything: the trees, the grass, the ground. Millions upon millions of driver ants swarmed through the field in a loose black column. It had to be at least a mile long and six feet wide. The ants were the size of a baby's fingers and the color of red wine.

Zoo

I flicked off the bug and squashed it under the heel of my boot.

Now, I love animals as much as the next biologist. But I do not like bugs. They don't do it for me. My subcortex says: *Ick. Get 'em off me.* I'd always known that entomology was not my bag. And the *Dorylus* is an especially nasty customer.

The frenzied column of ants connected two dark masses in the field. I realized they were Cape buffalo calves. My guess was they'd wandered into the path of the ants and been overwhelmed. Already dead, with most of their hides stripped, they were now in the process of being consumed by the living sea of bugs.

The *Dorylus,* or *siafu,* as it is called by the Bantu, can sometimes have colonies of fifty or sixty million. Like a foraging army, the colonies live on the march, attacking anything they come into contact with, including animals and sometimes children. Death often results from asphyxiation—when the flood of bugs crawls down the victim's throat. I cringed as I looked at the shiny, squirming black carpet extending into the distance. It was truly incredible.

Then I turned away and went to the river.

Chapter 26

I HAD JUST made it back to the trail when I heard a scream. It was hard to make out over the wind and splashing water, but it was definitely a human scream, coming from the direction of the river dock.

Apparently I was not alone out here.

I heard it again, and then once more as I ran back across the field, away from the ants. It sounded like a woman. I remembered the bloody clothes from the massacred animal-spotting safari and picked up my pace.

I arrived at the end of the dock and stopped short at the edge of the riverbank. There was a white woman with dark hair clinging to a large rock in the middle of the river. What the hell she was doing up there was a mystery. She was wearing khaki pants, but was barefoot. Her clothes were soaked flat against her skin. She clung to the pinnacle of the rock, scrambling for balance with her feet and hands.

I cupped my hands and shouted across the water: "Can you move?"

In retrospect it was a strange thing to say.

She glanced over at me, seeing me for the first time. The look she gave me was as if she'd never seen a person before. I didn't know whether she knew English or not. Then she let loose another scream, pointing upriver, to my right.

I followed the direction of her point with my eyes and saw what looked like a fifteen-foot-long clump of grayish mud appear on the surface.

It wasn't mud. This thing had more teeth than the average mud clump.

It was a Nile crocodile: the largest and most aggressive species of crocodile in Africa. As I watched, its scaly, spiny, and very powerful tail flicked, and it began floating out into the middle of the stream toward the woman clinging to the rock. I didn't know how the hell she'd managed to get herself into this situation, but I ordered myself to help her out of it.

I had four rounds left. Make them count, Oz.

I dropped to one knee and lined up the Mauser's sights with the crocodile's paddle-shaped head. I balanced the barrel against my arm, held my breath, and pulled the trigger.

The gun cracked and kicked hard into my shoulder, and I saw a splash in the water in front of the crocodile. I'd missed.

I sighted again and squeezed off two more shots. There was no splash. I'd nailed the son of a bitch, twice. I couldn't see where, but I'd heard bullets hitting meat.

But it didn't die. That would have been too easy. All it did was turn toward me with a quick sideways jerk of its surfboard-size head, as if I'd tapped it on the shoulder.

I blasted one more bullet at it and got the sucker right on the crown of its head. That did the trick. It stared out from the muck a moment, then sank and flopped over, belly-up, in the river.

I looked to my right again: a second crocodile, racing downriver in our direction.

Then I noticed the rest of them. In a lagoon some distance upriver was a bask of at least four crocodiles, and another three sunning themselves on the shore. No wonder they were riled up. It looked like the woman had entered a nesting area.

I aimed at the next approaching croc. It was coming at us like an animated hunk of driftwood. I pulled the trigger.

On nothing. I'd spent my last round, and the gun clicked on an empty chamber.

Chapter 27

HMM. THE CROCODILES glided through the water toward the woman while I sat on the bank with an unloaded gun. A lightbulb appeared over my head, and I threw down the gun.

I cupped my hands to my mouth and shouted across the water: "Be right back!"

I turned tail and began running back the way I'd come, into the field behind me.

I peeled off my wet shirt as I ran into thrashing brown grass. Just to clarify: I was about to dive into a horde of army ants with my shirt off. I ran through the glittering black carpet, feeling ants crunch under my boots with each step, to the corpse of the Cape buffalo calf. With my wet shirt I slapped ants from its gnarled, stiffened hooves, grabbed the body by the leg, and began dragging it back toward the river as fast as I could.

The ants went mad. A softly clicking, chattering swarm of ruby-dark ants followed after me. I could see the column shift and darken as millions of insects got new marching orders to deal with the intruder. I saw the message spread through the colony, borne on pheromones from one pair of antennae to the next. The only advantage I had was my legs.

The calf was lighter than I'd expected, as it had already been hollowed out some by the ants. The ants scampered up my arms and I swatted them off as best I could. I had ten or fifteen bites throbbing on my arms and chest by the time I made it back to the river dock. The pain was no big deal—it was only like being shot repeatedly with a staple gun.

The black swirling column had fallen a long way behind me by the time I arrived back at the riverbank.

Two crocodiles were swimming circles around the woman on the rock. I ran out onto the creaking wooden dock with the buffalo calf.

"*Hey!*" I shouted. "Dinnertime! Here!"

And I heaved the buffalo calf into the river. It splooshed into the slow muddy current below me like a fat kid doing a cannonball.

One of the crocodiles turned when it saw the heap of floating meat. A bird in hand is better than one on top of a rock, he probably thought. But the other one lingered, swimming a languid circle around the woman.

I snatched up the rifle and heaved it by its barrel at the crocodile. The butt of the rifle splashed next to its tail. Then it, too, turned and went toward the buffalo calf, following the other crocodile, who was now ripping into the dead meat. Confused ants stippled the thrashing water around them, flailing crazily on the surface of the river as the two crocodiles tore apart the carcass.

I ran along the shore until I was opposite the dark-haired woman. "Swim to me!" I shouted. "You have to swim to me now!"

She shook her head and closed her eyes, hugging the rock tighter.

"It's okay. You have to. You're running out of time. It's your only chance!"

She looked at me for a moment. She looked at the crocodiles, not far upriver. She climbed down into the water and pushed herself away from the rock.

She wasn't a good swimmer. Granted, conditions weren't ideal. Her arms slapped the water and her feet flailed. She seemed to take a day to paddle across the twenty-odd feet of calm water to the bank.

"Come on! Come on!" I said, my eyes flicking back and forth between her and the crocodiles.

I almost had to stifle the urge to clap when she finally arrived on shore. She stumbled when she tried to climb up the steep embankment onto the clearing, and fell to her knees in the mud.

"No, no! You've got it. Come on, take my hand."

I was lying flat on my belly, reaching my hand down to her. And then I felt a tickling cloud of insect legs skittering up my bare back.

"Hurry! *Hurry!*"

My backside was already flaming with pain.

The woman grasped my hand and I nearly ripped her arm off dragging her to her feet, up the embankment, and onto the clearing.

"Move!" I screamed, yanking her into a run with one hand as I slapped at myself with the other.

The ants were everywhere. On my neck, in my hair, my ears. I spat one out that had crawled into my mouth. The sound that involuntarily rose out of me was what I might call a shrill shriek of revulsion, like a woman standing on a chair screaming at a mouse.

I didn't stop running until I tripped over the tire

tracks and fell to the ground. Clear of the pulsing red-black column, I threw off my backpack and rolled over in the dust as though I were on fire, spitting and slapping at myself. I very literally had ants in my pants. With panicky, fumbling fingers I jerked at my boot laces and kicked off my boots. I tore off my pants and leaped out of them, yelping as I hopped up and down, flapping my pants as though they were a flag, ants flying out of the legs like flung pebbles.

After swiping them all off my legs, I thumbed the waist of my boxers for the most vital check of all. Clear.

"Thank God!"

Ant-free now, I squeezed my feet back into my unlaced boots and went about stomping the little bastards as they tried to scatter.

"Not so tough without your friends, are you?" I screamed at them, hopping like a crazed leprechaun, doing a little ant-killing jig in the dust. "Die! Die! Die!"

When the last ants scampered away, I caught my breath and inspected my arms, my legs, my chest, and back. My flesh was pebbled with welts, welts on top of welts, each about as red and juicy-looking as a maraschino cherry.

Suddenly, as though shaken from a dream, I remembered the woman. I turned and looked at her up close for the first time. She was petite—tiny as a child, with slender, birdlike bones. Even covered in river mud, she was undeniably good-looking—olive skin, bitumen-black hair slightly dusted with premature gray, sharp brown eyes, and high, distinct cheekbones.

"You saved my life," she said softly. She was still gazing somewhere into the middle distance. Her English had an elegant European lilt, what I thought was a French accent—vowels in the front of her mouth, consonants brushed with feathers. She hugged her knees, her body a seesaw anchored on her tailbone, rocking back and forth in the dirt. She definitely wasn't all there yet, but the lights were coming on.

Then I recalled I wasn't wearing pants. I slapped them into the dirt to knock any stray ants out of them and worried them on over my boots. I checked my camera in the backpack to make sure all was fine and sat down on a rock to lace up my boots.

"You saved my life," she said again, more lucid now.

"Actually," I said, grabbing her hand to pull her up, "I'm not done."

Chapter 28

WE HALF JOGGED the rest of the way back to the camp. It took us a little over an hour. In silence, the woman followed, still somewhat out to lunch in her brain, off somewhere else. It was late afternoon now, verging on gloaming, what photographers call the golden hour. The sinking African sun was huge above the darkening horizon, hanging there like a ball of burning blood. Bats had come out, flittering, swooping, and diving to catch insects. The world was beginning to chatter with twilight noises.

"Find some dry clothes and get changed," I said, guiding her into the first of the camp's platform tents. "We're not out of danger yet. I'm going to need your help barricading this place before nightfall."

After I left her, the first thing I did was look for

another gun. I couldn't find one, not in any of the other tents or the storage container. Not anywhere.

So I went to the next item on my priority list. I headed straight for the camp's centrally located bar and dining area and cracked the seal on a bottle of twelve-year-old Glenlivet—for medicinal reasons. I poured some on my smarting arms and legs and took a swig.

I was trickling Scotch down my back when I heard the unmistakable mumbling drone of a plane. Thank God. I ran out onto the little road that led to the airstrip and waved my arms as a single-engine plane buzzed low over the camp.

The plane waggled its wings in response as it flew past. It cut a wide arc around the camp and came circling back. As it roared overhead again, something fell from its window and landed in the reeds beside the airstrip. I searched thrashingly in the reeds and found it: it was a note crumpled around a stone.

"Staff informed us of situation. Need to check on camp farther upriver," the note said. "Back in twenty minutes."

I jogged back to the bar. Maybe we weren't dead after all.

I'd switched the Glenlivet for a bottle of Veuve Clicquot when the woman came in carrying a bag.

She was wearing fresh khakis and a faded white polo, but she was still filthy, scratched up, hair bedraggled, muddy, wet.

"Was that a plane?" she asked.

"Yeah," I said from behind the bar, unwinding the wire cage around the cork. "They saw us and dropped a note saying they'll be back soon." I thumbed out the cork. It popped and hit the drum-tight inner wall of the tent. The bottle smoked and white foam cascaded over my fingers like a science-fair volcano. I slurped Champagne off my wrist and took a swig.

"*Vive la* being out of here in twenty minutes," I said, offering her the bottle.

"Twenty minutes?" she said, eyes brightening with panic. "But we need to get out of here now!"

I looked at her hands: they were shaking like a machine about to break. I put the bottle on the bar and walked around to her.

"It's okay," I said. "We're going to be okay, Miss . . ."

"My name is Chloe. Chloe Tousignant," she said. She slumped and gripped the counter with one hand. She began to look sick, the color draining from her face.

"Listen, Chloe," I said, guiding her onto one of

the bar stools. Her thin shoulders were shaking. I tried to rub them, but the muscles under her skin were so tensely knotted it was like massaging sponge rubber.

"You've been through hell, but you're okay now. I promise you. Nothing's going to happen now."

She didn't reply. Her color wasn't getting better.

"Come on, Chloe," I said. "Stay with me. Can you talk to me? Who are you? Were you with the safari that was attacked? Were you on vacation?"

"No, I'm not a tourist. I'm a scientist. Population ecology." The words came out of her in a rapid, piqued flutter. Talking seemed to help, at least. "Our group came from the École Polytechnique in Paris."

That's an impressive institution. École Polytechnique is basically the French MIT. Female biologists I knew usually didn't look like ballerinas. They tended to favor Morrissey T-shirts and combat boots.

"Have you seen anyone else?" Chloe said. "I was with two colleagues, Jean Angone and Arthur Maxwell."

"No, I'm sorry," I said. "You're the only other person I've seen, besides some Botswanan cooks who threatened us with machetes and the guy I came in with, and he's dead."

She shook her head and bit her lip as she stared, glassy-eyed, at the floor.

"Why were you here?" I said. "A field trip?"

"Yes," she said, nodding. "We were collecting data on migratory birds at the Moremi Game Reserve. We came here to the delta two days ago. The lions attacked at dusk the day before last. They fell from a tree. The guide died first, and then everyone ran. I don't know how I escaped. I fled across the water and spent the night in a tree. When I heard your truck, I climbed down and headed for the sound. I was wading back across the river when I saw the crocodiles, and climbed onto that rock, and then just stayed there waiting for them to go . . ."

She closed her eyes and took a shivery breath. When she opened them again, I suddenly realized I'd been wrong about her. She wasn't just good-looking. There was something else, something austere and regal about her face. She was beautiful.

"And you are?" she said. "An American reporter? A documentarian?"

"My name is Jackson Oz," I said. "I came here to try to document aberrant behavior in lions. I got a tip that the lions in Botswana were acting weird from a guy I know—well, knew—Abe Bindix, who guides safaris here. Or did. His brother ran this camp, but he'd been out of contact for days, and we came to check on him. We were searching for you when the lions attacked us today. I escaped, but Abe died. There was nothing I could do."

Before I knew what was happening, Chloe softly took my hand in hers. She leaned forward and gave me a soft kiss on both cheeks.

"Thank you so much for what you did," she said, starting to tear up as she continued to hold my hand. "I was so tired. I was in despair. If you hadn't come along right then, I'm not sure if—I don't know if I would have lived."

"Well, you're here now," I said. I found myself wanting another brush of her lips. I squeezed her hand back, swiped the Champagne bottle from the bar, and offered it to her. "You made it. We both did."

"So you're not a documentarian. Who—I mean, what are you?" she asked.

"I'm actually a scientist, too. A biologist."

"From Columbia University?"

"Yes," I said. "How'd you know?"

She took a swig of Champagne.

"It was written on your underwear."

Chapter 29

"JACKSON OZ. COLUMBIA University," Chloe said. To my great irritation, I felt my face reddening. "I thought I knew all the names from Columbia. Do you know—er . . ." She put a thin finger to thin lips and her eyes turned up, trying to think of a name. "Michael Shrift?"

"Mike was my adviser," I said.

"Oh, so you are—er—a student?" Chloe said.

I liked her accent. This woman somehow made being confused sexy.

"Well, actually, I dropped out," I said.

She gave me a cockeyed glance, the needle of her WTF-ometer twitching.

"You dropped out? Um . . . let me guess. You have a blog."

"Yeah," I said, brightening. "Do you read my blog?"

"No," she said, taking another sip from the Champagne bottle. "It was just a guess. But I will now. Since you saved my life."

I didn't like the faint note of sarcasm in her voice. When things aren't going your way, change the conversation.

"What was your population study about?"

"Over the last few years, there has been a big change in some migratory bird populations," Chloe said as she shifted the bottle to her other hand and looked at the label. "Changing very rapidly. We do not know why."

"So you're saying what?" I said. "Birds are dying?"

"No," Chloe said, picking at the foil on the bottle with her thumbnail. "It's just the opposite. Bird populations are increasing at incredible rates. Exponential. It is very, very strange."

I thought about that. Like frogs, birds are often indicator species—animals whose population stability is a good measure of the stability of an ecosystem. Changes in the environment affect them quickly. Did this have something to do with HAC? I wondered.

"Tree nesters?" I said raising an eyebrow.

"Yes, and shrub and ground nesters as well," she said. "The phenomena are so unprecedented that many of the faculty in Paris refuse to believe it. That's why my colleagues and I came here. To gather data. I think something very, very wrong is happening to the environment."

"So do I," I said, talking fast now, getting excited. "It's not just the birds. There's been a massive outbreak of animal attacks on human beings over the last three years. The lions that killed your friends and mine, that wasn't just an isolated incident. Human beings are being increasingly attacked by animals. There's something that's gone completely haywire with the lions in this area. And other species, too. I think there's something badly wrong with the environment that's changing their behavior."

I rooted around in my backpack for the camera and set it on the bar.

"Look. This happened this afternoon."

Her face betrayed shock as she watched the footage.

"Oh, my God! That can't be right. I was so busy running for my life, I hadn't noticed. The lions were all male? How can that be? That has never happened before."

She shook her head at the screen and looked up at me with dinner-plate eyes.

"You need to show this, Jackson," she said. "People must see this."

"They will, Chloe." We began to hear the low thrum of a plane engine in the distance. "And please. Call me Oz."

Chapter 30

SIX HOURS LATER, wearing my good shoes and scratching one of those maraschino-cherry ant stings below my ear, I went clattering down the back stairs of Riley's—Maun's largest, and as far as I knew only, hotel.

Dropping my packed bags beside the scuffed brass rail of the outdoor hotel bar, I looked around for Chloe, whom I was supposed to meet for a quick drink before my midnight flight out of Botswana.

I did a double take when I spotted her talking on her cell phone, her luggage bunched beneath her feet at the bar stool. We had both been so bitten, bloody, and dirty we'd looked like mud idols when we came out of the bush a few hours before, but now, in a pale yellow dress with her hair still damp from the shower, Chloe was stunning.

I was struck by how happy I was to see her. Besides her obvious assets, I couldn't get over the toughness, the dogged will to live that this tiny slip of a woman had shown in surviving the trials she'd been through over the last few days. Meeting her had been one of the only good things to come out of this whole situation. That and the footage I had caught.

It was late, and there was almost no one in the bar: a group of tourists keeping quietly to themselves in one corner, a couple of gruff-looking drunk men at one table, and a piano player at a baby grand striking notes that tinkled over the steady sploosh of a fountain in the middle of the enclosure. The marble bowl of the fountain was lit from below, and the water flashed veins of blue-green light.

I turned away from Chloe when a tall, gaunt, red-haired man walked into the bar. It was Robinson Van der Hulst, Abraham's business partner and the pilot who'd found Chloe and me and flown us out of the bush.

"What's the word, Robinson?" I said as we shook hands. "Are the authorities collecting the lions for autopsies?"

Robinson shook his head regretfully and looked over his shoulder.

"The government game rangers are so busy they won't even help me retrieve the bodies. There's a lot going on, Mr. Oz, none of it good. For one thing, yours wasn't the only attack today."

Robinson glanced over his shoulder again.

"The whole delta is in chaos, man," he said. "Two other camps were attacked by lions and another two have been out of radio contact for twelve hours."

I blinked at him. The animal crisis that I'd been trying to convince people was coming for years seemed to have arrived full-blown in a single day.

"I even heard that the largest camp in the delta, Camp Eden, was attacked by jackals, of all things."

"Jackals?"

The implausibilities kept compounding, one on top of another. Jackals are basically coyotes. They occupy the same niche in the ecosystem. Once in a blue moon you'll hear about a jackal making off with a baby or something like that, but it's so rare that if it happens, it makes the news. Jackals don't attack adult humans. They just don't. Jackal attacks on humans are so rare that there isn't even any data on them. Feral dogs, wolves, dingoes, and so on might attack people now and then, but even those attacks usually occur because the animals are rabid.

That thought clicked on another lightbulb over my head.

"Listen—do you think there's any chance these attacks might have something to do with a virus? Like a massive outbreak of rabies? Robinson, you have to ask the authorities again. Hell, you have to *tell* them. The bodies of the lions, the jackals, all these animals need to be collected and studied. We need to do autopsies, tests for rabies—yesterday."

"You don't understand, Mr. Oz," Robinson said, shaking his head at me. "The authorities here aren't scientists. They're politicians. Which in Africa means they're thugs. Believe me, they're not in a listening mood right now. There must be close to a hundred people missing, and they're panicking. It's so bad, I hear they're going to issue an evacuation order for the entire delta. I've heard rumors the military is on its way."

At that moment, we saw a pickup truck roar up beside the hotel and come to a squealing, jerky halt. The smoky diesel engine of the parked truck hammered and chugged. A middle-aged African in a crisply ironed white shirt got out of the passenger door and marched into the bar. His head was roughly the size and shape of a basketball. Two young soldiers carrying AK-47s hopped out of the truck bed and filed in behind him. There was an immediate and palpable tension in the bar. The two drunk men at the nearby table quit talking.

"That's Assistant Superintendent Mokgwathi," Robinson whispered to me. "Maun's top cop. What now?"

The piano player stopped playing, and the vacuum of silence was louder than the music. The fountain splashed, glass clinked behind the bar.

"I must speak to a Mr. Oz," Mokgwathi said to the room in a deep and musically sweet African accent. "A Mr. Jackson Oz."

My legs twitched, and I was about to step forward when Robinson squeezed my shoulder and kept a vise grip on it. Chloe's eyes flashed at me from the bar and quickly looked away. Robinson didn't let go until the policemen, getting nothing from the room but vacant looks, pivoted on their jackboots and left the bar.

"What's up?" I said. "Why would they be looking for me?"

"Do you have your plane ticket?" he said.

I nodded.

"Good," Robinson said, grabbing my bags and jerking his head in the direction of the street. "My truck's around the corner. It's time to get you to the airport and onto your plane."

"I don't understand," I said.

"Someone in the hotel must have seen your camera and alerted the police," he said. "Tourism is big business here, man. One of the only businesses. If word gets out that animals have gone bonkers and are killing tourists, that's bad news for Botswana's GDP, isn't it? This is very dangerous for you."

"What is dangerous?" Chloe said. She'd watched the episode with the cops over the rim of her drink and now stood beside us with her bags.

"I'll tell you on the way to the airport," I said, shouldering her carry-on as I led her toward the street.

Chapter 31

AT THE AIRPORT, all the seats were taken in the Air Botswana waiting area. The terminal was filled to capacity, crowded with tourists coming in from evacuated safari camps.

The air buzzed with fear and nervous excitement. The tourists looked scared and confused, though I was glad to see that many of them were texting or talking on their cell phones. With the threat of a government cover-up looming, I hoped word of this craziness was already leaking to the press.

It took no small amount of persistence, as well as a folded hundred-dollar bill, and then another, to snag Chloe a seat on the midnight flight to Johannesburg with me. From there, we'd be going our separate ways. I was headed back to the US, I hoped for a press conference at which I would show the lion footage. Chloe needed to return to Paris.

I was glad I'd decided to leave the camcorder with Robinson when the airport scanners pulled me out of the security line for a more thorough search. I held my breath as the inspectors tossed my bags and wanded me. They missed the DVR tape I'd hidden in my pants, taped against the inside of my thigh. No TSA-style pat-downs out here, thank God.

As I was standing by the window at the gate, looking out onto the runway, my stomach dropped like an anchor when what looked like a military cargo plane blasted in. It was thick and snub-nosed, painted brown. Was the Botswanan military really crazy enough to try to quarantine this thing? I didn't want to find out.

Things were changing right in front of my eyes, I realized. Whatever this phenomenon was, it was spreading, getting stronger, catching hold. The jittery feeling of a rising crisis was in the air, like the feeling before a hurricane.

But I was convinced HAC wasn't a local problem. It was a global one. Governments and military forces have enough trouble dealing with large-scale problems one at a time. How were they going to be able to assist everyone everywhere, all at once?

This problem would call for an unheard-of amount of global cooperation. And I didn't see it happening yet.

"So you really think this thing is real, Oz?" Chloe said. Her eyes were focused out the window. Outside on the rough tarmac, soldiers spilled from the plane, Trojan Horse–style. "All around the world, animals suddenly attacking humans for no reason? And not other animals? I mean—how can that be? Why? Why now? It sounds—er—completely crazy."

"I don't know how or why, Chloe," I said. "All I know is that bird populations don't just double in the course of several years, and lions don't just suddenly, radically, inexplicably change their hunting behaviors. Something very weird is going on."

The temporary cell phone I'd bought in Maun that day rang as we were standing in line to board the plane. It was a voice mail from Gail Quinn, a former professor of mine at Columbia. It was good news. She'd shaken some trees and managed to arrange a meeting about HAC with Nate Gardner, the senior senator from New York.

"What is it?" Chloe said when I hung up, smiling. We were on the small passenger plane, hunching under the low ceiling.

"Good news. I have a meeting with one of the most prominent leaders in Congress about all this. With the videotape, I might have a real shot at getting the US government to help."

A depressing thought hit me as I was stowing my bag in the overhead. What if Senator Gardner reacted to me the same way Chloe initially had? Since I dropped out of Columbia before I received my doctorate, what if he thought I was just some wacko blogger, spinning Internet conspiracy theories between naps on my mother's couch? Sometimes I forgot to step back and look at how nut-jobby I could seem.

"Hey, I have a crazy idea," I said as I sat down next to her. "Because I'm crazy. Chloe, I know you have a lot to do after all this, but would it be possible for you to come with me?"

"What?" she said. "Go with you to the US?"

"You're right," I said, facing forward. "Like I said, it's crazy. Forget about it."

"No, wait," Chloe said. "I mean why? Why do you want me to come?"

"Well, your credentials, for one thing," I said. "Your degree. The École Polytechnique. You're a credible expert. Even better, a credible European expert who's seen and experienced the same things I

153

have. I'm concerned that the senator might initially react to me the way you did. He'll think I'm a crackpot. He'll probably look at me like I'm wearing a tinfoil hat. But if you're there with me . . ."

She raised an eyebrow.

"But please," I said. "Don't worry about it. I'll figure it out."

I took out my phone and pretended to play with it. Out of my peripheral vision, I picked up her aquiline nose doing a little crinkling thing as she squinted at me.

She leaned back in her seat as she let out a deep breath.

"It isn't a choice," she said as the plane began to taxi. "There really is some sort of environmental disaster happening. What kind of biologist would I be if I didn't do everything I could to solve this? Besides, you saved my life. I owe you a favor. So I'll go. On one condition."

"Anything."

"I hate flying. Can I just—er—hold your hand as we take off?"

I smiled as I slipped her fine-boned hand in mine.

"Twist my arm," I said.

Chapter 32

THE BROADWAY LOCAL clatters past on the elevated subway track when Natalie Shaw arrives at the door of Oz's building.

It's just past five a.m., still dark, though the sky is beginning to turn blue, and the steel-shuttered Harlem streets are empty. New York City actually does sleep after all, she thinks. The backs of her knees and armpits are misty with sweat in the already warm predawn summer air. She yawns as she keys herself into the dingy lobby. She's stopping by on her way home from the hospital, having just put in a thirty-hour shift, and she's half dead on her feet.

Trudging up the building's coffin-width stairwell, she still doesn't know why she's doing this. She pretty much broke up with Oz in her e-mail, and told him to find someone else to look in on Attila. It's the fact that he hasn't gotten back to her. Annoyed as that makes her, she can't help but wonder if maybe he never got the message, and now Attila is starving or something.

Getting closer to Oz's apartment, she doesn't have to wait long to find out that that's not the case. She can hear Attila by the time she gets to the third floor. Christ, she can actually smell the damn thing as she climbs onto the fifth-floor landing. She's baffled by the fact that Oz's neighbors haven't petitioned to kick him out of the building.

But then again, she put up with him for a long time, didn't she? I'd do anything for love, she thinks, but I won't do that. What? Take a detour home after a thirty-hour shift to go clean up chimp shit? Well, apparently I will do that. Except it's not for love; you already broke up with the bastard. To hell with the chimp—you're a chump.

In and out, she thinks, fishing Oz's keys from the pocket of her turquoise hospital scrubs. Five minutes. Feed the monkey, clean the monkey— maybe—then get the hell out.

Attila goes apeshit as she comes in. Natalie winces as she approaches, and the chimp goes berserk with shrieking. It's a piercing, nails-onchalkboard *EEE-EEEE-EEEE* sound, the edge of it like a pocketknife slicing her eardrum.

"Nice to see you too, asshole," Natalie says, lifting the pooper-scooper as she unlatches the door of his cage. "Your face could make a freight train take a dirt road, did you know that? Anyway. Lucky me is here to gather your droppings."

She bags her rubber gloves along with the crap before coming back with the food. Tangerines, a stack of Fig Newtons, and a pound of deli roast beef. Not to mention the goddamn applesauce with the crushed-up vitamins and Zoloft. All of it on a tray. Surprised it wasn't silver. Oz takes better care of this chimp than he took care of her.

"Bon appétit, monsieur." Natalie sets down the tray and latches the cage again. "Breakfast is served. Don't choke on it."

Her hand is on the doorknob when she hears a noisy thump come from Attila's direction.

"Ugh. What now?"

She hurries back into Attila's room. She stops short in the doorway.

Attila is on the floor of the cage, the food scattered pellmell all around him. He's lying facedown, his hands under his chest. He isn't moving.

What in the hell? Did he have a heart attack or

something? That's all we need, she thinks, undoing the latch. To have the thing die on her before Oz comes home.

She bends down, nudges him, tries to turn him over. Attila spins around and wipes a reeking handful of shit across the shirt of her scrubs. He shrieks and smears it down her chest and onto her pants. Then he jumps back into the corner of the room, pant-hooting, howling, "*EEE-EEEEEEEEEAHHHH!*"

Natalie stands, looking down at herself in disgust.

"You evil little bastard!" she shouts at the chimp.

Then Attila quits screaming. He shuts his mouth, and with his sweet, expressive brown eyes he gives her a cold, quizzical look that makes her begin to slowly back away.

Chapter 33

HOT, GLARING LIGHT bores through the diamond-shaped spaces between the links of Attila's cage as he lies, unmoving, on the cluttered floor of his room, all alone again.

Slowly, he rises to his feet and crosses the hallway into Oz's bedroom. He yanks out the drawers of the dresser. After upending the drawers, he ransacks the closet, hooting and screeching as he tosses jeans and shirts across the floor.

Then he pisses over everything. He drenches the clothes and continues on to the bed, training the hot yellow stream on the pillow.

That done, he snatches the fire-engine-red hat from a bedpost and knuckle-walks into the hallway bathroom. The wall bolts of the sink creak as he pulls his weight onto it.

He looks at himself in the mirror and positions the red hat on his own head at a rakish angle. He crouches on the edge of the sink, opposable toes gripping the porcelain rim, staring at himself.

Attila sits blank-faced on the sink, motionless and tense, as he stares into his own glassy brown eyes, his rubbery, masklike face. Attila is confused, becoming more agitated by the moment. Something strange and awful is stirring in his soul. He feels alienated by his own reflection.

From the moment Natalie arrived, Attila had detected an odd, unsettling smell—a mixture of the apricot scent of her shampoo, her minty deodorant, even the slight acrid whiff of nail polish on her toes. There was something queasy, bad, sickening about the combination of smells on her. All those grubby odors mingled with the worst smell of all—the scent of her, her resentment of him, her disgust. He smelled that. He had smelled her contempt.

That's why he had tricked her.

Attila returns to his cage. From the corner he retrieves what looks like a children's toy tablet. It is a PECS—a Picture Exchange Communication System—a talking touchscreen laptop designed to help teach language to autistic children, which Oz has used in his experiments with Attila.

On the screen are rows of pictures, things that Attila might want, such as bananas, peanuts, balls, and dolls. Also scattered among the columns are pictures of faces displaying various expressions.

Again and again, Attila presses the picture representing himself, and then the face in the lower right-hand corner of the grid.

"Attila, *angry!*" says the chipper, computerized female voice to the empty apartment. "Attila, *angry!*"

BOOK THREE

HOME SWEET HOME

Chapter 34

MAUN TO JOHANNESBURG, Johannesburg to New York, New York to D.C. The chirping of the jet's landing gear and the accompanying jolt of bumping wheels woke me up as we touched down at Reagan National Airport.

As we thudded along the runway I gaped out the window at the majestic and welcome sight of the Washington Monument's ivory spire across the Potomac. I remembered coming down to D.C. from New York on Amtrak with my dad to see the sights when I was a kid. We would visit the Lincoln Memorial, throw pennies in the reflecting pool. Everything had seemed so solid then. So rational and safe.

I reached into the seat-back pocket in front of me

and took out the DVR tape of the lion attacks that I'd smuggled out of Africa. That was then, I thought, shaking my head at it. This is now. Then I slipped the tape into my shirt pocket.

I turned on the iPhone I'd bought in the airport: my in-box was flooded with e-mails, and there were nineteen voice mails. During the layover in Johannesburg I'd been contacting every scientist I could think of who might have any interest in HAC.

I'd put out the Bat-Signal all over the world, and had managed to scramble together a last-second rendezvous with several of my allies before my meeting with Senator Gardner. This was our first shot at getting HAC taken seriously by the world, and I wanted to go over everything one last time to make sure we had our story straight.

I looked beside me at Chloe, sleeping peacefully with her head against my arm.

No wonder she was exhausted. We'd talked pretty much nonstop on our transcontinental trip back to the States, going over all possibilities about HAC. I was a little amazed at how quickly we also slid into more personal matters. Our childhoods, families, the kinds of things that really mattered.

Chloe's mother had died when she was five.

Her father was a career military man, an officer in the French Foreign Legion, who often left her on her grandparents' isolated cattle farm in Auvergne. Her grandfather, a retired civil engineer turned farmer, opened her eyes to the wonders of the natural world—farming, gardening, and especially animals.

As the plane wheeled toward the terminal, Chloe woke up and, seeing me watching her, sat upright as she rubbed her eyes.

"I'm sorry," she said.

"Nothing to be sorry about," I said as the seat belt light bonged off.

When we'd made it off the plane, I stopped in front of a breaking-news feed scrolling across a newsstand TV.

"What is it?" Chloe said.

"I don't know," I said. "I was hoping CNN picked up on the animal attacks in Botswana."

It was craziness, all right. But not ours. A girl with a shaved head, some sort of pop singer, was attacking a car with a broken umbrella while a dozen paparazzi recorded her every move.

KITTY KATRINA SHAVES HEAD, ATTACKS PAPARAZZI. HAS KITKAT GONE OFF THE DEEP END? shouted the crawler at the bottom of the screen.

"Who's Kitty Katrina?" Chloe said, looking at the screen, confused.

I shrugged.

"Welcome to America," I said.

Chapter 35

THE ROCKFORD HOTEL, where our meeting was scheduled to take place, is situated in a run-down, slightly sketchy area of southeast D.C. across the water from Buzzard Point.

We checked into separate rooms and dropped off our things. I showered and used the quick moment of peace and solitude before the meeting to call Natalie. It was early afternoon on a Wednesday, and I was pretty sure she was off work at the moment. Her phone rang until I got her voice mail.

"You've reached the voice-mail box of"—said a robot, and then a pause, and Natalie's bright bell of a voice carefully saying her own name—"Natalie Shaw."

"Please leave a message after the tone."

"Hi, Natalie," I said into the void, looking out the hotel window at the Potomac. "I'm back in the States. I saw your e-mail. I just wanted to talk things out. I'm in D.C. right now, but I'll be back in New York tomorrow, I hope. Let me know what's up."

In fact, I was mainly worried about Attila. It had been almost a week since I'd left him. I hadn't heard back from Mrs. Abreu, either. I hoped he was all right.

I had work to do.

"Are you sure we're in the right place?" Chloe asked as we entered the shabby hotel ballroom. The carpeting was criminally ugly—stain-mottled and worn thin in the heavily trafficked spots.

There was a small crowd milling around a table set with cheap hors d'oeuvres, water pitchers, and coffee urns. It was a sea of flannel, glasses, and beards, swarming around the free food as enthusiastically as the vultures I'd seen in the Okavango Delta.

"Believe me," I said. "We're in the right place."

On our way to the front of the room, we passed a young, skinny white guy with intense blue eyes and blond eyebrows that disappeared into his face. He was wearing a red tracksuit and a white Kangol hat, and was bent in ferocious attention over the glowing oracle of his iPad. Spotting us, he jumped out of his seat and gave me an awkward fist bump.

"Word to your moms, Ozzle," he said.

"Dr. Strauss, thanks for coming," I said, introducing him to Chloe. "Eberhard was just awarded the microbiology chair at the University of Bonn."

Chloe and I walked on. "You see why I need you now?" I said, gesturing at the rows of World of Warcraft diehards we passed. "These guys are all beyond brilliant, but, as you can see, PR is not their strong suit. That's why it's so important that you agreed to come with me."

"And I thought you wanted me for my mind," Chloe said, smiling.

"Give me the tape, Oz. The audiovisual is in operating order," said a fresh-faced kid dressed as though he were ready for a rodeo. His shoulders were hunched up to his ears and his long arms dangled stiffly at his sides. He turned and sniffed loudly at Chloe's hair.

"Your hair smells good," he said in a too-loud voice, half Okie and half machine, as if Robby the Robot had grown up in a Steinbeck novel.

"Jonathan, thanks, man. Here you go." I handed him the tape and ushered Chloe along.

"Don't mind him. That was Jonathan Moore. He's

an autistic savant, and one of the best agricultural engineers in the world. He's a renowned animal communicator. He was one of my first contacts when I started researching HAC. He helped me work with Attila."

I had rolled the dice and told Chloe about Attila on our flight. I even showed her my wallet pictures. She said she thought I was brave for having rescued him. So she seemed cool with it. Go figure.

Chapter 36

SOME MINUTES LATER I found myself on the stage, tapping the podium microphone. The feedback squealed and settled down. The murmuring room went silent, and all heads swiveled in my direction.

"Without further ado, folks," I said, nodding to Jonathan, who gave me a thumbs-up by the projector. "This is what is happening in Africa. It speaks for itself. I recorded this two days ago in the Okavango Delta in Botswana."

I stepped back into the dark to watch the room watch the video. I was pleased to see that they were stunned. When the male lions' heads appeared in the field, a wave of whispers rose up in the room. These were some very smart folks, and I'd definitely gotten their attention.

When Jonathan turned the lights back on, the roomful of whispers broke into a full-blast cacophony of forty people trying to shout over each other all at once.

"Come on, folks," I called over the din as I waved the legal tablet in my hand and stepped up to the microphone. "My meeting with the senator is only a few hours away. His first question is going to be, why is this happening? We have proof not only of this inexplicable hyperaggressive behavior in lions but also of an unprecedented change in their social behavior. We need to come up with some workable theories."

"How can this be, Oz?" my former evolutionary biology professor, Gail Quinn, said. "How can this have happened overnight?"

"I don't know, Gail," I said. "That's what I called you all here to try to help me figure it out. My best guess so far is that it may be some sort of radical new adaptive zone. I'm thinking that there may be a dramatic change in the environment that for some reason we haven't been able to pick up on yet."

"Which aspect of the environment is changing, though?" somebody said.

"My money is on a viral agent, Oz," Eberhard Strauss said. "As I said before, these behaviors, especially the hyperaggression, are symptomatic of rabies. I am not saying it is rabies, but it may be some virus that attacks the nervous system."

"I considered that," I said. "But for one thing, rabies is transmitted from animal to animal through bodily fluids. That might explain what's going on in the wild, but in the recent L.A. lion attack and escape, the animals were completely isolated."

"Assuming that incident has anything to do with this," someone said.

"That's right. Assuming it is, though—bear with me—how could isolated zoo animals have been affected?"

"It could be airborne," Strauss pointed out. "Or carried by parasites. Mosquitoes, fleas." He ticked off possibilities on his fingers. "The meat they were feeding the lions in the zoo could have been infected. You name it. Many possibilities."

"Let me throw out another argument against the virus theory," I said. "An animal with rabies, or similar diseases that attack the nervous system, usually exhibits more symptoms than hyper-aggressive behavior. Erratic muscle movement, mange, dermal lesions, hydrophobia. The lions that killed my friend looked quite healthy to me. Physically, at least. And the zoo lions in California weren't displaying any physical symptoms, either. I certainly wouldn't rule out a virus at this point, but it would have to be one we've never seen before."

"Has there been an autopsy on any of these animals?" asked Dr. Quinn.

"No," I said. "The African authorities won't allow it. That's one of the first things I'm going to bring up with the senator."

"What about an autopsy on the zoo lions in L.A.?" somebody shouted.

"Good question," I said.

"If it's not a virus, then we may be talking about a cascade change in the environment," said Alice Boyd, a regal, silver-haired septuagenarian, a MacArthur fellow from the University of Washington. "Have you thought about solar flares? A geomagnetic reversal? I'm only thinking of the way that animal behavior sometimes changes rapidly before a major geological event—earthquakes, tsunamis. Maybe something's coming. A cosmic event that these animals are somehow sensing."

"Good point," I said, dashing it down on my tablet. I liked the idea of geomagnetic reversal—well, actually, I hated it, as it was scary as hell, but I liked it as a suggestion. Geological data show us that every once in a while the earth's magnetic field reverses itself: basically, after such an event, your compass needle will point south where before it had pointed north. These switches seem to be random as far as we can tell. There's a lot of disagreement about how long these shifts last—recent evidence from the USGS suggests that one of these shifts in the past lasted only four years. But a geomagnetic shift's potential effect on the biosphere is unknown—for the simple reason that it has never happened in human memory.

"Are you people this stupid?" someone shouted in the murmuring crowd. I looked: it was a lean, handsome young man I didn't know. He was the only person in the room wearing a suit. "Those lions could have been trained by Siegfried and Roy. This footage doesn't prove a thing."

There was a hush in the crowd followed by the buzzing can-opener hum of an electric wheelchair.

I nodded at Charles Groh as he piloted his iBOT wheelchair down the ballroom's center aisle. Charles was one of the world's leading gorilla experts, although he was effectively retired these days, unfortunately. Three years ago he was suddenly attacked by a four-hundred-pound gorilla whom he had known and worked with for ten years. The ape broke all the bones in his face and tore away his nose, lips, one of his ears, one of his eyes, and one of his hands. He also took off Groh's right leg from the knee down.

The primatologist stopped in front of the handsome skeptic.

"That tape is as real as my face," he said.

I smiled in relief as the group continued debating among themselves. A terrific dynamic was forming now. What had once been mere tolerance of my HAC obsession by my friends and colleagues had now suddenly become scientific respect. The debate was shifting from the question of *whether* something was happening to the more important questions of why it was happening and how to fix it.

But what Alice Boyd had said about geomagnetic shifts stuck with me. It lodged itself in the back of my mind and refused to go away. I had a feeling she was barking up the right tree. It wasn't exactly the suggestion of a geomagnetic shift affecting the biosphere in unforeseen ways as it was the general direction of her thinking: a massive but invisible change in the environment that animals could sense but we could not.

Do you remember the Indian Ocean tsunami? Yes, we live in interesting times. As the wars and natural disasters fall one upon another like a hard rain, they get buried in the quickly overlapping layers of mud in our shitty memories. Which catastrophe was that? December 26, 2004. The giant tsunami that ripped across the Indian Ocean from the epicenter of a 9.0-magnitude earthquake off the coast of Sumatra, drowning more than two hundred thousand people in Indonesia, Sri Lanka, India, and Thailand. I was in Iraq at the time. I remember crowding around a cheap little TV in our base camp, watching the news. I remember how I was struck when I heard that, in Sri Lanka, a full day before the first wave hit, the animals began to disappear inland. Birds, lizards, snakes, mongoose—gone. Elephants ran for higher ground. Dogs refused to go outdoors. Flamingos abandoned their low-lying breeding areas. Although the tsunami killed hundreds of thousands of people, relatively few animals were reported dead. Animals' more acute hearing and other senses might have enabled them to hear or feel the earth's vibration, tipping them off to the approaching disaster long before humans realized what was going on. The animals knew something bad was up. They could feel the vibrations, feel it in their bones. The people, though? Oblivious. Even when the sea mysteriously retreated by a mile and a half, gathering itself for the eighty-foot wave that followed—what did they do? The children went down to the exposed ocean floor to gather seashells.

Chapter 37

RED AND BLUE lights flash against the walls of the dark apartment as a howling fire truck roars down Broadway, far below. The siren dissipates, soon replaced by the grating, music-box tinkle of an ice cream truck.

Sitting on the edge of the sink in the stifling yellow bathroom, Attila glances at the window idly for a moment, as if trying to remember something. Then he shifts his weight forward and goes back to studying himself in the mirror.

He's been looking in the mirror for hours. With meticulous fascination, he gazes at his deep-set, burnished, golden-brown eyes rimmed in black, the wide pink saucers of his ears poking out from beneath the red woolen cap. Periodically he opens his wide, protrusive mouth and thumbs at his long canine teeth. He looks down at his arms, examines the coarse brown hair, the thick leathery skin of his hands, his black fingernails, his long, knotty-knuckled fingers and stubby thumbs.

He closes his eyes and sucks in a deep, meditative breath through his nose. Attila tilts forward until his fingertips and his forehead press against the cool sleek glass of the mirror, his mind trying to right itself, trying to quit roving crazily over the swirling, sickening landscape of strange sounds and strange smells.

There's the scent of crackling grease from the chicken place across 125th Street. The damp, chalky smell of Sheetrock from the church renovation around the corner. The rancid stink of a water treatment plant. The oily, garbagey, fishy smell of the Hudson River.

If there were an EEG monitoring his brain waves, it would be showing a spike of activity in the amygdala, the part of the primate brain responsible for smell, memory, and learning.

Then the Bad Smell comes again.

It comes from the buildings and rooms and pipes, from the streets and alleys and sewers, from the cars and buses. From everywhere, all at once.

Zoo

The Bad Smell is people. And as he stands here in the epicenter of one of the most densely populated places on earth, this frightening, stifling, choking stench closes in on him like a noose, like a bag over his head.

He is shaking. His hands are trembling. The wind shifts, and he smells the psychiatric center a block north. He hears screaming and smells horror, unbearable pain.

All this terrible foulness collects in his mind like smoke in an air filter. Attila plugs his nostrils with his fingers. He stops shaking and opens his glassy brown eyes. He shudders.

A cracked coffee mug with two toothbrushes in it rests on the soap dish. Attila picks it up, shakes out the toothbrushes, and flops the mug back and forth in his hands, wondering what to do with it. He looks again at his reflection in the mirror, wearing the red hat. He rocks back and flings the cup hard at the mirror, smashing it to smithereens and splintering the mirror into a fractured starburst. It feels good. It scratches an itch inside of him.

Then the itch comes back.

Huffing, panting, yowling, he leaps from the sink into the hallway, hurling and smashing everything he can reach. He goes into the room with the computers and smashes them all. He rips them from the wall, yanking out their electrical cords, and tosses them into each other. Sparks crackle and fizz, bits of machinery fly about the room like handfuls of flung sand.

Soon he hears a noise: a repeated thumping on the wall near the door.

"SHUT THE FUCK UP IN THERE!" comes the muffled voice of a person. Next-door neighbor. "You stop that shit right now or I'm calling the cops!"

Attila screams back as he rushes over to the wall and begins pounding it as hard as he can. Plaster particulates rise in the air like white smoke as the mirror on the wall jumps once, twice, then breaks free of its moorings and crashes to the floor near his feet. Glass scatters across the hallway.

When he sniffs again, he catches a new scent emanating from the adjacent apartment.

Attila pant-hoots and shrieks as he scampers through the ruined room.

There is one human smell he enjoys, and he can smell it now.

The scent of human fear.

Chapter 38

THE HAC MEETING was still in full swing that afternoon when an e-mail popped up on my iPhone from Elena Wernert, Senator Gardner's senior staffer.

The senator couldn't meet with me today, she informed me, and my heart sank like a stone before I read the bit that followed: if I was interested, she could "squeeze me in" for five minutes at a conservation hearing that the Senate Committee on Environment and Public Works was holding tomorrow at ten.

I thought: a congressional hearing—*booyah*. That was better than a meeting with the senator. I couldn't have rubbed on a bottle and asked a genie for a better way to get the word out.

So: was I interested?

Absolutely interested, I wrote back, tapping letters on the phone's glowing screen under the table.

As the meeting wore on toward evening, something strange happened. More people kept arriving, prominent geneticists, biologists, people whose names I'd known for years but whom I had never met. I did a double take when Jonathan Eley walked in—a popular astronomer who hosted a New Agey PBS series on the origins of the universe.

They all wanted to see the lion attack footage, which by then had been set up to run continuously in a cordoned-off section of the meeting room.

The Botswana zoological anomaly, as many were starting to call it, was attracting scientists like moths to a flame.

This whole thing was on a new level now, I realized. The buzz on this was intense. Also, in a strange way, I'd won a kind of respect that I'd never really had before: as the meeting gradually segued from the ballroom to the hotel bar, well-known scientists from top-shelf institutions—Harvard, MIT, Johns Hopkins—who normally wouldn't have given me the time of day shuffled over to shake my hand or offer to buy me a beer.

As the attaboys accumulated, I took five from worrying about the end of the world to allow myself a golden moment of self-congratulation. Even after people had called me crazy, I'd stuck to my guns with HAC, and now I felt vindicated.

"Well, aren't you quite the celebrity?" Chloe said, picking at the shoulder of my sport coat after I'd said good-bye to a frosty-haired Princeton microbiologist. My hand was pink and hot from handshakes.

"Yep," I said. "Ladies and gentlemen, Jackson Oz, rock-and-roll biologist. No autographs, and easy on the flash photography."

After the meeting broke up in the early evening, Chloe and I went upstairs to her hotel suite to prepare for the Senate hearing. Sharing a pot of coffee, we cranked out a five-minute statement to the committee that emphasized the dire nature of the problem. I gave several specific policy suggestions, such as broadcasting warnings to every local department of animal care and control to be on alert for increased aggression. But the most important request was for funding to research the problem. We needed to get the best people we could, as fast as possible.

After rereading it, Chloe collapsed in a chair and nodded her head.

"This is good, Oz. With the tape, it should cause quite a stir. We've already grabbed the attention of scientists. Now we're going to tell the world."

We called room service and had the coffee exchanged for a late dinner. Skate wing with capers and cauliflower farro and a bottle of Vouvray (Chloe's suggestion). It was delicious.

She was oddly quiet as we ate. She swirled her wine and gazed distractedly through the window. Outside in the bluish, luminous dark, the Frederick Douglass Bridge, lit up like a birthday cake, spanned the Anacostia River.

When Chloe finally looked at me, her brown eyes were glistening with moisture.

"Back in Africa," she began, her voice quiet, "when night fell, I had resigned myself to my death. I started praying to my grandfather, saying that if I had to die, that maybe he could help somehow. That it would be quick. The next day, I was about to give up hope. Then I looked up, and you were there."

"And now we're here," I said, raising my glass.

"Exactly," she said. "I never believed in fate before, but now I don't know. One moment, I'm about to die in Africa, and the next, I'm in America. And in the middle of a storm. Something that might be one of the biggest events in history. This doesn't often happen to a girl from Auvergne. It doesn't seem real."

"It is real," I said. "You want me to pinch you

to prove it?" That's when she leaned across the tiny table and touched my face.

"No," she said. "I want you to kiss me."

I leaned toward her from across the table and we kissed for the first time. It was soft and right. Then the image of Natalie floated across my eyelids, and though it was the last thing on earth I wanted to do, I broke it off.

"No?" Chloe said surprised. "I thought—"

"I should have told you. I'm sort of, uh—"

"You're married."

"God, no."

"Petite amie? Une amante?"

"No, no. I mean, it's, uh . . . it's hard to say. I think I just broke up with someone," I said, avoiding her eyes.

Chloe harrumphed. "You *think?*"

"Yeah."

Chloe lifted her glass, took a sip of wine. "Well, I appreciate your honesty, Mr. Truth and Justice," she said.

"I guess I should go back to my room," I said. I wadded my napkin on my plate and stood. "We have a big day tomorrow."

"Are you completely crazy? You are here now," she said. Then she sipped more wine and added:

"Besides, I've already seen your underwear."

I gave her a look.

"No, I'm serious, Oz. I don't want to be alone tonight. Please stay?"

"I'll sleep on the chair."

She rolled her eyes.

"Sleep in the bed, with me," she said over the rim of her glass. "Don't worry. Just sleep."

It turned out she wasn't kidding about the just sleeping part. She was sawing logs by the time I came out from my shower.

I watched her in the dim light from the window—her dark eyelashes, her pale face, her thin, delicate arms. Lying there, she looked lovely, so girlish and birdlike. I was already kicking myself. What were you thinking? Natalie broke up with you. It's done. You're a free agent now. Go for it.

Chloe had come all this way for me, I realized. She trusted me and believed in me, which Natalie never really did.

After I tucked her under the covers, I lay beside her and looked at the ceiling.

"Good night, you dumbass," I said to myself, and shut my eyes.

Chapter 39

MY EYES OPENED I don't know how many hours later. The room was so dark I almost couldn't tell whether or not I'd opened my eyes. Not even an orange glow from the city outside. It was as if someone had put blackout curtains on the windows, which I hadn't remembered doing.

Then: shaking. Some sort of clicking, metallic rattle. My eyes flitted around the dark room. It took me a moment to realize it was the doorknob.

The rattling became louder—and more violent— as if someone were trying to wrench the doorknob out of the door. A grinding, scratching sound soon accompanied it. Then came a tentative *whump* against the door.

My first thought was that it was one of the other

scientists playing a joke. After the meeting, the beer had been flowing like water.

There was a second *whump*. Harder now. Something big and heavy behind it.

I sat up. I didn't think it was a joke. It wasn't funny enough.

The blow that followed made the top of the door crack. I heard wood splintering.

What the hell?

I threw back the sheet and was on my feet as the groaning hinges ripped free from the door frame. The door exploded inward, smashing against the floor.

An enormous shape filled the doorway. Then it didn't. There was movement in the room. Then another huge shape darkened the door for an instant and was gone, inside the black room.

"Oz? Are you there?"

Behind me, Chloe sat up in the bed, reached over to the bedside lamp, switched it on, and screamed.

They were bears. Two bears—two massive fucking grizzly bears—filled the room, maybe five feet from the bed. The two bears moved forward on stout, powerful legs, their fur rippling over their bodies in waves. Drool swung from their open mouths, and their beady little black eyes stared outward, as blank and indifferent as death.

I could not move. It was as if my feet had been nailed down. There was no thinking. No fight-or-flight. Even my lizard brain had checked out.

Bear One reared back on his hind legs and swiped at me with his paw. I tumbled backward and felt bright hot wetness I knew was blood on my cheek and neck. My hand flew to my face: blood poured between my fingers, covered my face, stung my eyes.

Then I woke up on my back in the bed, screaming. My hands were flailing at the empty air above me. I reached for my neck. No blood. No pain.

It took me a moment to realize Chloe was screaming, too, beside me in the bed.

"Recevez les de moi!" she yelled in the dark.

I grabbed her shoulders.

"Get them off me! No!" Chloe said, pushing me away. Her eyes were open, but still seeing her nightmare.

"It's okay, Chloe! It's a dream! Just a dream!"

Her lungs sucked at the air. I held her and felt her body slowly loosen.

"But it was so real. We were sleeping, and then the door broke down and bears rushed in. I watched one of them kill you."

"What?" I clicked on the light. "You dreamed about bears?"

"Yes. They were huge. Two huge grizzly bears broke down the door and came in the room."

"Bullshit!" I hopped out of bed and began pacing.

"What is it?"

"I had the same dream. Two grizzly bears knocked down the door and came in, and one of them ripped my face off!"

"How is that possible? How is it possible we both had the same nightmare?"

I had heard of mutual dreaming before, but I'd always been skeptical, never having experienced it. Only in the most extreme cases were there reports of people dreaming the exact same thing. Was it because we were exposed to the same stimuli, or was it something else? Did it have to do with HAC? Surely not . . .

"*Mon Dieu*," Chloe said. "What is this? I'm so scared, Oz. What is going on? What is happening to the world?"

A feeling like a vein of ice sliced from my toes to the top of my head.

"I don't know," I said, holding my head in my hands.

Chapter 40

WHEN MY EYES opened again the next morning, Chloe was curled up against me, her head nestled in my armpit and my hand in her hair. Looking down at her, I thought about the night before. The shared nightmare, dreaming the same dream.

I didn't know what to think. A definite first for me. Chloe didn't seem to want to talk about it, either. She didn't mention it as we got ready and went down to get our cab.

Outside, it was a crisp, sunny summer day. Sharp light, cloudless blue sky. Taxis and bike messengers, businesspeople going to work, sipping coffee, looking at their watches, Kindles out and earbuds in to isolate themselves for the commute. Seeing them made me think of the animals in

Sri Lanka heading for the hills days before the tsunami while the people stayed behind, gathering seashells on the newly extended beach and wondering where the elephants went. Chloe and I exchanged a dark look as we rode. We didn't have to say it. You could practically taste it in the air. Something bad was coming. Something the world had never seen.

The Dirksen Senate Office Building was in the northwest part of the Capitol complex on First Street. I was heartened when I spotted some national media trucks at the curb outside the majestic white marble building. At least we had a shot now at giving people a warning.

I also noticed some familiar faces waiting on the sidewalk beside the building's steps. I shook hands with my old professors Gail Quinn and Claire Dugard. Dr. Charles Groh was there in his wheelchair. I patted his shoulder and squeezed it.

"Go get 'em, Oz," Groh said, turning the pat into a hug. "You can do this."

Chloe and I continued into the building, where white-shirted Capitol cops manned metal detectors. In the sweeping marble atrium behind them, spiffy Senate staffers, lobbyists, and press people swarmed about like bees in a hive, making honey and royal jelly. More shabbily dressed groups of people waited in line behind velvet ropes and looked bored.

As we headed for the security desk, we had to walk around a massive public art installation, a thirty-foot-tall sculpture that looked like a stainless steel oak tree. "Hi, I'm here for the ten o'clock hearing for the Committee on Environment and Public Works," I said to the cop behind the desk. He was a big handsome black man with a shaved head and a face as hard to crack as a bank safe.

He sighed as he lifted his clipboard. "Name?" he said.

"Jackson Oz," I said. "*O z*, Oscar Zulu."

He tsk-tsked as he shook his head at his clipboard. "Hmm. No Oz," he said, and stared back up at me.

"There must be a mix-up," I said. "I was invited by Senator Gardner yesterday at the last minute. Could you double-check with his office for me?"

The crime dog looked at me as if I'd asked to borrow his gun.

"Please?" tossed in Chloe, sweetening the sauce.

"Fine," he said, leaning back in his squeaky leather chair and chinning the receiver of the desk phone. "Now I'm a receptionist, I guess."

He punched some numbers. Then he turned in

his chair and mumbled into the phone. He had a slight smirk on his face when he hung up.

"Just what I thought. They told me to watch out for you activist crazies at dispatch. Sorry, buddy. You're not on the list, and you need to go now."

My stomach fell inside me like an elevator that had snapped a cable. I exchanged a baffled look with Chloe.

"Did they say why?" I said.

"Don't push it," the cop said. "There's the exit. Use it."

I thought quickly. "The website said that some seats are open to the public. Can't we just attend as spectators, then?"

He gave a dismissive noise through his nose, half chuckle and half snort. "How long you been in D.C.?" he said, pointing down the corridor behind him at the line of people behind the velvet rope.

"You see those folks?" he said. "Lobbyists have been paying those sorry individuals twenty bucks an hour for the last two days to wait on line in order to snag a seat for that hearing. First come, first served here, buddy, and it's been served for some time."

He turned to Chloe with a genuinely sorry expression on his face. "Sorry, sweet cheeks. A pretty face can only get you so far in this town. 'Bye, now."

Chapter 41

THE SPECTATORS WEREN'T the only ones who'd been served, I thought, fuming as we walked away from the desk.

I couldn't believe what we were being told. Was this some sort of sick joke?

On the steps outside the building I took out my phone and dialed Senator Gardner's office.

"Yes?" said a quick, impatient female voice.

Elena Wernert, the staffer who had called me the day before.

"This is Jackson Oz," I said. "There's been a mistake. Security's not letting me into the hearing."

"Yes, well. I've been trying to contact you, Mr. Oz," Wernert said. "We're not going to be able to accommodate you after all. The hearing is full."

"Bullshit," I said. "Bull. *Shit!*"

"Funny you should use that term, Mr. Oz," Wernert spat. "Because bullshit is exactly what we've been hearing about you. We were led to believe that you were a Columbia scholar, but we've looked into your background. You neglected to inform us of some of the more radical claims on your blog. We need some insight into the animal conservation problems we've been having, not some lunatic with a conspiracy theory about animals taking over the planet. We're sorry, but Senator Gardner doesn't need to associate with wing-nut bloggers."

I knew it. More politics, more people covering their asses rather than actually trying to understand what's happening in the real world. It was Washington at its finest.

I took a deep breath.

"There is an imminent threat, ma'am," I said. "Perhaps if you'd taken time out of your busy day, you could have come by the meeting yesterday and seen for yourself. Animal behavior is changing radically and alarmingly, and people are dying. I can prove it."

"It doesn't make the slightest shred of sense," Wernert said. "Why is it happening?"

"I'm not sure. Not yet. That's one of the questions

we need to figure out. But the why of it is not what's at stake at the moment, Ms. Wernert. You don't have to know why your house is on fire to run for the exit. Warnings need to be sent out right now for people to be wary of animal aggression."

"Right. I'm afraid that'll fly like a lead balloon on CNN," Wernert said. "Senator Gardner tells the public, 'Lock up your killer Shih Tzu.'"

"Please. At least let me show Senator Gardner the film I have." I was irritated to hear a new note of begging in my voice.

"The senator has more important things to do than become involved with your fringe theory. He's booked solid for the next month. Good-bye." Wernert hung up.

I stared at my phone. To come this far just to be sold down the river was unacceptable. I didn't even care about all the time and effort it took me to put this presentation together. It was the fact that the public needed to hear what I had to say, and that the facts were being hidden by the very people who were supposed to be protecting the populace.

Senator's blessing or not, a warning needed to go out. No one else was going to do it. It was up to me.

I looked at the media people down by the door,

gathered for the environmental hearing that was starting to get underway, and a plan came to me.

As I walked back toward the metal detectors, I turned and stopped. Then I climbed up on the platform base of the giant indoor sculpture, jumped up, and caught the first branch of the stainless steel tree.

Lawyers and politicians and even some real people stopped and started pointing as I scurried up to the top.

"Excuse me!" I called to everyone through cupped hands. "Excuse me. I have something important to say."

"Oz?" Chloe said, looking up at me from the lobby floor. "What are you doing?"

"The only thing left to do," I called down to her. "The people need to know."

Chapter 42

"EXCUSE ME!" I shouted. "Everyone—I am a scientist. My name is Jackson Oz, and I was invited to speak at an environmental hearing for the US Senate before I was mysteriously uninvited."

I glanced down to see the cop who'd just eighty-sixed us standing beneath the tree, his gun in one hand, his radio in the other.

I paused, swallowed, continued.

"An environmental disturbance of global proportions is happening. Three days ago, in Botswana, more than a hundred people were killed by wild animals. I believe this epidemic is spreading worldwide. Everyone may be in jeopardy. Be on the lookout for sudden aggression in animals—"

An alarm sounded. I paused. A piercing white

light strobed, and the hallway reverberated with clanging bells. From deeper inside the building, I could hear an approaching herd of stomping footfalls.

I bit my lip. I thought maybe I'd grab a little attention from a reporter or two before I was arrested, but now I was worried. After 9/11, this was probably one of the best-guarded places on earth. Maybe my plan wasn't as brilliant as it sounded a moment before.

That thought was confirmed as a team of men in black fatigues appeared from an interior hallway, swinging M16s and riot shields. As the SWAT team came through the ringing metal detectors, I could see the letters CERT flashing in silver tape across the backs of their flak jackets.

"Get down from there! *Now!*" a mustached man in a tactical helmet called from the skinny end of a crackling megaphone as he trained the business end of his M16 at my chest.

I was doing just that, kneeling down to hang-jump off the metal branch, when I heard a boom, and what felt like an A-Rod line drive hit me in the back of my right hand. My grip faltered and I dropped to the marble floor like a bag of meat.

I looked at my hand. It felt broken. It looked like I'd been stung by a hornet the size of a kitten.

I'd been shot with some type of nonlethal round. A rubber bullet, I guessed.

But that was the least of my problems. Two blinks later, there was a violent, zinging pain in the backs of my legs and my teeth involuntarily clenched as I started shaking.

"You are being Tasered. Don't move, you squirrely little prick," said a voice so close to my head I could smell the onions on his breath.

That was easy: I couldn't move, as my muscles were being zapped into paralysis. Even after the Taser's fish-hooks were ripped from my back, it still felt like someone was boring into my skull with an electric drill. My brain was numbed.

Now four cops were on top of me, wrenching my arms behind my back to cuff my wrists.

"That's what you get for dicking around," the cop said in my ear. "You're in trouble. Like federal homeland security–style trouble."

I was hauled to my feet and shove-walked toward an open double door in the marble wall. I tried to get my feet under me, but the muscles in my legs were still wobbly. I stumbled, they dragged me, I got my legs back, and then they fell out from under me again. I looked down at my useless, jellylike legs. It was like they were somebody else's.

"Oh, so now you're resisting arrest," the cop sneered, and a boot blasted into my spine.

"Get off of him! Stop hurting him!" A woman, screaming. I heard it as if I were underwater, registered it as if I were in a coma.

I saw Chloe out of the corner of my eye. She was rushing forward, pushing at the cops as she screamed.

I also spotted Gail Quinn, Claire Dugard, and Charles Groh beside her, shouting at the Capitol police. The hallway resounded with the cacophonous echoes of shouting, scuffling, stomping boots.

Two dream moments later, they were all cuffed and trussed on the floor beside me. They even cuffed Charles Groh to his wheelchair. Clearly a very dangerous man, him.

We were yanked up and dragged toward a side door opening onto a dingy back corridor.

"Hey, look, Larry," said the cop to one of his buddies. "It's the attack of the retards. Where's the bearded lady? Outside keeping the short bus running for the getaway?"

Right then was when I truly lost it. I turned and tried to kick the cop in his balls. I missed, though I did manage to land a pretty good blow on his shin.

Zoo

Then my view was blocked by a fist, showing me a sweeping vista of some guy's fingers and knuckles. I took in the scenery for a leisurely fraction of a second before being disturbed by the noisy crunch of my nose breaking, which echoed numbly in my ears as the lights above me dimmed and sputtered out.

Chapter 43

AFTER THE PANDEMONIUM, the Capitol cops brought us to an MPDC holding tank. We were processed and conveyed into a cell in the rear of the building. The walls were cluttered with peace signs, anarchy signs, and pot leaves that previous occupants had keyed and Sharpied onto the grimy tiles. This room had seen its share of troublemakers.

We spent the night in the cell: Gail Quinn, Claire Dugard, Charles Groh, Chloe, and me, as well as a few cockroaches I at first mistook for Yorkshire terriers. I leaned against the wall with two scraps of paper towel twisted in my nostrils and my sinuses clogged with blood.

We used the time wisely. After I was done apologizing profusely for landing us all in jail, we stayed up half the night in the windowless concrete room, trying to piece together the potential causes of HAC.

We kept bumping up against the same barriers we had encountered at the meeting. We decided it was unlikely that it was a virus. Whatever it was, for it to similarly affect various different species in diverse areas argued against that possibility. We all agreed it was more likely that this sudden and aberrant shift in behavior was probably a response to some change in the environment. Obviously the best thing to do now was to perform autopsies on affected animals and look for any anatomical or physiological peculiarities that might point us in the right direction.

Dr. Quinn pledged the help of the Columbia University biology department, if and when we could get a specimen.

"Who needs the government anyway, Oz?" she said from where she sat, campfire-style, by the jail cell door. "Even if they'd listened to you today, they would have formed a committee to hire a research team to come up with a study on the personality types of the best people needed to come up with an action plan."

We were freed the next morning after our

arraignment. The others got off with a misdemeanor charge of public disturbance and a five-hundred-dollar fine, and I was charged with criminal trespass and had to enter a plea and pay three thousand dollars in bail.

Though I now had a federal record and a court date, I wasn't terribly worried about it as we pushed Dr. Groh's wheelchair down the ramp beside the courthouse steps in the early morning sunlight. I had bigger fish to fry—we all did, whether anyone realized it or not. The government was about to be overwhelmed with a lot more important things than me.

"What now? We go hunting?" Chloe said after we had helped load Dr. Groh into the back of a wheelchair-accessible cab with Claire and Gail and said our good-byes.

"First, the next portion of your vacation package," I said, pointing to a restaurant down the street. "Allow me to introduce you to an American gem: the twenty-four-hour diner."

"I have another suggestion," Chloe said, pointing at my nose. "Your nose looks crooked. Very crooked. You might want to think about seeing a doctor."

So our breakfast wound up being eaten in the waiting room of the George Washington University

Hospital's ER. After wolfing down an Egg McMuffin while John Hancocking half a dozen documents, I stood on a chair and blitzed through the channels of the wall-mounted TV, trying to see if there was any word of our protest on the news. Two trips around the horn and I left it on ESPN, where they were recapping a game last night in which the Celtics had lost to the Knicks: a small glimmer of good news.

"This is ridiculous," I said to Chloe. "There's nothing. Not a single word about Botswana or the protest. We were arrested for nothing."

Another hour of waiting and I was taken for some X-rays. When Chloe and I came back into the treatment room, we noticed a prisoner in an orange jumpsuit surrounded by armed guards in the bay across from us.

"Look. Another troublemaker," Chloe whispered to me. Her smile was sweet and impish.

I smiled back. That she could keep up a sense of humor through all this bullshit was incredible.

"Yeah, well," I said. "This must be the mad, bad, and dangerous-to-know section."

After a while a handsome doctor came in with my X-ray, the glossy sheet of black film flopping in his small, smooth hand. He looked young enough to be a George Washington University undergrad.

He glanced at Chloe a beat too long for my liking and smiled cheerily as he told me that my nose was indeed broken.

"I didn't like your nose before anyway," Chloe said as Dr. Feelgood snapped a pair of latex gloves onto his tiny porcelain hands to set my nose back into its proper form.

"I am kidding," said Chloe, smiling behind her hand. In a moment I was lying with my shirt off on a crinkling sheet of gurney paper.

"I'm going to have to rebreak your nose before I set it," the doctor said as he pinched down hard on my face. "It's been a number of hours since you were injured."

I didn't like the sound of that. My face betrayed me.

"It'll only take a second," said the doctor. He was talking to me as though I were a child afraid of needles.

"Ready?" He snapped his glove. Bastard was whistling.

I was struggling to sit up, and then I felt a soft hand in mine.

"You can do this, Oz," Chloe said, squeezing my hand. "I'm right here."

A funny thing happened then. I actually did calm

down. This was becoming a theme for us, helping each other out, anticipating each other's needs. As I looked at Chloe and felt her cool hand in mine, I realized I was falling very hard and fast in love with this woman. I had a suspicion it was happening to her, too.

Then the doctor broke my nose and I screamed like a baby.

Chapter 44

WITH A BANDAGE X-taped across my face and bloody cotton balls peeking rakishly from my nostrils, I left the hospital with Chloe and caught a cab back to the hotel. We showered, packed, checked out, and went to Union Station to catch the next New York–bound Acela train.

New criminal record or not, I needed to return to the Big Apple to regroup and try like hell to broadcast my lion footage to the world. Get it on the Internet, see if I could get it on the network news.

As we were settling into our seats, I tried calling Natalie again. The phone went straight to voice mail, and I hung up. I'd left her a message almost forty-eight hours before. What the hell? Was she icing me out?

Half an hour later I was coming back from the snack car with a beer and a half bottle of wine. Chloe was shuffling a deck of cards on the tray table in front of her.

"Go fish," I said.

"These aren't playing cards," Chloe said. "These are tarot cards."

"Tarot cards?" I said, giving her a quizzical look. "What scientist carries tarot cards?"

Chloe shrugged.

"I think they are very beautiful," she said. "They belonged to my mother. I found them in a box of her things after she died. It's my—how do you say it?—good luck charm. It's superstitious, I know."

She slipped them back in their box and reached beneath her seat for her purse.

"Lemme see those," I said, putting a hand on hers. "Do you know how to . . . do whatever it is you do with tarot cards?"

"We can do a reading," she said, sliding the cards back out of the box. "You shuffle the cards and then lay out ten of them in what is called the Celtic cross. The best kind of reading is the question reading. First you write down a question, then deal out the cards to find the answer. The tenth card in the sequence will give you the answer."

I uncapped a pen and scribbled out on an Amtrak cocktail napkin:

Will HAC destroy the world?

I handed her the napkin, but she waved it off.

"Don't show it to me yet. Just turn it over and shuffle."

So I folded it and put it down. I shuffled the cards and carefully slipped them off the top of the deck one by one, laying them down on the tray table in the places where she pointed.

The formation complete, Chloe began turning the cards over. The first one showed an old man in a cloak, holding a staff and a lantern.

"That's the Hermit," she said. "It represents, er—how do you say?—introspection, searching."

Chloe's voice had a slight note of seriousness in it. How did a scientist become a closet mystic? I was intrigued. It made me think of Isaac Newton doing alchemy experiments in his spare time, trying to turn lead into gold when he wasn't busy laying down the foundation of classical physics.

She turned over the other cards. One card was called the Tower, another the Lovers, which I liked the sound of.

"Now, this is the one that will answer the

question," Chloe said as I arrived at the tenth card. She flipped it over.

Outside, the eastern seaboard clattered by in swaths of gray and brown; snatches of the ocean sparkled weakly in the failing afternoon light.

I looked at the card. It looked like a picture of an angel with birdlike wings. Feathers and red and yellow triangles splayed out from the cloud he was sitting in, and the angel seemed to be blowing through some sort of straw.

"What is it? The angel?" I said.

Chloe bit her lip as she kept staring at the card. "This card is *Le Jugement*." She pointed at the angel. "This is the angel Gabriel, blowing his horn." She pointed at the red and yellow triangles. "This is fire."

I didn't need a crystal ball to know what that meant.

I showed her my question.

"Duh-duh-*duh* . . . " Chloe playfully hummed ominous movie music. She smiled, laughed, and scooped up the cards. But as she did, I saw that her hands were shaking slightly.

We sat in silence as the Acela train blasted like a switch across the miserable ass of Delaware. Gazing out at the blur of tract housing and strip malls, for some reason I started thinking about the book *The*

Little Red Caboose, which my mom used to read to me when I was a kid.

How wonderful the illustrations had made the world seem. Shiny cars and friendly policemen as the train went through the city; apple-cheeked farmers driving corn-filled pickups in the country; painted Indians on horseback as the train chugged up the mountain. I remembered looking at the pictures for hours, at the world that was waiting for me, happy, colorful, safe.

As we went into a tunnel, I closed my eyes and saw the card again: the Judgment.

What kind of storybooks would I be reading to my children? I wondered.

Chapter 45

IT WAS ABOUT nine at night when we emerged from Penn Station onto the bustling expanse of Eighth Avenue in midtown Manhattan. The dark mood that had gripped me after the tarot reading hadn't let go. The city was wet. The clouds had broken into rain during our journey, and now the weather alternated between drizzle and bursts of harder rain. We stood on the curb, burdened with our luggage, without umbrellas, getting wet. Steam rose from the streets, and the headlights of the cars were mirrored in the shimmering asphalt.

We flagged down a cab. I opened the door for Chloe and dumped our bags in the trunk. I got in and told the driver my address. On the seat beside me Chloe was gaping through the window at the looming Empire State Building. It was lit up in tiers of white and blue.

"I have not been in New York City in a long time," she said.

The rain gathered new momentum and drummed on the roof of the car like flung handfuls of gravel. Chloe was quiet. She snuggled into the crook of my arm, and I listened to the rhythmic rubber-on-glass squeals of the windshield wipers. The city lights blasted past us, twinkling like hazy underwater jewels in the dark.

"It's leaving, isn't it?" she said quietly, into my chest.

"What's leaving? What are you talking about?"

She sat up a little. Her eyes were moist. "I'm afraid that Claire Dugard is right," she said. "The world is ending. Everything that everyone has worked so hard for, our parents, their parents. It's all going away, and no one is going to do anything about it . . . and it's just so . . . so sad."

"You can't think like that," I said, softly squeezing her shoulders. "This is crazy, I know, but we can solve it. We're going to figure it out."

"I don't know what to think anymore. We dreamed the same dream. That's impossible. And then seeing that tarot card on the train. It's silly, I know. But it scared me to death. I feel strange. I feel very strange."

I didn't know what to say, so I just held her as she dissolved into real, racking sobs. We'd been through a lot lately. I hoped it was the jet lag.

I thought what the grandmotherly Alice Boyd had said about the eerie, seemingly precognitive animal behavior right before natural disasters. I thought about the elephants and the birds heading for the hills days before the tsunami.

What was the term Alice had used? A "cosmic event"?

After a moment, I looked down at Chloe, and she reached for my face, a hand on each cheek, and kissed me deeply. Her face melted into mine. She kissed me.

And I kissed back. I kissed back.

Chapter 46

YELLOW. A YELLOW car stops downstairs, in front of the building. Attila arrives at a thumping run at the front window of the apartment, gazes down at the street below. He looses a wild, piercing shriek as the cab door opens and he sees Oz. He hops up and down, howling in excitement.

He stops, and is quiet. His dark, glistening brown eyes glide downward and see something else.

Oz is reaching into the cab. Now another person emerges from the yellow thing. Even from five floors up, Attila can see it is a female. A woman.

Attila's face drops. He begins to whimper. The black tips of his long leathery fingers press against the glass. He blows from his nostrils in soft, sorrowful puffs as he stares down at his friend and the newcomer.

His sadness sours into a feeling of betrayal. Of jealousy. The yawning gulf in his chest becomes filled with a new feeling. It pours in like floodwater.

Hot, ugly rage.

Rage gushes up inside him like an urge to vomit.

Attila leaps up, pounding at his chest. Growling, gurgling noises erupt from his throat as he begins to tear back and forth through the ruins of the apartment, smashing and tearing everything in his path. He smashes and tears things not yet smashed and torn, and further smashes and tears things that have already been smashed and torn.

Today is a day for biting and smashing.

He begins pounding on the walls again, knocking down the few remaining pictures. Their frames clatter and crash. More glass scatters across the floor. He grabs the radiator in the hallway, begins to shake it. He winces as he pulls and pulls. The pipe that connects it to the wall whines. There is a shriek and a groan as he rips it free of its moorings. Attila hurls the radiator into the bathroom, the door to which he wrenched off its hinges a few days ago. The radiator bashes the bathroom sink and shatters it. The sink crumbles into chunks of porcelain rubble.

Attila knuckle-walks to the front door. He sniffs. He hears Oz coming up the stairs now, with another pair of feet walking in tandem beside or behind him. He has an idea. Quickly, deliberately, he runs through the apartment, clicking off all the lights.

The apartment is dark except for the orange glow from the lights outside filtering through the windows. The torn blinds cast orange tiger stripes of light across the room. A train rumbles by outside, and sets the room to shaking. Attila listens to the approaching, ascending footsteps. He yawns with his enormous jaws. He waits.

Chapter 47

CHLOE WAS STILL smiling, her body loose, soft, and warm in my arms, when the cab dropped us off in front of my building on 125th Street. Then she took a moment to absorb the squalid streetscape. Beside us, two homeless guys in a bus shelter were yelling and shoving each other for some reason as a rat the size of a Chihuahua looked on.

"Home sweet home," I said, as the Broadway local thundered by above us on the elevated track. "It's not as bad as it looks. I promise."

"It is very, er . . ." She spun a finger in the air, searched for a word.

"Urban?" I suggested.

"*Non, non.* More, eh—what is the word? *Misérable?*"

Huffing and puffing after hauling our bags up five flights of stairs, I was turning the key in the lock of my front door when I heard an unusual sound. It was coming from behind the door. It stopped, then started again—loud and rasping, some kind of hiss. I opened the door. I looked out into the darkness of my apartment. I was struck by the smell. Not good. It smelled like shit.

I heard the sound more clearly: it was coming from somewhere beyond us through the unlit threshold. I moved in front of Chloe, and the darkness in the doorway seemed to collect together and form into a broad shape.

"Attila?" I said.

What in the hell? He should have been in his cage.

"*Oo-oo-oo-oo ah-ah-ah heeaagh heeaagh hyeeeaaaaaghhhh!*"

The shadow bulged, and then the weight slammed into my chest like a train. The blow knocked me on my back.

"Attila!" I barked.

Chloe was somewhere behind me, screaming. I was on my back in the doorway, my wind knocked out, tailbone smarting like hell, trying to process what was going on. Attila had knocked me over, and now he was tumbling in crazy circles around the apartment.

"What the fuck is wrong with you?" I said. I gathered myself to my feet, fumbling for the light switch, glancing behind me for Chloe.

How had he gotten out of his cage?

He was just scared, I thought, frantically trying to assess the situation. He must have thought I was an intruder or something. I needed to calm him down.

I stepped into the apartment and snapped on the light.

"Look, Attila," I said. "It's me. Oz. You're safe, kid."

The cold white fluorescent light slowly buzzed on, illuminating my apartment.

It was a horror show. It looked exactly as though a wild chimp had been let loose in my apartment for a week. The whole place was in shambles. The refrigerator door was open, trickling feeble blue light into the room and humming, the food that had been in it rotten and scattered across the floor. The cupboard doors were wrenched off their hinges, all the dishes raked out and smashed on the floor, the faucet running in the sink for God knows how long, sticky puddles of dried piss on the linoleum, shit smeared in streaks on the walls. This sight proved to be a preview of what the rest of the apartment looked like.

And then Attila was barreling toward me again from out of the darkened, ruined apartment. He seemed to know exactly who I was. And he was wearing my red hat.

"ATTILA!" I screamed, and he sank his jaws down on my knee.

I fought. I kicked. I punched him in the back of his head. He didn't even seem to notice. My fists bounced off his skull like rubber balls. He wasn't the same chimp. Something inside him had snapped.

Chloe was screaming—I heard her distantly, as if I were underwater.

There was a pan lying overturned on the edge of the kitchen counter, just within arm's reach. It was a hefty black cast-iron skillet that had belonged to my Polish grandmother. I'd eaten pierogi that had been fried in that thing, and that day it may have saved my life.

I snatched it up and brought it down on the crown of Attila's head, half strength at first, which did nothing, and then I swung it as though I were Roger Federer hitting a Dunlop crosscourt. The gruesome sound of the skillet bonking Attila's skull made me wince. I felt his bite loosen. I hit him with it again, and he let go.

He was dazed from the blow. He stumbled back into the corner by the refrigerator. His face was damp with blood. He cowered in the corner, shrieking.

"Heeaagh! Heeaagh! Heeaagh!"

"Oz!" said Chloe. "Are you okay?"

Attila turned toward her. His eyes were blank and dangerous. He began to skulk toward us.

"Stay away from her!"

I heaved the skillet at him. He raised an arm and swatted it off, and the skillet went sailing behind him and smashed through the kitchen window almost as easily as if there hadn't been any glass there. Shards of glass tinkled to the floor.

For a moment I thought he'd snapped out of it. I dropped to the floor on my knees, and grimaced in pain. Attila had chewed up my knee badly.

"Attila," I said. My hands were palm up, open. I was using my lullaby voice. "Attila. What's gotten into you? Relax! It's me."

Chloe stood in the open doorway still, as if she were ready to bolt.

Attila looked at me. He stood on a pile of crumbled dishes on the kitchen floor. He cocked his head and fixed his gaze on me from under the brim of my red knit hat.

Attila's face changed then. For a second, he seemed like himself again. As he looked into my eyes, his expression was an unnerving gaze of unbearable sadness—betrayal, knowing.

Then he jumped onto the countertop and out the window onto the fire escape. He was gone.

Chapter 48

AN ELDERLY HISPANIC man in rumpled janitor blues is waiting for a bus. He sips a brown-bagged can of Tecate and hums half a tune. He's on his way home from work. He nudges up the brim of a sweat-stiffened Yankees cap. Then a chimpanzee drops off the bottom of the fire escape of the building beside him. The chimp is wearing a red hat. The can of Tecate lands on the sidewalk.

"Heeaagh!" says the chimp. *"Heeaagh-heeaagh!"*

The chimp scrambles past him, an explosion of hairy limbs, feet, fingers. He sniffs, looks around, tears down the sidewalk with a bouncing, loping gait, propelling himself forward with long, powerful arms.

The world is suddenly a wild swirl of strange

231

lights and sounds—and a new sense of openness. Blindly knuckle-running down the sidewalk, Attila does not even pause as he bolts into the commotion of 125th Street. It's a circus of honking. Attila streaks in front of a minivan, and the driver lays on the brakes and horn half a moment before the eastbound M104 bus behind it crushes its rear end. There's a crunch of plastic, metal, glass. More honking.

Now on the other side of the street, Attila races alongside the long and brightly lit window of a Duane Reade drugstore before he banks the corner and passes a fried-chicken restaurant.

He pant-hoots at a number 1 train as it blasts by high overhead on the shaking iron latticework of the elevated tracks. He runs along the sidewalk, past benches and fire hydrants, scrabbling for a place to hide.

A group of teenagers are halfheartedly punting around a battered soccer ball on the sidewalk in front of a bodega. A tiny, grizzled Hispanic man sits on a plastic folding chair by the door of the store, smoking a cigarette and watching the kids playing soccer. A sleek black car with tinted windows idles on the corner, a rap song blasting from its radio in fuzzy thumps that shake it on its springs.

A chimpanzee wearing a red hat rushes headlong

through the soccer game. The girls point and shriek. The soccer ball skitters away into the street.

A patrol car from the Twenty-Sixth Precinct is just pulling away from the curb in front of a deli on Lenox Avenue when they get the call.

"Repeat that, dispatch. Who's on the roof of a candy store?" says Sergeant Timothy Perez, a tall, fit, five-year veteran who was promoted to his position the week before.

The radio squeals, static crunches.

"A chimpanzee," says the bitch box.

"Come again?" says Officer Jack Murphy, at the wheel.

The growing crowd on the corner of Broadway and 123rd is spilling into the street when the police arrive on the scene. The lights paint the scene red and blue. Murphy gives a half whoop with the siren and curtly parts the crowd by climbing the cruiser onto the sidewalk.

Sergeant Perez rolls down his window and shines his Maglite at the red plastic awning of the bodega. Bright eyes flash back at him in the pale ring of light.

"Heeaagh heeaagh hyeeeaaaaaghhhh!"

"Well, I'll be a monkey's uncle," says Murphy.

Okay, so dispatch isn't on shrooms, Perez thinks. What appears to be a chimpanzee is indeed standing on top of the awning. Wearing a red hat.

Perez and Murphy step out of the car.

"Ooh, the po po's here," somebody says. "What'd the monkey do, Officer? He rob a bank?"

One of the kids in front of the store whacks at the bodega's awning with a broom handle.

"C'mon, Bubbles," the kid says in a high-pitched voice. "Quit messin'. It's me, Michael." He drops the impression. "Get down here 'fore I beatcha ass."

The kids are laughing. It's a circus atmosphere.

"Gimme that," Perez says, snatching the broom from the kid.

Perez looks up at the chimp. Noticing what looks like blood on the animal's face, he lightly lays his hand on the handle of his Glock.

He knows it's not a funny situation. His brother-in-law, a New Jersey state trooper, once told him about an escaped pet chimp in West Orange who had turned some guy's face into a Picasso. These guys can be very dangerous animals. Not to be fucked with.

Perez puts the radio to his cheek.

"We got the monkey over here on 123rd and Broadway. He's perched on the awning over a store. We need to get animal control up here. Someone with a tranquilizer gun or something. We can keep watch in the meantime."

"Ten four," says the radio, and Perez clips it to his belt.

"Whatsamatter, Magilla Gorilla?" says Murphy. "You want a banana or somethin'?"

Perez can't believe it. It looks like talking a chimp off a ledge is going to be the first test of his command.

Above the crowd, Attila cowers against the building's bricks, paralyzed with fear and confusion. He scrambled up to escape the crowd of screaming people, and now he can't go up or go down. Adrenaline surges in his nerves as more and more voices cackle and shout from below, and more cars with piercing colored lights arrive.

Soon a large van joins the three police cruisers parked on the street. Two men in crisp tan uniforms step out of the van.

Attila peeks out over the edge of the awning, then darts back into the corner against the brick wall. He shrinks into himself, trying to make his body as small as possible. He wants to disappear.

Scrunched against the bricks, he finds a bundle of coaxial cables strung along the corner of the six-story building. He wraps his fingers around it, then his toes.

The animal control officers—one of whom is

a former horse trainer—aren't city workers but independent contractors hired on a case-by-case basis. The one who's a former trainer chambers a dart into his tranquilizer pistol while his partner unhooks the ladder from the van's roof. Too late. The chimp is climbing.

"Hey, hey, yo!" One of the street kids points. "He goin' all King Kong up in this shit."

Sergeant Perez and the animal control guy exchange a look and a groan as the chimp scurries up a bundle of cables that runs along the side of the building. The speed with which he zips up there is pretty amazing. Dude is boogying.

"Go, monkey, go!" the kids start chanting. The ape makes it to the top of the six-story building and disappears over the ledge of the roof.

After waiting a respectful moment, Officer Murphy shrugs at his boss and joins in the chanting.

Chapter 49

CHLOE WANTED ME to go to the hospital right away. I waved her off. I'd been in enough waiting rooms lately. Still keyed up with adrenaline, I dumped half a bottle of hydrogen peroxide over my knee and taped wads of paper towels to it. Clutching my leg, I hobbled around the apartment surveying the rest of the wreckage.

It was as if everything I owned had been fed through a wood chipper. There was hardly an object in the apartment that Attila hadn't found a way of smashing. To say nothing of the suffocating, nauseating stench of rotten food combined with the piss and shit spattered everywhere. I figured I shouldn't count on getting my deposit back.

I had known that before long Attila would

become unmanageable, and I'd have to find a more suitable home for him, but he was only five. Chimps generally don't get too unruly until they're a bit older. I couldn't help but wonder if what I was looking at here showed rage, a personal anger toward me. What had made Attila do this? Separation anxiety? And how had he escaped from his cage?

With our bags still piled in the hallway outside the door, Chloe stepped gingerly amid the wreckage, afraid to touch anything.

"Oz, I'm so sorry," she said.

Maybe it was Chloe's presence that had set him off. Chimps are fiercely territorial, and have often been observed to kill over boundary disputes. Had Attila perceived Chloe as some sort of territorial threat?

On the other hand, he'd clearly taken a lot of time to do this much damage to the apartment.

I was walking past the doorway of the back bedroom when I smelled something especially foul. Even worse than the potpourri of rotten food and fecal matter that the rest of the apartment reeked of.

In the bedroom doorway I smelled something so concentratedly dense, so horrific, that I was afraid to turn on the light. But I did turn on the light.

I stood there for a moment, stock-still, breathing heavily.

"What is it, Oz?" Chloe called from behind me, in the hallway.

It wasn't just that the room was a wreck. It wasn't just that the stripped mattress was torn to tattered fluff and sodden with urine—though there was that.

I could feel my heartbeat hammering in my ears as my eyes scanned the room. There was blood on the walls. In thin streaks and freckles. In wide, heavy smears. Handprints.

Huge, long handprints—chimp handprints. There was one right there beside the switch plate, which also had blood on it. Four very long, thick fingers and a small stubby hook of a thumb.

I looked up. There was dried blood misted on the light fixture in the ceiling. It gave the room a slightly pinkish cast. All this blood had been there for days. It was dry and dark, the color of brown rust.

With my eyes, I followed the blood smears to the far corner of the room.

"What?" Chloe said in the hallway.

There was something on the floor in the corner of the room opposite me, between the bed and the wall. The streaks of blood led there, just as all roads led to Rome.

I could feel Chloe behind me.

"Stay there," I said. "Don't come in."

I covered my face with the collar of my shirt and I stepped farther into the room. I tasted bitterness in the back of my mouth. Bile was rising in my throat.

It was a human body. Most of one, anyway. It was a decomposing—and what looked like a partially eaten—human body. I couldn't identify it by the face, because the face was gone. As were the feet and hands. But there was long red hair. Red, red, Irish girl's hair, and the body was wearing turquoise hospital scrubs.

A rectangular plastic card was clipped to the breast pocket of the blood-stiffened shirt.

I unclipped it and looked at it. Under dirt-brown streaks of dried blood, there was Natalie's deer-in-the-headlights mug shot on her hospital ID badge.

NATALIE MARIE SHAW, it said beneath the picture.

I hardly noticed Chloe as I brushed past her in the hallway. I'd made it to the front door when Chloe grabbed my arm.

"What is it? Tell me, Oz. Please. What's in there?" I babbled. "My—uh, my girlfriend . . ."

She balked, scrunched her face up. Her face

showed confusion, with the possibility of anger in it.

"I thought she was your ex-girlfriend."

"She is now."

We called the police from Mrs. Mullen's apartment. Mrs. Mullen, my next-door neighbor—a sweet little Irish lady who was so old she'd probably come over in the potato famine. I wasn't terribly shocked when Mrs. Mullen said she hadn't heard anything in the last week. The lady was deaf as a stone. She didn't even know I lived with a chimp.

The first cops to arrive were already aware of Attila. They told me he had been spotted on the street but that he was still on the loose. Something about hiding on the roof of a bodega.

What now? What did I do with my life?

My home was destroyed. If I hadn't zipped off to Africa and asked Natalie to take care of Attila, she would still be alive. My fault. If I didn't have a fucking chimp in my apartment she would still be alive. Also my fault. She was a saint—even after breaking up with me, she'd still come over to check on Attila. And he had killed her. I went further and further back down the chain of decisions I'd made, thinking about what I could have done differently.

A lot. Regret sucked at my heart like a leech.

Chloe sat beside me and held my hand as I sat in the stairwell while police radios squawked and crackled in my apartment and all down the hallway neighbors had come out to stare.

What now? What indeed.

And the nightmare wasn't over. Not even close.

BOOK FOUR

THE NATIVES ARE RESTLESS

Chapter 50

FIVE YEARS LATER

WHEN I FELT the train slow, my eyes fluttered, bringing me out of an impromptu nap.

Outside the window of the Acela, I could see we weren't in D.C. yet. We were going through a seemingly abandoned industrial town in South Jersey, or maybe northern Maryland. These decaying towns all looked depressingly the same: windowless brick factories; deserted, rusting bridges; a main street lined with plywood-boarded windows and overgrown with weeds. Going back to nature, slowly.

Turns out an apocalypse actually comes on pretty slowly. Not fire and brimstone but rust and dandelions. Not a bang but a whimper.

Perhaps it was due to the continuing economic downturn, but rumors abounded on the Internet. People were dying in these in-between places. No one knew why.

I had my theories.

Gazing out at the orphaned town, I thought of those lines from Yeats:

Things fall apart; the centre cannot hold;
Mere anarchy is loosed upon the world . . .

For a moment I stared blankly at my reflection in the black screen of the sleeping laptop that was open on the tray table in front of me. You could have packed for a long weekend in the bags under my eyes.

So much to do and so little goddamn time to do it.

For the last five years, I'd been working nonstop with my friends at Columbia to try to get a handle on HAC. A lot of the work consisted of collecting the corpses of affected animals and performing autopsies on them.

We'd seen a lot of specimens. Too many. Tigers from India. Russian bears. Beavers, wolverines, even ground squirrels. The unusually aggressive behavior had spread to so many mammal species we were starting to lose count.

It wasn't rabies. As far as we could tell from the specimens we'd studied, it didn't seem like a virus. We had noticed something interesting, though. The brains of the affected animals were a little heavier than normal. Not only that, but they were heavier by the same amount, about 1.3 percent. The increase in brain matter seemed to be concentrated mostly in the amygdala, the part of the mammalian brain generally thought to be responsible for memory and learning.

The finding was unusual enough to finally get the government on board. For the last year, we'd gotten decent funding and had been working with a liaison from the Department of Health and Human Services.

So the good news now was that we had provided the world with proof that something was causing abnormal mutations in mammalian amygdalae that were triggering this aberrantly aggressive behavior. The bad news was that we didn't have a clue what it was.

There were other questions. Why were some animals affected and not others? And why were humans entirely unaffected by these mutations?

Were there other symptoms associated with the mutations? Yes, and they varied from one species to another. In some species—lions, for instance— the mutations seemed to affect only male animals. Not so in other species. There had been an ugly episode of bizarrely psychotic behavior among a group of female elephants in Thailand. Every hunch we got about every question opened up a fresh jar of questions. Questions that had been answered sprouted more questions, like the heads of the Hydra: cut off one and two grow back in its place.

I stared out at the wasteland that America was becoming, rusting under the hard, pitiless summer sky.

Chapter 51

AND THERE WAS more bad news that morning—special, just for me. I had to interrupt my research in order to head down to D.C. to do my Chicken Little dance at another time-suck of a congressional hearing. For all the scientific evidence we were amassing—and in spite of the exponential increases in animal attacks, which were irrefutable—many people, both in the government and in the citizenry our elected officials are supposedly beholden to, were still refusing to accept that anything out of the ordinary was happening.

I wasn't the only voice screaming in the wilderness anymore—but still, not everyone had heard the call. In those first few years, it was a long, uphill battle to get people to recognize what was happening.

I had frequently been at loggerheads in the op-ed pages with Harvey Saltonstall—yes, the Harvey Saltonstall: evolutionary biologist, popular science writer, holder of the Henry Wentworth Wallace chair at Harvard. I had a couple of public debates with him, too. Harvey and I had shared a few split screens on news shows. He was my most prominent public critic, and his opposition to HAC must have delayed public acceptance of it by years. It drove me nuts debating him—he had the academic cred, the name, the CV, and who the hell was I? I looked like your office's IT guy standing next to that stately, handsome man, twiggy in his tweeds, with his pipe-smoky baritone, his Boston Brahmin accent, and that obnoxious tic of swiping back his silver hair. Twit.

I rubbed circles on my throbbing temples with my thumbs, my gathering headache coming at me in fuzzy radio waves of pain, and was more astonished than alarmed when a guy I didn't know came in and sat down across from me. He looked like an ex-husband of Britney Spears: skinny arms blue with bad tats, houndstooth Sinatra hat, a goatee that looked drawn on.

A small part of me wondered if I was still asleep.

"Can I help you?" I said.

"You Jackson Oz?"

I might have rolled my eyes. Here we go.

So, then. I'd written a book about HAC, which had become a controversial bestseller. On the one hand, it was the best thing I'd done yet to spread the word about HAC: it led to appearances on the major media outlets, where I tried to warn people about the growing danger and the increasingly dire need for immediate, coordinated action. On the other hand, I was sort of famous—or, rather, infamous. Pet owners didn't like me much. "Dog people," especially, despised my message, now even more so since we'd gotten Congress and the president to consider a national quarantine.

"Actually, no," I said. "But I get that all the time."

The man was unfazed.

"Why you gotta hate on dogs, yo? Why you gotta be getting people all crazy and shit? To sell your stupid-ass books? My rottie ain't evil. She's a sweetheart."

"Everything okay here?" said a behemoth of a black man in a tailored pin-striped suit who had just materialized in the doorway beside K-Fed.

"We havin' a conver*sation* here," the guy said with righteous indignation. "A private conversation."

"Not anymore," said my sometime bodyguard, FBI special agent Nimo Kade. He flashed a winning smile and a badge. "Would you like to find your seat or do you need some help?"

Nimo shouldered the dipshit out of the train car and I let out a long breath of relief.

Working with the government has its perks.

This sort of thing happened a lot. My e-mail in-box was so full of death threats that these days I just deleted them without being curious enough to open them.

"You bring out the best and brightest, don't you, Oz?" Nimo said when the guy was gone.

"It's my sparkling personality," I said. "Where is everyone?"

Chloe appeared in the doorway of the train car. The best thing about the last five years—five unrewarding years of slaving away in the lab, constant traveling, constant frustration—was having Chloe by my side. She'd been working as hard as I was. Harder, actually. And somehow, instead of sporting my burned-fuse chic, she was her same self, with silky skin and owlish eyes, her body willowy and elegant as a stroke of calligraphy.

Then there was a noisy, porcine squeal, and something giggly and sticky shot through the open doorway, scrambled onto the seat, and landed in my lap.

Zoo

"Egads! A monster!" I said in my 1930s radio drama voice as our three-year-old son, Eli, climbed me as though he were Sir Edmund Hillary and I were Everest. I put him in a mock headlock and kissed him on the top of his fuzzy blond head.

Eli wasn't only a rambunctious kid who loved wrestling and snapping together LEGO guns, he was smart. As a whip. At eighteen months, he could write words on the fridge with magnet letters. And he was bilingual in English and French.

Chloe and I had gotten married in a quickie job in the city clerk's office the day after she found out she was pregnant. Then we'd held a ceremony for friends and family a couple of months later. Eli was born eight weeks prematurely, and had to be put in the NICU. We were afraid he might not make it. But a week later, he bounced back. Started getting bigger and healthier.

As I watched him hop up next to Chloe in the seat across from me and open his favorite book, *The Jungle Book*, my depression was replaced with a rejuvenated sense of determination.

The hell with Yeats, I thought. The center would hold. It would have to. For my wife and son, I'd make it hold or die trying.

Chapter 52

TRAFFIC WAS STOPPED dead on the way to the Capitol from Union Station. In the backseat of the sleek black government sedan, Eli fidgeted in my lap, gnawing like a gremlin on a fruit leather we had gotten at Trader Joe's. He was getting cranky. Chloe was already cranky because they didn't have the car seat for Eli that they had said they would. The afternoon sun sparkled on a sea of chrome and glass and glowered like a fat yellow bully above us, a problem that the car's anemic AC alleviated exactly not at all.

I was getting pretty cranky myself. Another worthless hearing? What was the use? Nothing ever happened at these kangaroo courts but a jamboree of choreographed histrionics. Worst of all, Senator

Charlie Chargaff, my avowed archenemy, was going to be on the inquiry panel today. I couldn't wait to get grilled by a hair-plugged good ol' boy with a spray-on tan who was going to try to ride his demonization of me into the White House.

When at long last we rounded a corner, I could see the reason for the clogged traffic. A block from the Capitol complex, a smattering of young people in black hoodies and black masks were squaring off against riot cops. Several of the protesters were waving black flags with the circle-A anarchy symbol sprayed on them in cracked white paint. Billowing plumes of pink smoke sprayed up around them. Car horns honked all around us like the bleating of bored sheep.

"What are these fools protesting now?" Chloe said, watching from the corner of her eye as Eli whacked a Batman action figure against the seat, making blow-up noises with his cheeks. "They already have what they want. Anarchy is here."

The driver peeled off into a U-turn and brought us around the back of the Capitol building. I felt the tickling buzz of my phone vibrating in the inner lining of my suit jacket.

The caller ID said US GOVERNMENT.

"Who is it?" Chloe said.

"Uncle Sam," I said.

"Mr. Oz?" said a resonant voice.

"Speaking."

"Are you at the hearing yet?"

"Bad traffic, on my way. Who is this?"

"This is Stanley Marshall, the president's chief of staff. Something's come up, a matter of national security. We need your help on it. Take a detour and come for a meeting."

"Now? I'm scheduled to speak in half an hour."

"I understand that, Mr. Oz. The president would like to speak to you instead. This is more pressing. Put one of the agents on the phone; I can give him directions."

I lurched into the front seat and handed Nimo my phone.

"What was that?" Chloe said as we pulled another U-turn. Eli dropped his Batman figure on the car floor as we turned.

"Mommy! Get Ba'man!"

"I don't know," I half whispered. "I guess we're going to meet the president."

Ten minutes later the car was pulling into a municipal parking garage in Dupont Circle. Seemed fishy. I leaned up front.

"Are we meeting Deep Throat?" I said. "I thought we were going to the White House."

Nimo looked back at me and shrugged.

"They told us to come here," he said as we wheeled onto the garage's ramp.

We slowly circled up to the roof. I was confused. It was deserted.

"What is this?" Chloe said. "There's no one here."

"Damn," I said.

"Mommy!" said Eli. "Get Ba'man!"

"What?" said Chloe, ignoring him.

"This must have been a ploy. Senator Chargaff. He must have found my number and had someone call, pretending to be the chief of staff, so I wouldn't show up to the hearing. Make me look like a flake. Bastard."

I tried calling the number that had just called me. I was listening to the phone ring, unanswered, when we heard a low, chopping mumble—like an industrial fan heard through a pillow.

A plastic bag drifting along the concrete wall beyond the windshield fluttered and took flight, graceful as a bird blown across the cityscape of D.C. Then we heard the deafening suck-and-throb tattoo of a landing helicopter, cottoning the air like a migraine in the head of a god.

The whirlybird that landed five empty spots to the left of the sedan was a massive Black Hawk with military markings. An army colonel in mirrored aviators and a jacket as decorated as a Christmas tree hopped out of it and jog-walked toward the car.

"Daddy!" Eli yelled in my ear.

"What?" I yelled above the throbbing din.

"Get—Ba'man!"

Chapter 53

AND WE'D BEEN worried about no car seat for Eli *in the car*.

Strapped into the wailing, shuddering army helicopter a few minutes later, we pushed off the parking-garage roof and swung low as a sweet chariot over downtown Washington. We picked up altitude, and before long it was no longer concrete and highways but rolling jewel-green Virginia swampland that rushed by beneath us. I looked over at Eli, who was strapped in on Chloe's lap, clutching his Batman, eyes big as Frisbees, in awe.

We banked hard and thundered due north for twenty minutes or so and then began descending again. An office park of stark glass buildings emerged from the forest. From the vantage point of a few thousand feet above, they looked like blocks of ice melting on the grass. We dove toward the central building. I thought we were going to land on the red H of the helipad on the ground next to it, but instead the pilot guided us onto the flat roof of the building.

"Thanks, Colonel," yelled a silver-haired man in a navy Windbreaker who was waiting for us on the roof as we disembarked. "I'll take it from here."

The colonel flicked a salute at him, and the chopper picked up behind us and rose skyward.

I noticed the letters NSA on the electronic badge clipped to the pocket of his crisp white dress shirt as he led me, Chloe, Eli, and Nimo across the sun-baked asphalt of the roof toward a door.

The National Security Agency: the department that does worldwide electronic surveillance for all the intelligence services—so cloak-and-dagger that some people call it No Such Agency.

"Section Chief Mike Leahy," the man said, shaking my hand as we entered the building. "Thanks for agreeing to come."

He led us out of a stairwell into a long, blinding-white corridor.

"Sorry for all the drama, but when"—he glanced at Eli—"the you-know-what hits the fan, things tend to work pretty fast around here."

We turned a corner and entered a semicircular room that had rows of seats and a podium in front. It reminded me of a college lecture hall. Behind the podium was a shiny, sleek television screen the size of a billboard.

A side door opened and a middle-aged black man entered the room. Leahy was in business attire, but this guy wore a black polo shirt with black jeans and Chuck Taylors that squeaked like balloon animals on the shiny white floor. The gold Rolex at his wrist added a splash of bling to the ensemble.

"Are you the president?" Eli said, gazing up at him.

"No, I'm not," the man said.

"Actually," Leahy said, smiling stiffly, "the president has been detained. This is Conrad Marlowe from the Defense Department."

"Don't jerk their chains, Mike," Marlowe said. His teeth could have been mah-jongg tiles, and his voice was like a velvet cello. "Mr. Oz here is smarter than that. He saw this coming back in 2012. Hell, back in 2011, 2010. The president's not coming. They say that to get you on the bird. And technically, I'm not from the Defense Department. I work for a think tank. War games. That kind of happy crap.

They think I can solve this Rubik's Cube, but I'm having my doubts."

"But we really do need your help, Mr. Oz," said Leahy.

Now standing in the doorway was a severe-looking sparrow of a woman with threaded brows and hair yanked back as tight as a figure skater's. She clicked her knuckles twice on the open door. Leahy cleared his throat.

"This is Jen, my assistant," he said. "Would it be all right if she brought Eli across the hall to have some ice cream and play computer games while we talk shop?"

"Heck, if he doesn't want to go, I'm down," Marlowe said, glancing at Jen, a speck of fire in his eye.

"Can I go, Mommy?"

"No ice cream without the magic word, okay?"

"Pleeease!" Eli beamed bright as a headlight as Jen herded him out the door.

"Hard to find a sitter on short notice," I told Leahy.

"Okay," Chloe said after they were gone. "Let's cut to the chase, yes? What is this? Why are we here? What's happened?"

"It's here, Mrs. Oz," Leahy said.

"What's here?" I said.

"HAC has arrived in the United States like gangbusters," said Marlowe. "The animals are on the warpath. It's spreading. A pandemic."

"We're calling the unfortunate new environment Z-O-O," Leahy said, spelling out the word. "Those letters stand for something, but fuck if I can remember what."

Marlowe snickered. "And we're just one of the animals."

Chapter 54

ANNAPOLIS, MARYLAND

DR. CHARLES GROH lets the hiss and crackle rise to a frenzy, and then, sensing their undersides beginning to burn, reaches a fork into the cast-iron pan and turns over the slices of bacon one by one. The bacon strips tremble and buckle, spitting a mist of fat flecks and smoke above the pan.

Behind him, sprawled on the patterned floor of Mexican Talavera tiles, his chocolate Lab, Charlie II, whines pitifully and drums his tail against the side of the kitchen island. His whining erupts into a yelp.

"Patience, Charlie. Patience," Groh says, waving his fork in the air like a maestro. "With the important things in life, it's all about the timing. And bacon is a very important thing."

Zoo

After draping the bacon on a paper towel, Groh hobbles to the sink with his cane and washes his hand. The male gorilla who had attacked him in his primatology lab at Johns Hopkins eight years ago took his left hand as well as his nose, his lips, his right eye, left ear, and his right leg from the knee down. Groh uses a prosthetic hand and leg.

The incident had actually been a perverse godsend, in a cosmic sense. Back then, everything had been put on the back burner but his career. He was tenured, secure in his career, with a CV thick as a phone book. He had written academic books and several popular books on gorillas, and had been awarded a "genius" grant from the MacArthur Foundation. He was the toast of intellectual circles— but as his career floated higher and higher into the ether he had been spending less and less time with his wife, Adrianna, and his son, Christopher Robin. He was growing distant from his family, and Christopher was growing up without him. He was even neglecting his teaching, sloughing off most of his classes on TAs.

For all its pain and horror, the mauling and his grueling recovery had saved him, in a way—it brought him back down to earth. Yes, he now wears sunglasses in public, and his potential career as a foot model is shot. But he can still teach. Although certain positions are off the table, he can still make love to his wife. He can still fry bacon.

All things considered, Groh thinks, lifting a steaming mug of coffee to his surgically reconstructed lips, he is a relatively lucky man.

Groh folds a strip of bacon into his mouth and switches on the radio beside the sink. The needle's zeroed in on some nattering morning talk show, and he paws around the dial until he lands on some classical music. Verdi. That's better. He hears the clink of crockery against the marble counter of the kitchen island and turns. His twelve-year-old son mumbles a good morning as he tilts a box of Lucky Charms into a cereal bowl. He's a handsome kid, currently brown as a nut from hours of outdoor play at his summer day camp.

"Hey, kiddo," Groh says. "Cease and desist with the Charms. I made us bacon."

"Bacon and what?" says Chris, turning on the MLB Network on the kitchen TV. He mutes it, letting his dad's Verdi score the recap of the Braves losing to the Orioles the night before.

"Bacon and bacon so far," Groh says, opening the fridge. "How about an egg?"

"Can I have bacon with Lucky Charms?" says his son, staring at the screen.

"I don't know. Would your mother let you do that?"

Adrianna is in Baltimore for a few days with her elderly mother, who just had her gallbladder removed.

"Are you nuts? Hell no," Chris says.

Groh smiles as he brings over the steaming pieces of swine.

"Then have at it, boy," he says. "She'll be home soon."

Groh makes his way across the floor between the kitchen and the front door when he hears a truck pull up outside. He glances out the window and sees that it's a Lawn Doctor truck in front of the neighbors' place across the street. A couple of childless yuppie lobbyists who pull down some long green, apparently, judging from their matching Beemers. They certainly aren't landscapers. Crabgrass and brown spots mottle their sickly lawn like mange. Hence the Lawn Doctor truck.

When he turns from the window, Charlie II is looking out the open front door, panting as he spies with him on the neighbors through the glass of the storm door. Groh galumphs back toward the kitchen on his cane, patting the dog on top of his sleek, brown, dopey head. A flurry of shiny red cartoon hearts is floating out of Charlie II's expression.

"Okay," Groh says, scooping up his keys with a jingle from the kitchen counter. "I'm off to work. You're on your own for another hour, Chris. Mom left Nana's already and will be here to take you to camp. Love you."

"Dad, wait. I almost forgot," Chris says.

Groh watches his son ransack the backpack dangling from a hook on the wall by the front door. He fishes something from the bag and hands it to him—what looks like a red-and-white plastic necklace.

"It's a lanyard. I made it at camp yesterday," says Chris. "I thought it could hold your sunglasses, you know, like, around your neck, when you're working or something. I made it red and white for the Nats."

Groh looks at it, then at his son, his one eye threatening to fog up.

"Hey, thanks, kiddo," Groh says. "It's awesome. Are the Nats playing tonight?"

"At home. Versus the Diamondbacks. Seven tonight. Strasburg's starting."

"You want to go?" Groh says.

"What? To the stadium? Heck, yeah!" says Chris, slapping him a high five.

Lucky man, Groh thinks again as he pats his son on the shoulder and then steps into the garage.

Chapter 55

"HEY, CHARLIE. WANT some bacon?" Chris says to Charlie II when his dad is gone. "Hear that, boy? The Nats game. Stephen Strasburg throws like a hundred miles an hour." He heads back into the kitchen. The dog's claws click on the floor tiles behind him.

No one in the family loves Charlie II more than Chris. They've practically grown up together, having been "pups" at the same time. The family has moved three times, following Charles's new jobs, and each time, Charlie II was Chris's best friend until he managed to make human friends. Chris remembers how hard it was to make the dog stay home when he went off to play with his friends. Charlie II would whine in sadness, his eyes forlornly watching Chris from the window as he left the house. And if Chris looked back, he might not be able to leave. To *not* be with Chris seems to be the hardest thing for the dog to do. They are close as brothers.

Chris kills the Verdi on the radio, turns up the volume on the TV, and zaps through the channels with one hand, searching for ESPN. With the other hand he picks up a slice of bacon from the grease-dampened paper towel and offers it to Charlie II under the counter.

A hot shock of pain in his hand. Chris drops the remote.

"*Hey!*" He yanks back his hand and looks at it. Charlie bit him. There are puncture marks in his hand.

"*Ow!* What the *fuck?* What'd you do *that* for?"

Chris looks agape at Charlie II, standing beside him in the kitchen. The piece of bacon lies untouched on the floor tiles. Something is—something is not right. There is some weird look in the dog's eyes—some knowing, almost angry glaze in them that Chris has never seen before. Charlie begins to growl. His jowls flap against his teeth, spit percolating deep in his throat. The eighty-pound Labrador crouches, coiling back, the fur bristling high and stiff as steel wool on the back of his neck.

He is growling, sounding like a guard dog, his teeth bared, a gloopy white thread yo-yoing from his lower lip in a pool of saliva.

"What in the *hell*? What's wrong, boy? Stop it. It's me. What's wrong with you?"

It looks like one of his eyes is messed up. Charlie's head keeps jerking to one side, as though he were a boxer shaking off a punch. Something is *wrong*.

Charlie curls in on his hind legs and lets loose with a string of the loudest, most threatening barks Chris has ever heard him make. He sounds like a junkyard dog warning off intruders, not the family pet he's known more than half his life. Charlie is in a rage—lungs heaving up quick, loud, guttural barks that sound like "WAR-WAR-WAR-*WAR*—*WAR!*"

That's it. Chris gets scared. He panics. He tumbles from his chair and starts running. He feels Charlie's hot breath on the backs of his knees, hears jaws snapping behind him.

The closest door is the hallway pantry. Chris dashes inside and slams the door, and feels the *whump* and rattle of Charlie throwing his weight against it. He leans with his back against the pantry door, holding it shut.

On the other side of it, Charlie smashes his body

into the door, the thing shuddering on its hinges under the impact. Charlie scrabbles his toenails at the door, clawing and barking, heaves himself into it in manic thumps, seemingly wanting to rip him to ribbons. In all the years they have owned the dog, he's never sounded like—like a *wild animal*.

He's gone crazy, Chris thinks. He saw it in his eyes. The dog is off his rocker. He no longer seems like Charlie II. He is something else. Another dog entirely. A bad dog.

He feels himself beginning to cry. In the hallway, he can hear the dog skulking in circles, still rumble-jawed, occasionally sneezing, occasionally breaking into a fresh wave of furious barking.

"WAR-WAR-WAR-*WAR*—*WAR!*"

Chris looks down at his hand. The punctures in his palm aren't huge, but they're deep, and bleeding. There's blood all over his shorts.

Chris shakes his head, swiping at his eyes. He has to calm down and think. He's still bleeding. He has to deal with that.

He crouches down and reaches for a package of paper towels on the bottom shelf. On the paper towel package, a handsome mountain man in a flannel shirt smiles. He tears open the bag with his teeth, wraps a wad of paper towels around his hand,

and tightens the makeshift bandage with a strip of plastic wrap.

He sits in the hot, cramped darkness, listening to the dog pace and growl in the hallway. He is thinking about maybe using the broom to beat back the dog for long enough to run for help. Then the phone in the kitchen rings.

The machine bleeps and someone starts leaving a message. He hears Charlie II skitter back into the kitchen.

Chris bolts from the pantry and races up the back stairs. He's halfway to his room when Charlie arrives on the stairs in front of him.

Chris dives sidelong into his parents' bedroom. Charlie comes through the doorway a moment later, forcing Chris into the bathroom. He whams the door shut a split second before the dog crashes against it, and Charlie again goes berserk with barks and snarls.

Damn it. His plan had been to call his mom or dad from the cell phone in his room. Now he's stuck again.

"Charlie!" he calls through the door. "There's something wrong with you. It's me. It's Chris."

He can hear a note of pleading in his own voice, and it seems only to spark the dog's contempt.

Charlie either can't hear him or it doesn't matter. He continues barking, clawing, snarling.

"WAR-WAR-WAR-*WAR*—*WAR!*"

That's when he remembers that his mom is on her way home. She doesn't know Charlie II has gone berserk. If she comes in the front door, Charlie might bite her, too.

He needs to call her. His cell phone is in his bedroom. He starts pacing back and forth across the bright bathroom floor. It's still steamy from a shower. He suddenly remembers the box in his dad's closet. His dad's a gadget guy; has trouble tossing out spare parts and computer cables and stuff like that. Chris remembers the box has some old cell phones in it. You can dial 911 on old cell phones, right? He remembers hearing that somewhere. He hopes it's true.

His parents' closet is right next to the bathroom. And the walls are made of Sheetrock, right? He stepped through the ceiling once, dicking around in the attic when they'd first moved in, and knew firsthand how that stuff is surprisingly soft and crumbly.

Plan. He will make a hole in the wall, try to climb through it into the closet. Get the old cell phone from the box. Call 911.

He unscrews the metal shower curtain rod and begins to bash at the wall with it. He works at it for a while. The hole is about the diameter of a basketball when he hears the rumbling electric moan of the garage door opening from the floor below.

Charlie II stops barking and bolts from the room.

Chris panics. He's too late. His mom will get bitten. He thinks of his dad's gun. He's been duck hunting a few times with his dad; sometimes with his uncle, too, when his uncle is visiting. He knows there's a shotgun in the closet. He's not sure if there are shells.

Chris drops the shower curtain rod to the bathroom tiles with a clatter, yanks the door open, and then goes into the closet. The shotgun is on the top shelf, lying on a pair of folded orange hunting vests. He can't quite reach the shelf. He kick-scoots a chair into the closet, scrambles on top of it. He fumbles through the orange vests. He finds a box of ammo in one of them. He knocks out a handful of shells, pockets them, races downstairs with the shotgun.

He fiddles with the gun on the stairs. How the fuck do you load the stupid thing again?

Slow down, he tells himself. *Think*.

He's shot the thing like three times in his life, always with his dad, and his dad has always done the loading. Remember. He flips the gun over and notices some sort of closed slot on the side. He fiddles with a little catch underneath it and works the slide forward, opening it up. Then he slips the slug in and pumps the slide back. It goes *chik-clack*.

He can hear his mother coming through the door as he slides around the hallway corner, slippery in his socks on the glossy hardwood floor, shotgun heavy and awkward in his hands.

"Hello?" he hears his mom call. "Chris?"

"Mom!" he shouts down the hallway. "Look out! There's something wrong with Charlie!"

The dog appears. He turns the corner at the opposite end of the hallway. His toenails click on the wood floor. Spit hangs in frothy strings from his mouth. He does that crazed head-twitching thing again, sneezes.

The dog moves forward slowly, growling, loose pulled-back lips flapping against bared teeth.

He watches the dog approach. He doesn't want to shoot. Charlie isn't just a pet. He's a brother.

"WAR-WAR-WAR-*WAR*—*WAR!*"

The dog breaks forward into a run and leaps.

Chris raises the barrel of the gun and pulls the trigger. The kick of the gun butt knocks him on his back. The dog falls.

Blood peppers the walls.

The blast has taken off the Labrador's face. His skin is gone; blood pumps from the place where his eyes used to be.

Chris rises to his knees, then crumbles back to the floor, crying. He drops the gun. He hears his mom come running.

"What the hell is going *on*?" she shouts.

The dog's legs twitch wretchedly as blood gushes on the floor, dampening Chris's socks. The animal lies dying just feet away from him.

"I'm sorry," Chris half whispers. "Oh, I'm so sorry, so sorry."

Chapter 56

THE NEXT FEW hours didn't seem real. We sat in squeaking, uncomfortable chairs that were bolted to the floor facing the massive TV. Leahy dimmed the lights to show us footage of attacks that the NSA had picked up throughout the country. The most chilling one was from California.

The footage began with an aerial shot of an accident taken from a traffic helicopter. A jackknifed FedEx truck was half overturned alongside a sun-bleached highway. The traffic was at a near standstill as drivers slid by, rubbernecking at the mounds of boxes and packages spilling into the roadside ditch.

"This is news footage from this morning out of Petaluma," Leahy said. "That's US 101 just north of San Francisco."

"News footage?" I said. "You're showing me something the public has already seen?"

"Grow up, Jimmy Olsen," said Marlowe. "It's taped. The feds snatched it up before it could get out."

The camera cut out and came on again with a shot from a slightly higher elevation. Alongside the same highway, what looked like dirty brown water rushed along a service road drainage ditch.

As the chopper lowered toward the scene, I could make out that it wasn't floodwater—there were things moving in it.

"What in the hell?" I whispered, mostly to myself. I squinted and leaned forward, trying to make out the fuzzy footage.

It was a flood of fur.

"Mon Dieu," Chloe said. "Are those . . . *dogs?*"

Leahy nodded.

I kept watching. The camera zoomed in.

"What in the shit is going on here?" said the staticky voice of the cameraman, talking to somebody else in the helicopter, apparently. His voice threw the sound levels out of whack for a moment.

It was hard to tell—some of the dogs looked feral, but most of them looked like pets: fat, awkward, with collars on. They were filthy, crazed, scrambling all over each other like migrating lemmings. The camera panned back. This was something altogether new. The roaring column of animals went on for miles, it seemed.

"There must be . . . ," Chloe said.

"Our estimates are between five hundred and a thousand dogs in there," Leahy said.

"Wait. *Shh!*" Marlowe hissed. "We're getting to the good part."

The chopper swung in lower and sped along the ditch until it came to the spearhead of the bulging, running line of animals.

"The dogs at the front of this horde we think are Dogo Argentinos," said Marlowe. "They're enormous, aggressive dogs, bred for fighting in South America. They're banned in some countries."

The Dogos suddenly swerved a sharp turn, up out of the drainage ditch and then down an embankment to the right. The column followed, shifting direction en masse, like a flock of birds.

The cameraman zoomed way in, trying to get a close-up shot. The frame jittered. There was a squall of barking. Then an outburst of shouting among the people in the helicopter. The chopper abruptly lifted. There was a growling sound, and the camera swung sharply downward: a pit bull was stuck absurdly to the helicopter, jaws clamped down on the skid, shaking as if he were trying to kill it. The animal dangled crazily from the flying machine before letting go, tumbling back down through the air into the river of hair and teeth.

Leahy put the lights back on.

I turned as Chloe looked at me with eyes wide and bright as tealights. This was worse than we could have imagined.

She closed her eyes.

"I want to get Eli, and I want to get out of here," she whispered.

I rubbed her hand powerlessly, not knowing what to say.

Chapter 57

THAT AFTERNOON, MARLOWE and Leahy shuffled us into several other meetings. More government people kept arriving by the minute. There was someone from the CIA, Alicia Swirsky, a tiny middle-aged woman whose elfin features were offset by her serious-as-a-heart-attack demeanor, and two FBI agents in midnight blue—Rumsy, a young guy still wet behind the ears with enthusiasm, and Roberts, a guy with pockmarked cheeks and the old-school look of a man who knew his barber and tailor by name. The latest arrival was a four-star army general named Albert Garcia, who had just stormed in with the fuck-you bluster of someone accustomed to everybody rising and saluting when he enters a room. He was flanked by two uniformed aides. Garcia had a magpie's nest of shiny objects weighing down his uniform, a body like a backyard brick oven, and a head that looked like it'd been carved out of a tree stump with a chain saw.

After the video of the giant dog pack—dog horde, maybe?—was shown for what seemed like the fifteenth time, this Garcia guy cleared his throat.

"Now, according to ground reports, all the animals in this attack are male," the general said. "Why is that again?"

"Mass male grouping is one of the fundamental aspects of this phenomenon. We're not sure why," I said. "Male mammals—well, actually, any animal species in which males compete for females—usually display more aggressive behavior."

"In the report it said thousands of house pets had gone missing," said Agent Rumsy as he thumbed through the binder splayed open in front of him. "Is it just male animals that are missing?"

"That's another mystery," Mike Leahy cut in. "The female dogs are running away same as the males, but they're not the ones causing trouble. In fact, no one knows where they are."

"What *have* you learned on the research end, Mr. Oz?" said Alicia Swirsky, the CIA lady.

I gave them the elevator pitch about the research

we'd done at Columbia—the discrepancy in brain weights, the strange mutation in the amygdalae of affected mammals.

"Coming to the point," said Agent Roberts, wiping his bulbous nose with his thumb, a trace of backcountry in his voice, "do we have any theories as to cause?"

He didn't phrase it as a question.

"We're still trying to crack it," I said.

General Garcia clapped his binder shut and tossed it on the table. He sat back in his chair and folded his hands. His fingers were thick and brown as sausages.

"All well and good," he said. "But I believe, ladies and gentlemen, it's time to get down to brass tacks."

He jerked his head at the aide sitting next to him, who went fishing in a briefcase and came back with a file folder the size of an encyclopedia. He slammed it on the table, from which a cloud of dust would have risen if the room weren't clean enough to build microchips in.

"We need to talk contingency plans. The president has already signed directive fifty-one and issued an executive order initiating Garden Plot," Garcia said.

"Garden what?" I said.

"Domestic security contingency plan," Roberts explained in his Lone Star drawl. "They used it during the L.A. riots in the early nineties, and after nine-eleven."

"Affirmative," said the general. "It's SOP in a situation like this. The military assists local law enforcement in times of emergency. It gives the secretary of defense and the attorney general authority to deploy all appropriate mission sets required to restore order."

"What about the Posse Comitatus Act, which restricts the military from enforcing domestic law?" Swirsky said.

"I believe it doesn't apply in a situation like this, ma'am," Garcia said with a curt nod. "As point of contact for the DOD, I'm going to go ahead and issue orders to start mobilizing the National Guard's ready reserve."

I was ready to pull my hair out. HAC wasn't a riot or a terrorist attack. It was more like an environmental disaster. What a load of bureaucratic bullshit. Were they going to declare war on the animals? Why were they focused on *offense*? We needed to be thinking *defense*. This was insanity.

"We need to focus on finding the root of the problem, not killing animals," I said, trying to remain calm. "I mean, I'm sorry—I just don't get what your plan is, exactly. Bomb animals or something? What? Why don't we issue a nationwide warning to watch out for animals, especially pets, to limit the damage until we figure this thing out?"

"Because that would cause a nationwide panic even more destructive than this epidemic," Garcia said. "And because you boys've had plenty of time to 'figure this thing out,' and here you've come to us with zilch. Wild dogs were a problem in Iraq until we started exterminating them. You remember that, don't you, Staff Sergeant Oz?"

I flinched. He'd done his research.

"We put enough boots on the street, we can nip this thing in the bud in a few weeks. A month, tops."

I sat there, stewing in rage. I was about to try to point out how irrational the notion of simply exterminating dogs was, but I stopped myself. It was time for me to go. I needed to get back to New York and redouble my research, do everything in my power to figure this thing out before the army started trying to napalm the animals.

I caught Leahy's eye at the front of the room as I stood.

"If that's all you need me for, folks, then I've done all I can do for you. I'm sure my son must be getting restless. If you have any more questions, you have my information."

Leahy escorted us out. We picked up Eli and went downstairs. A black Lincoln Town Car was waiting for us, engine panting in the parking circle. Nimo was already in the passenger seat.

"Everything you heard today is top secret, Mr. Oz," Leahy said as we stepped outside into cuttingly bright sunlight. "So, in the interests of national security, we trust you'll be discreet."

"Of course," I said as we climbed into the back of the black car.

Half an hour later, the woodlands beginning to give way to the D.C. metropolitan area, I felt the tickling buzz of my phone again, vibrating in the inner lining of my suit jacket.

It was a message from Charles Groh. He sounded —well, upset.

"Oz, listen. HAC is here. My own dog went crazy today. My twelve-year-old son had to kill it."

"What is it?" said Chloe as I shook my head.

I wanted to lie to her, but I couldn't.

Chapter 58

FROM THE REAR of *Leda Lady Queen,* his rust-caked twenty-two-foot fishing boat, Ronnie Pederson lights his fourth cigarette of the morning and squints as he stares out at the gently slapping surface of the Gulf of Mexico.

The coast of Texas—Galveston Island and, beyond it, the southern suburbs of Houston—is now just a flat brown line on the horizon to the north. To the south, the moisture in the air blurs the line between the sky and the sea. Somewhere in that blue-gray blur, the water bends out of sight over the surface of the earth. Although the radius of visibility at sea on a perfectly clear day is only twelve miles, for some reason you grasp the bigness of the world when you're out on the open water, more than you ever can on land.

The sky looks clear enough, and the water is flat as a drum skin to the horizon, but Ronnie keeps his eyes open nonetheless. Out here in the Gulf you have to watch the weather carefully. This late in August, a storm can brew up at the drop of a hat.

The boat is silent. The way Ronnie likes it. Just the chug of the old diesel and the hiss of spray off the bow. Duane and Troll, his old high school football buddies turned commercial fishing partners, are at their positions aft and starboard, lost in their own early-morning thoughts.

An hour later, as the sun finally peeks above the horizon, they're ratcheting in the first net lines. Looks like a good catch, from the way Troll's netting the fish out of the drink, his arms working like a ditchdigger's. Soon the deck pens are filled with shrimp, the little things squirming like slimy pink bugs as Duane sprinkles ice over them.

They had taken on another hand a couple of weeks before, but it didn't work out. The college kid had come on all tough, but the guy was green as a sapling. The rocking of the boat had gotten to him.

He was still puking the second day—feeding the seagulls, as they called it—and they had to let him go. Now it's just the three of them again.

As the sun gets higher, they decide to try their luck farther out. For a moment, there's a breath of coolness in the air, promising more, and Ronnie is struck with a good feeling. It's the same feeling he used to get on the football field. That same pregnant sense of peaceful isolation right before you knock a fullback ass over teakettle into the sidelines.

"Hey," Duane calls from the other side of the boat. "Look at 'at!"

Ronnie steps across the clanging sheet-metal deck, ducking beneath rigging and machinery.

"What?"

He looks at where Duane's pointing.

Up ahead of them, moving fast but seemingly not moving at all because of the wideness of the sea, are several dolphins. They look like saddlebacks, but he isn't sure. They hop in and out of the water in graceful arcs. There are three or four of them. Their sleek, silver bodies weave in and out of the water in perfect sequence, moving together all at once. How the hell do they know how to do that? Where'd they learn that? Why do they all jump out of the water and dive back in again at the same time? There must be a reason for it. An animal's body does everything it can to maximize results by minimizing energy, Ronnie knows. Everything like that has some kind of reason. Animals don't do things without a reason. It is a beautiful sight.

Ronnie is awakened from these thoughts when he hears a loud, heavy thud in the boat.

"*What* in the *hell*—," Ronnie hears Troll say behind him.

The three friends stare at what is now in their boat, and then up at each other. It is a dolphin. A full-grown saddleback dolphin has leaped out of the water and into the back of their boat, where there's an open drop-off to bring up the trawling net, and is slapping and writhing on the deck, wiggling like a maniac.

They would only be slightly more surprised if a mermaid had jumped into their boat.

Thing looks silly, absurd, out of the water. It's about six feet long, and squealing like a pig.

"Well, look at that," says Duane.

Ronnie cuts the engine and walks to the back of the boat.

"This is the damnedest thing I ever seen," says Troll.

"Well," says Duane. "I reckon we should put him back."

He moves to start pushing the dolphin back into the water. The dolphin bucks and giggles.

"This is a story to tell our grandchildren, ain't it?"

They are laughing as they try to roll the lashing dolphin off the deck.

They all startle, and jump back, as another dolphin races headlong out of the water, arcs through the air with a trail of jewel-like water droplets behind it, lands with a wild slapping thud on the deck right beside them, and slides down half the length of the boat.

The friends look at each other, then burst into laughter.

"Is this some kind of dolphin joke?" says Duane.

That's when the weird shit really starts happening. In come the dolphins. One after another after another, the fat, sleek, shiny animals leap out of the water and land in the boat.

Ronnie stands there on the deck, looking down at the now seven or eight dolphins, squirming like crazy in the boat. Suffice it to say he has never in his life seen this sort of behavior. Bizarre. Completely fucking bizarre.

Soon it goes from funny to scary.

Now there are dozens of dolphins on the boat. This is when Ronnie turns from bewilderment to fear. Something not only very strange but very wrong is happening. The dolphins tunnel deeper across the deck, sliding all over each other. An avalanche of heavy, slippery silver bodies, a chorus all around them of squeals, squeaks, giggles.

It is as if the sea is throwing them up, heaving the animals from the sparkling depths of the Gulf.

After a while, it's not just the deck pens that are full; the deck itself is a mess of dolphins. The men are desperately heaving and kicking the animals off the back deck, but more keep coming.

There must be more than a hundred now. Ronnie slogs through the wiggling dolphins back toward the wheel and gives her some throttle.

In response, the thirty-year-old trawler, weighed down more than it has ever been, tipples like a drunk on a three-day bender and capsizes.

Ronnie, treading water, feels himself going into a kind of slow-motion shock.

Troll is the first to panic. He's doggie-paddling beside the overturned trawler, splashing like mad and making huffing sounds.

"Calm down, damn it," Ronnie shouts to him.

"Kick off your boots. Conserve your energy."

Dolphins are pressing up against them like cattle, splashing, chattering, squeezing, suffocating them.

Troll is still splashing, clawing at the rim of the sinking boat, fighting the herd of dolphins. In another minute he goes down, pops back up, and goes down again. This time for good.

Duane goes the same way a few minutes later.

Before too long, *Leda Lady Queen* is gone beneath the waves.

Ronnie, doing the dead man's float, lasts a little while longer. When he is sure he has nothing left, and no one is coming, he faces it like a man. He stops fighting and, drinking as much salt water as he can, slides beneath the dark, cool water, letting it rush over him like a blanket, letting the Gulf swallow him.

Though the three men are dead, the dolphins continue to play. They leap, they splash, they giggle, they frolic and jump.

Seemingly for joy.

Chapter 59

BARBARA HATFIELD DOESN'T know what time it is when she emerges into consciousness on top of the covers of her bed beneath the misty canopy of mosquito netting. Inside the dark, rough clapboard room, and outside the windows, it is gray now. All time, space, matter comes in shades of sad, heavy, leaden gray.

She's still wearing her shorts and shirt and mud-encrusted jungle boots. She scratches at the hardened pus of a mosquito bite under her greasy hair, scratches the skin on her arms and legs. She hasn't bathed in four days.

Her eyes fall to the empty side of the bed beside her. She leans over and takes Sylvia's pillow in her hands, presses it to her face.

The scent of her still clings to the fabric. Sylvia's smile as she's coming back from her run, flesh glowing, slick with sweat. Her nimble hands always doing something, fixing the forty-year-old compound's leaking roof, changing the Land Rover's oil. Tending the garden—she looked so gorgeous with her arms and legs stained black with dirt up to her elbows and knees and her hair held back, Rosie the Riveter–style, in a bandanna. She'd come through the door in that bandanna and her weathered leather gloves, holding her clippers and a twine-bound bundle of weeds, and Barbara would want to grab her and kiss her so long and deep that Sylvia would have to push her away just to come up for air.

This year-long grant was a once-in-a-lifetime scenario, a golden ticket for a primatologist. It provided enough money to live for a year in Rwanda, working at the mountain gorilla research camp that Dian Fossey had made famous.

Sylvia had thought it would be too dangerous, but Barbara had begged and cajoled and finally convinced her to put the community garden on hold for a year and follow her to Africa.

They'd been returning from doing the yearly UN-required endangered species census of the mountain gorillas when the unspeakable occurred. Barbara was walking up the path to their cabin behind Sylvia when three silverback male gorillas emerged from the open front door.

A moment later, there were gorillas everywhere. Silverbacks and younger males. There was an electric fence around the camp, but the gorillas had somehow penetrated the camp's perimeter. They grunted, threw debris, leaped off the roofs of the cabins and outbuildings. Cargo crates clattered; the air was a swirl of pounding, panting, huffing.

Barbara remembers running into the jungle, her lungs burning, as leaves and branches crunched and cracked behind her. Then she had looked back and noticed that Sylvia wasn't with her anymore.

She mustered up her courage and came back to the camp that night—to find everyone gone. All three Rwandan trackers, the four young men from the antipoaching team, and Sylvia. All gone.

In the bed, Barbara moans as she grasps at her throbbing head with her hands, trying to wring the memory from her brain as though it were a sponge. She had been quick to dismiss the fringe-level, paranoid racket about HAC, the absurd buzzing of Internet lunatics. She believed the theory was crackpot because she knows animals—gorillas in particular. But now she is having doubts. The behavior of all mammals, even mountain gorilla behavior, seems to have undergone a meltdown.

She's in dire straits. The radio and generators have been smashed, along with the guns. The nearest village is thirty miles away, through mountain jungle so impassable they had to be airlifted here by helicopter. The next supply run is forty-eight hours away.

Two more days to get through, Barbara thinks. If the gorillas return, she will have no chance.

She is sitting up in bed, rocking back and forth. In despair.

Then she feels something. It is a distinctly felt presence, as if Sylvia were there in the room beside her, watching, invisible. Not only that, but her lover seems pissed off at Barbara for doing the damsel-in-distress act, panicking, giving up.

Have I taught you nothing? Sylvia's presence seems to say. *Buck up, girl. Grow some ovaries.*

Barbara climbs to her feet, ripping aside the gray film of mosquito netting. Sylvia is right. She needs to do something. In a moment she knows what.

Behind the storage shed are barrels of gasoline for the generators. Barbara can fill up some canisters, douse the tree line, set it on fire. She hates thinking about damaging such a precious ecosystem, but it is a life-and-death situation. Her life and death, specifically. Perhaps the smoke will attract attention from the villages in the valley, and perhaps someone will eventually come to investigate. And get her out of here.

She is coming out from behind the shed with two gas cans sloshing tinnily in her hands when she hears the crunch of branches off to her left. She turns. Her eyes fall on the tree line. She drops the gas cans. They tumble at her feet.

Coming through the trees is something that defies imagination.

About two hundred yards away, rhinos are entering the clearing. Half a dozen massive horned rhinos.

Which is impossible. How did they get here? Rhinos graze in the plains. They have to be within walking distance of water. Why would rhinos migrate seventy miles laterally and several thousand feet vertically from their natural habitat? What would she see next? Polar bears?

The animals keep coming. There are more than

a dozen rhinos now. The scene is so out there, so upside down—so wrong.

As the creatures approach, a memory comes to Barbara. She is eleven years old, sitting in the front pew of a Baptist church with her family in northern Florida. The fire-and-brimstone preacher points a gnarled finger at the small crowd in the pews as he reads from the Book of Revelation.

"And the first beast was like a lion," he says histrionically, turning his eyes to heaven. "And the second like a calf. And the third had a face like a man."

End times, Barbara thinks, watching the giant animals step curiously amid the jungle underbrush. She is in such desperation that she almost begins to pray.

Chapter 60

MOBILIZED OUT OF Fort Drum, New York, Captain Stephen Bowen's Tenth Mountain Division consists of two four-man fire teams, a small but elite unit.

Arrayed in the standard wedge formation, the men move as one up the wooded hill in their camos. Using hand and arm signals, they are silent, all but invisible. Standard operating procedure for combat patrol.

The fact that their combat patrol runs alongside a bike path in Hapgood Wright Town Forest near Walden Pond in Concord, Massachusetts, is definitely not SOP, though. It's more FUBAR than snafu. In Captain Bowen's opinion, this is about as screwball as it comes.

Bowen knows for a stone-cold fact that what they are doing is illegal. They're supposed to be helping the cops direct traffic, not going out on a search-and-destroy mission in a public park. And the orders, if you could call them that, are truly out there.

Bowen, though only twenty-seven, was hard-core even before he did his three tours neck-deep in the shit of Afghanistan and Iraq. The word INFIDEL is tattooed across his chest in an arc of Gothic lettering, and inked on his back, under the Mountain Division insignia of crossed swords, is his credo, KILLING: THERE IS NO SUBSTITUTE.

"Cap, down the hill," says King, on point. "Movement. Six o'clock."

"What are you waiting for, soldier?" Bowen says. "Drop it like it's hot."

King opens up with his M16A4.

Bowen's eyes twinkle like Strawberry Shortcake's as the familiar, ripping, heavy-metal clack of gunfire echoes across the hills.

Is there anything better than guns unloading? he thinks. What else can make your eyes water and your dick get hard at the same time?

"Shit," King mutters after three three-round bursts. "Missed. I think it's still coming."

"That's what she said," says Chavez.

"Lemme show you how it's done, Poindexter," Bowen says, parting leaves as he steps forward.

When he gets to the crest of the hill Bowen mentally does a little Scooby-Doo: *Eeuooorr?* Directly in front of them, down the incline of a patchy deer path, are three—what are they? Bowen thinks. *Dogs?* He glasses them with the 10X binoculars. Hmm. Foxes? About a dozen or so. Now, how about that? Rabid, bloodthirsty foxes. Whatever.

"Tallyho, motherfuckers," Bowen says, dropping the glasses and lifting his rifle smoothly to his shoulder.

The new gun pulls left a bit when he pulls the trigger, but he manages to adjust.

The men start laughing as they come down the hill.

"Shit, Cap. Didn't think we'd be going hunting today," says Chavez, poking at one of the dead foxes with the muzzle of his gun. "Hope you understand PETA will be gettin' a e-mail."

They camp for the night by a creek under an old train bridge three clicks to the north. There's a battered old couch there, a couple of sun-faded Coors boxes, torn condom wrappers, amateur graffiti.

"This night air's making me feel romantic," Gardner says, popping open an MRE. "Any you guys wanna take a moonlit stroll?"

"How about a weenie roast, boys?" someone says in a falsetto.

Bowen sits Indian-style beside the fire, zeroing out the rear sight of his rifle with an Allen wrench. He wonders if or when he should tell them the real reason they're here.

Two nights ago there was an incident. A whole cul-de-sac off Cambridge Turnpike was massacred. He's seen the photos. Some of the scariest shit he ever saw, which was saying something. One of the pictures he's having trouble getting out of his mind. A little boy on a racecar-shaped bed, entrails ribboned out onto the carpet.

"Wire that shit tight, ladies," Bowen says, glancing out at the dark beyond the firelight. "I know this is fun, but this ain't a frat party. This is a military op, so act like it."

The attack comes a few minutes north of 0130. Bowen wakes to screaming and gunfire. Between three-round bursts comes howling. Guttural, snarling, inhuman noises. Fairy-tale monster-type shit.

"We got a fuckin' ogre out there?" he shouts, rising to his feet and grabbing his gun in one movement.

If that isn't bad enough, Bowen hears the whine and tiny crack of bullets singing by his ears.

"Watch your goddamn shooting lanes!" Bowen barks. "Watch your lanes!"

Someone throws a flare. The sudden light throws long shadows high onto the spindly black trunks of the trees.

Some twenty feet away, galloping on all fours up the shore of the creek, are bears. Four of the biggest goddamn brown bears he has ever seen.

Bowen doesn't think. He yanks an M67 frag grenade from his vest, snaps off the safety clip, fingers the pin, and pulls the grenade away from the pin the way you're taught to. He holds the grenade for a moment, thumb off the safety spoon, letting it cook.

"Frag out!" Bowen hollers, and dives to one side as he tosses it.

There is a flashing soft thump. Followed by silence.

When someone chucks another flare, they can

see that all four bears are down for the count. Off in the darkness, they hear the sound of other bears retreating, their paws splashing in the creek.

Bowen scans his men, does a quick head count. Everyone in the squad present and accounted for. He puts a hand to his chest, feeling his heartbeat hammering *bang bang bang* against his ribs like a goddamn elf making shoes in somebody's basement. Bears in the wire? Good holy shit, that was close. This animals-rising-up-against-man bullshit isn't bullshit after all.

He turns. Out there in the darkness, beyond the firelight and across the water, Captain Bowen can feel eyes on them.

A lot of eyes.

Chapter 61

I'D HAD BETTER mornings.

I awoke that day from a dream. Eli and I had been walking through New York's Museum of Natural History. The light was eerie, watery, pale blue. We stopped before the diorama of the gray wolf. Eli's favorite. The wolves were posed in midhunt, racing through timberland snowdrifts in pursuit of an elk. This elk was doing it wrong. You get attacked by wolves, you stay still. Stand your ground, you have a chance of surviving. Run, you're dead. One of the wolves had his jaws clamped on the hind leg of the elk. The wolves' eyes flashed winter-moonlight yellow, their lips curled back to show their teeth. I held Eli's hand. Then the wolves came alive, and suddenly there was no glass in the diorama. The wolves spilled from the diorama and were on the floor of the museum in an instant. Eli's hand slid from mine, and the wolves tore at his throat.

Then my eyes opened. It took me a long moment to realize who I was and where I was. When I realized these things, I wanted to go back to sleep. Maybe dream better dreams.

It was before dawn. I was in the Alphabet City apartment Chloe, Eli, and I had moved into a year ago.

I sat up. I placed a palm on Chloe's warm, still back, then looked across the dim room into the corner, where Eli slept soundly in his toddler bed, a curled hand clutching his stuffed bunny to his chest.

I wiped sweat from my face. My hand was shaking. My child and my wife. They were both safe. For now.

Since our return from Washington, things had been escalating. Day by day. Exponentially. Strange, extraordinarily violent animal attacks were on the news every evening now, happening everywhere from New Hampshire to New Delhi, from Sweden to Singapore.

There had been several bizarre animal attacks here in New York. Night before last, two kitchen workers in a chic French bistro in the West Village had been found dead. Mysterious circumstances. A Ninth Precinct cop who happened to live in our building had told us what the papers left out—at the government's request. The men had been killed by rats that had flooded in through the basement. They had been stripped to the bone. No word yet if this would affect their Zagat rating.

It was being called the Worldwide Animal Epidemic, and even my fiercest detractors were admitting that it was the worst global environmental disaster of all time. The phone rang off the hook with reporters asking me to comment, but I was too tired. I didn't take any pride in being right, in saying I told you so.

I blamed myself, really. I'd had years to prepare, to tell the world, to figure out why it was happening, to try to come up with a solution. I'd failed at all these things. Sitting there, staring at my son, I realized I had completely failed him—my son, my wife, everyone.

"Where's Eli?" said Chloe.

She sprang upright beside me in bed.

As I rubbed her back, I could feel her heart beating as hard and quickly as mine. Like me, Chloe was torn up inside, worrying about the increasingly bad news and about how we were going to protect ourselves and our son. Paranoia and sleeplessness were our new normal these days.

"He's okay. Everything's fine," I said. I pulled her close.

You know things are getting bad when you find yourself uttering empty platitudes that you don't even believe yourself.

"What time is it?" Chloe said, her slender olive-skinned arm fumbling for her watch on the bedside table. She was still gorgeous. That didn't change. "You can't be late for your meeting."

I'd gotten a call from the mayor the day before. He wanted a face-to-face. Though the National Guard had been mobilized for the first time since 9/11, the mayor's assistant said he needed all the advice I could give him on dealing with this wave of animal violence.

"Meeting's at eight," I said. "I'm going to get up in a second. How are we on food? I heard the Union Square farmers market is opening back up today."

Not just attacks but food was becoming a worry now. Some people said farming and trucking were being disrupted out west. There were rumors on the Internet of massive food shortages on Long Island. But no one really knew, or, in any case, no one knew what to do about it. Every day, people fled the city while others seemed to be flocking to it. We were approaching an end-times state of mind.

"We're still good," Chloe said. "We're out of milk, but that grocery store on Avenue A is still open."

"Fine, but don't stay outside more than you have to. And take the bear banger."

In addition to having an alarm installed and gates put on the apartment windows, I'd picked up some bear bangers from a sporting goods store on Broadway. The device looked like a pen but was actually an extremely loud explosive flare used by hikers to fend off wildlife.

I wrenched myself out of bed, gave Chloe a kiss, and headed for the shower.

Checking the locks on the gated window in the bathroom, I remembered the government code name for the environmental disaster, ZOO.

Why? I stood in the shower, letting the hot water roll over my head, staring at the tiles. Why is this happening? What has changed in recent history—what have we got now that wasn't here before?

Never in human history has there been a time when most people are so distanced from animals. So removed from them, both psychologically and physically. If you are a human being in a place like, say, where I live, New York City, you won't really have to interact with a nonhuman animal all day long. It makes me think about how the world must have been before the Industrial Revolution. You needed oxen to plow the fields. The fastest way between two points was a horse. Knowing animals, being close to them, used to be a way of life. Less and less so for more and more people now. Homo sapiens is so close to dogs that we even coevolved with them. The genetic difference between a human and a chimp is about the same as the difference between two subspecies of groundhog that evolved on opposite banks of a river—and yet even Attila had been affected. Surely the root of HAC was some very, very small, and very, very recent, change. And that change had to be something that humanity was up to, because we seemed to be the only mammal on the planet incapable of being affected. For whatever reason, whatever it was that was going on got along just fine with our brains, but simply did not gel with the brains of seemingly all other mammals.

It was a zoo, all right, I thought, shutting off the water, staring out through the bars down at Seventh Street. Only it was starting to look like the Homo sapiens were the ones who would be relegated to the cages from now on.

Chapter 62

TWENTY MINUTES LATER, my taxi driver cranked the reggaeton as we swam upstream through sludgy traffic on the Bowery for my early-morning meeting. Usually the noise would have driven me up the wall. But that morning, I actually found the only-in–New York aggravation oddly comforting. By the time we made it to the Flatiron district, I had begun to think affectionately of the swamp of traffic and gratuitous honking.

It meant that, disaster or no, people were going to work today. The Big Apple hadn't gotten the end-of-the-world memo just yet.

Then I saw a dog on the street. It was moving along the sidewalk just north of Thirty-Fourth Street.

On the east side of Third Avenue, coming off

the curb about half a block ahead, was what looked like a medium-size black-and-white Border collie mix with a dirty blue bandanna around its neck. The mutt was by itself, and as I watched, it began to thread its way through the traffic, from east to west, across the avenue.

What set my alarm needles to twitching was the animal's sense of purpose, of deliberate calmness. Stray dogs usually have a guilty, skulking look about them, especially in a big city in broad daylight. This dog wasn't going too fast or too slow, nor was it looking at anyone. It was focused, confident—looking like it was headed somewhere.

I had a sudden hunch.

I leaned forward. "Stop the cab, please," I said.

"Here?"

I threw him a bill. "Keep the change."

"You want receipt?"

I was out the door, narrowly avoiding becoming enmeshed in the grille of a beer truck as I jogged across Third Avenue and headed north in pursuit of the dog. I got to the corner of Forty-First Street and looked left, down the block where the dog had been headed. At first I couldn't see anything. Then I stepped into the street alongside the line of parked cars and saw a white tail wagging as it crested the top of the rise by Lexington Avenue.

"The hell do you think you're doing?" a traffic cop shouted at me as I played Frogger across the intersection.

I kept my eyes on the tail of the collie, its little white feet picking up into a trot, as it crossed Park Avenue, a block west.

Kicking it up to a full-blown sprint, I managed to keep track of the dog as it crossed Madison Avenue. It kept going west on Forty-First, heading toward Fifth Avenue and the front steps of the New York Public Library.

I got to Fifth just in time to see the dog heading north on the sidewalk on the west side of the avenue, toward the corner of Forty-Second.

Dodging my way through an asteroid belt of early-morning commuters, I ran on the east side of the avenue, parallel to the dog—who was really moving now, boogying—toward Forty-Second. When I got to the corner there was too much traffic to cross and I had to wait for the light.

It took ten ticks of eternity for the light to change.

When it finally did I bolted ass-on-fire across Fifth, scanning the avenue up and down and looking east and west on Forty-Second. The dog could have gone anywhere—maybe into Bryant Park, behind the library to the west. It could have slipped into one of the surrounding office towers for all I knew.

The dog was nowhere to be seen. Wherever it had gone, and whatever I might have learned from it, was lost now.

I was crossing to the other side of Forty-Second to catch another cab, glancing at my watch and trying to calculate how late to the meeting I would be, when another dog almost ran between my legs in the crosswalk. I wheeled around and watched as a white Yorkshire terrier made the corner and trotted west along the south side of Forty-Second. Little dude was on a mission.

Oz: follow that Yorkie.

There was a small ornate stone building on the perimeter of Bryant Park—not taking my eyes off it, I watched the little white dog scuttle on stubby legs and disappear into the recessed doorway of the little building.

In a moment I was standing by the squat, easy-to-miss building. The recessed doorway led to a small descending stairwell that ended in two black wrought iron doors hitched together with a padlocked chain.

I stood at the top of the stairs, blinking. I was completely bamboozled. Because there was nothing else to see. The dog had vanished.

Chapter 63

I HEARD THE echoes of my shoes clattering down the fetid concrete stairs. I pushed against the doors—they creaked and groaned inward easily, making a wide gap against the bight of the heavy black chain. I presumed the dog had slipped through the gap.

Why he had done so was a mystery.

I squinted, peering through the dim gap. I thought about going into the library and finding out who might have the key to the lock.

For about four seconds.

I abandoned that plan and popped two buttons off my oxford cloth shirt, squeezing myself feetfirst through the narrow gap.

Inside, I found a light switch and turned it on. A feeble orange lamp flickered on above. It was a storage room, full of lawn mowers, rakes, and other maintenance equipment for the park. Beside the equipment to the right were more stairs, leading to a downward-sloping corridor lined with ducts and pipes.

The arched tunnel was made of old-fashioned faded red brick. I vaguely remembered that Bryant Park stands on the site of what had been the city's main reservoir in the mid-1800s. The curving tunnel went on for ten feet and then opened up into a small round room filled with huge pipes, valves—everything gunked up with disuse and caked orange with rust. The largest of the pipes was open at the end and set sideways into the wall about a foot off the floor, like a tunnel.

I squatted down next to the pipe and caught a scent—rank, musky, unmistakable.

It was the smell of wet dog.

Wet dog and then some. It was mixed with a lush potpourri of garbage, skunk, dead animal, shit. It was a smell that could peel paint. There was some kind of moisture on the floor of the wide pipe, and the stench seemed to emanate from it like smoke from a tire fire. It was acrid, hideous.

I stared into the reeking blackness. For a long time. I thought of turning back, of dog attacks.

Something about the complete focus of the dogs I had followed told me I was safe. I went into the pipe.

It was like crawling into the asshole of Satan. Every five feet I had to stop and repress the urge to vomit. My hands, knees, and feet squelched in the sucking black muck as I slogged my way through the tube.

Darkness. Stench. Claustrophobia.

In the pipe, I could hear sounds coming from someplace I figured was at the opposite end. Yelping, whining. Dog sounds.

Eventually I ran out of pipe. I stood up in the dark of some new room. The smell was even more concentrated here. Had I climbed into the sewer?

There was a dim, barely luminous light on somewhere, a weak orange flicker. My eyes adjusted.

Below me, the sunken floor of the ballroom-size underground chamber was moving.

As far beyond me as I could see, there was a squirming mass of eyes, teeth, hair.

The dogs were moving around and on top of each other in a way I had never seen before. They were slithering against each other like worms in a can. I was within scenting distance for all of them, but not a single one even turned toward me.

Many of them were copulating. The dogs fucked

impassively, with slack tongues and unchanging expressions. Others looked sick, their hides mottled in what looked like a whitish mold. Small fights broke out here and there. A few dogs would come together in a sudden tumble of kicking legs, snapping jaws, and barking—blazing into sudden fits, one dog dominating and another surrendering with a pitiful whine, the other dogs skulking away quickly. The room was foggy and hot with moving bodies, wet with breath and tongues. Snorting. Sneezing. Heads twitching. Legs scratching.

Along the wall of the chamber to my right, galleries had been carved in the raw dirt walls and in them, female dogs were nursing puppies. The swollen bitches lay on their sides, their bloated bellies looking tender and thin-skinned, pink, jiggling with the weight of milk as the puppies suckled.

I looked out across the squirming underground orgy of dogs. These dogs were acting as if they were organized somehow, as if they had a hive mind. They were acting more like insects than like mammals.

Then that lightbulb clicked on again above my head. The hive mind. Bugs. That proved to be one of the keys to understanding what was going on.

The animals were all acting like social insects—swarming, teeming, feeding, breeding.

Zoo

The sight reminded me of something I once saw on a research trip to Costa Rica in grad school. The time I saw an ant death spiral. It's an amazing thing. We came across hundreds and hundreds of ants, all running together in a giant spiraling circle. It was as though they were running laps, spiraling and spiraling together, a squirming black whirlpool of ants. It shows you the power of pheromones. Ants follow one another by their pheromone trails. When you see a line of marching ants, it means that each ant is following the chemical trail of the one in front it, picking up the scent with its sensitive antennae. But every once in a while something happens that breaks the pheromone trail—a log falls on the middle of the line, for example. And suddenly some ant in the middle of the chain now finds himself at the front of a new one. He panics. (I'm anthropomorphizing here, but bear with me.) He runs around like crazy, searching for another pheromone trail to follow. Eventually he finds one, and starts following this other ant. But unbeknownst to him, he's just found the pheromone trail of the ant in the back of his own line. And then the column turns into a loop that winds and winds in on itself as the ants, blindly following one another, simply run around and around in circles until they die.

And I thought: pheromones.

Chapter 64

SCRAMBLING, HUFFING, NEARLY ten meters up in the tree, Cheslav Prokopovich stops climbing and tentatively leans out, distributing his weight carefully along the limbs of the Siberian pine, which are getting thinner at this height.

Through the mesh of crisscrossing branches, he can see for several kilometers down the rocky river valley, its horizontal visual panorama interrupted only by the tall and starkly looming transcontinental radio tower that is the reason for the village's existence this far north.

But sightseeing is the least of his concerns this afternoon.

Prokopovich carefully unstraps his rifle from his back and flicks a downward glance at the forest floor, looking for the other members of his hunting party. From this height, Sasha, Jirg, and Kiril look identical. The three Russians are wearing army boots and cheap camouflage hunting coveralls. All of them are stocky, bald, and chunky-featured, as if they're built out of rocks.

Lifelong friends and residents of Inta, the four men had worked together in the nickel mine that opened up in the heady times after the fall of the Berlin Wall. Their annual late-summer hunt is supposed to be a time of respite before the snow and ice come, before the arctic temperatures drive them inside and underground for six months beside the fire—six long, boring, maddeningly sedentary months of bottomless cups of vodka and endless hands of durak.

All year, Prokopovich anticipates this excursion, especially the sunny moment before he bags his elk—that full-body tremble of excitement, the childlike splashing of his heart inside his chest.

His heart is splashing now, Prokopovich thinks as he breathes on his rifle's scope and dries it with his sleeve.

The weapon Prokopovich presses to his cheek is a handcrafted Mosin-Nagant hunting rifle. Through the scope's reticle he scans the boreal forest of evergreens, firs, and pines that green the landscape. He is looking for any slight sign of movement.

Specifically, he is looking for the wolves. The wolves that have been chasing them since morning.

There are several dozen, maybe more. The biggest and most aggressive wolves he has ever seen. Why so many wolves have decided to pack together and come after them Prokopovich does not know. He only knows that if Kiril had not woken up early to take a piss and seen them in the distance, loping up the mountainside like lava flowing in reverse, they might already be dead.

Prokopovich rests the sight on the rattletrap rail bridge that spans the ravine they crossed earlier. The abandoned rail line was built by gulag prisoners in the 1950s, when Inta's network of government labor camps was still running. Their plan had been to head up the mountain across the dilapidated old bridge. They thought the wolves would be unable or too afraid to cross it. Up in the tree, he spies the bridge through the rifle scope, waits, and watches.

Prokopovich is thinking about his wife when the

wolves break cover from the tree line en masse and head for the ravine.

"*Tchyo za ga'lima,*" Prokopovich mutters to himself as the animals head straight for the bridge.

He watches as they begin to fastidiously work their way across, gingerly picking over the decrepit wooden ties and iron beams, one by one, paw by nimble paw.

"*Blya!*" Prokopovich says to the sky. "*Vse zayebalo!*"

Whore!

Fuck it all!

Chapter 65

SPITTING OUT A sticky pine needle, Prokopovich rivets his eyes on the approaching wolves. They are moving fast, but he tries to count them. Soon, the task of counting them becomes overwhelming. He can't. There are too many. What he sees is impossible. He has heard of packs of ten, maybe fifteen. Surely there must be fifty wolves spilling out of the trees, funneling over the bridge after them.

Prokopovich straps the rifle on his back and hurries down the tree.

"What now, hunter man?" Kiril says, soothing his nerves with a swig of vodka from his canteen.

Kiril's face is cauliflowered and enflamed with rosacea. His eyes are like raisins.

Prokopovich pauses for a moment, frowning. It

is not Sasha, who still plays hockey, or his cousin Jirg, the weight lifter, whom he is worried about; it is the largest of the men, his best friend, Kiril, who causes him concern. The big, boisterous fool is squatting against the trunk of a tree, wheezing like a concertina from the exertion of the morning's uphill march. Kiril is fat as a swine and smokes like a broken truck, and is as slow-moving as sap in January.

Dead weight, Prokopovich thinks grimly, looking at his friend.

"*Blya!* We run, you drunken pig. We run for our lives!"

The wolves are a swarm of gray dots down in the distant valley, slaloming between trees up the mountain. They make no noise. No barking, no howling. Only silent running.

"Hurry! Run, if you want to live!"

The men have one last chance. There is another bridge over the ravine, a little less than a kilometer farther north. It is in even worse shape than the first one, a mere skeleton of a bridge, with no ties at all. They will have to scale the outside of its rusted latticework frame. An almost suicidal enterprise, especially for poor fat Kiril. But there is no other choice. At least there is no way the four-footed wolves will be able to cross that. The problem is getting there in time.

They are within sight of the bridge when Kiril drops. He looks terrible. He huffs at the air like a fish out of water, hacks into a fist. His face is swollen, the color of borscht.

"*Bol'she—nyet!*" he says between gasps. "No. More. Can't. Not . . . one . . . more . . . step."

"Damn you!" Prokopovich gives him a savage kick. For all the good it does, he may as well have kicked a tire. "*Mudak!* Get up, you son of a whore."

"*Blya, blya,*" Jirg adds. "My wife isn't going to be a widow because you're a fat fuck."

"*Pojdite!* Go! Both of you!" Prokopovich says as his knees crunch in the pine needles beside Kiril. "Kiril just needs to catch his breath. We will catch up with you at the bridge."

Sasha and Jirg do not need to be told twice. In a breath, they are gone.

Prokopovich holds Kiril's heaving shoulder and gazes forlornly through the trees at the distant Ural Mountains, looming to the east.

"Go, Cheslav," Kiril pants. "Don't do this." His beady eyes look defeated and miserable. "Jirg is right. I am fat and useless. I am too weak. Always have been."

Kiril is a clumsy, bumbling fool, laughed at by one and all. What redeems him, what has always made him Cheslav's best friend, is that Kiril himself is always the one who laughs the hardest.

Prokopovich checks the ammo in his rifle as he sees the wolves beginning to race through the trees.

"I'm sorry," Kiril says as the panting of the wolves becomes audible now. Kiril is weeping. His voice is cracked and whimpery. "I always loved these hunts. You are my great friend, Cheslav. I never became a millionaire, but I am rich to have had you for a friend."

"*Zatk'nis!*" Prokopovich hocks a dismissive dollop of spit in the pine needles. "Shut up, you poof, and take up your gun. We are going to live."

As the wolves approach, Prokopovich looks down the valley. It is crisply sunny at this elevation, but the plain beyond the bridge, where the village is located, is overcast, bathed in a dark purple-red glow, as if lit by a black light.

So this is where I die, Prokopovich thinks.

Then the first wolf, a male with eyes as yellow as the moon, steps into the clearing.

It is a monster of a thing, fifty kilos at least. When he was a child on a hunt with his father, Cheslav saw a wolf smaller than the one now before him take down a bull elk.

Too bad I am not a bull elk, Cheslav thinks.

"Stand up, you fool," he says to Kiril.

Kiril heaves himself to his feet.

Together, they stand back-to-back, with their guns facing out.

Prokopovich knows what to do with wolves. Stand your ground. You stay put, they respect you, you live. You run, you die.

The wolves begin to gather around them. More and more come. The groups of wolves begin to mingle, merge, intermesh. Snarling, growling, teeth snapping, staccato bursts of threat-barks. The wolves form a circle around them. They advance, they retreat. The air is filled with a cacophony of barking.

Prokopovich can feel Kiril quaking against his back.

"Stand still, *mudak*," he grumbles at Kiril, behind him.

"We stand our ground, we live. We run, we die. They smell your fear."

"*Eto piz'dets, eto piz'dets,*" Kiril is half whining, half mumbling. "This is so fucked up, this is so fucked up."

Kiril squeezes the trigger of his gun and a shot goes off, from the hip, aimed almost at random into the crowd of wolves. Cheslav feels the gun crack against his elbow. A jet of blood leaps into the air, like a squirt of bright dark berry juice, and there's a whimpering howl.

"Kiril!" Prokopovich shouts. "No!"

He hears Kiril pull the trigger again. Another howl and a spurt of blood.

A wave of fresh agitation moves throughout the circle, a swell of freshly crazed barking.

Whatever, Cheslav thinks. Fuck it. And he, too, fires a shot into the crowd.

They kill about seven of them. More keep coming.

Then Kiril decides to run. He leaves their post in the middle of the circle and tries to bolt. A moment after he does—just a fraction of a moment later, a sliver of time so thin an eye blink does not describe it—the circle of wolves rushes in to close. Their bodies become a whirlpool of fur, roaring throats, thrashing legs, ripping jaws, all piling on top of each other. Prokopovich squeezes another fistful of bullets into the horde, but it is useless. The wolves swarm over the two men until they disappear beneath them.

It goes on for several minutes before the clamor dies down. The pack loosens and the wolves separate, rove the field, sniff the ground, begin to tumble and growl, not in earnest violence but in play.

Cheslav and Kiril are gone. There are no bodies left to speak of. There is blood smeared across the floor of grass and pine needles. Many of the wolves have bloody snouts and mouths, and some of them lick blood from their damp, matted fur. Some of them squabble here and there over bones. But the men themselves have disappeared.

Chapter 66

I'M SURE I looked like a zombie who had freshly clawed his way out of the crypt when I flung open the door of our apartment. I heard the clink and scuttle of Chloe putting away groceries in the kitchen. I left the keys in the lock and sprinted down the front hallway.

As I stood in the kitchen doorway, Chloe looked at me as though I had gone completely crazy. I looked it: I was slathered with black filth and breathing hard after running back from Bryant Park.

But I wasn't crazy.

For the first time in years, I knew I was right.

"Hi," I said.

"So," she said. "How was the meeting with the mayor?"

Her voice was sarcastic.

"Incredibly productive."

Chloe stood up from where she knelt beside the open refrigerator, closed it.

"The mayor's office just called. What the hell happened to you?"

I took the jar of salsa she was absentmindedly holding and set it firmly on the counter. I held her by the shoulders as I struggled to catch my breath.

"I've figured it out!" My voice was choked with excitement. I tried to calm it. "The reason for the attacks . . . it's not a virus . . . it's pheromones."

Chloe looked at me askance.

"You're not making sense, Oz."

I started to collapse onto a chair next to the kitchen table.

"Don't touch the furniture!" said Chloe.

I remained standing.

"On my way to the meeting, I saw a stray dog," I said. "I followed it into a tunnel beneath Bryant Park. Inside were more dogs. Thousands of them."

Chloe nodded, mental gears turning.

"You saw another dog pack?" she said. "Like the one on the video?"

"Yeah," I said, nodding. I started to wipe sweat from my eyes with filthy fingers, thought better of it, got to work on blinking it out instead. "But here's the thing. They were all grouped together, rubbing against each other, behaving in a way I've never seen before. They were mating, regurgitating food. They had these chambers where females were giving birth."

"Disgusting," said Chloe.

Then she began backing away from me, her hands flying to her face.

"*Mon Dieu!* What is that smell?" she said, finally catching the full brunt of the dog sludge I'd crawled through.

"Exactly!"

I shimmied out of my shirt. My pants followed a moment later. I was leaving black streaks on the kitchen tiles. I rummaged through the kitchen drawers in my socks and underwear, found a plastic bag, and threw the clothes inside, tying it tightly.

"We need to test my clothes. It's their smell. I think the dogs are emitting it. But they almost weren't acting like dogs, Chloe. I know this sounds insane. They were acting like insects. Like ants or bees or something. It's not a virus, like rabies, that's making the animals go haywire. We need to test for some kind of new pheromone in the environment."

"That's crazy," Chloe said, still covering her face.

"Is it?" I said. "This whole thing has been staring us in the face from the beginning. How do animals communicate? Subconsciously, I mean. How do dogs, bears, hyenas recognize one another, their environment, their territory?"

"Secreting and sniffing pheromones," Chloe said.

"Life, at its most basic level, is chemistry," I said. "Right?"

"Hmm."

"Groups of molecular compounds reacting to other groups of molecular compounds. When an animal sniffs a rival or a predator, it receives information that changes its behavior. That's what's occurring here. In some way. Except the animal signals are getting crossed somehow. The signals they're getting are making them act against their instincts. There's something new, something wrong—either with the pheromones themselves or the way the animals are processing them."

"It might make sense," Chloe said, getting into it now. "The mutations we found in the animals were in the amygdala, which usually governs the sense of smell."

I paced back and forth across the kitchen in my underwear, still holding the sagging trash bag full of my reeking clothes.

"I think it may even have something to do with that bizarre stuff that went on with Attila," I said. "A chimp's sense of smell isn't that great. But I rescued him from a perfume lab where they were doing chemical experiments on him. I think the pheromone or whatever it is in the environment somehow made him go crazy."

"Like a steroid or something," Chloe said. "Are the animals exhibiting a kind of chemically triggered rage?"

"Could be."

"But why all of a sudden?" Chloe said. "What's changing the way they perceive pheromones?"

"I don't know. But I do know that we need to find some pheromone experts and put them in a room, yesterday. More like five years ago. I'll call the lab, you call that government guy, Leahy. I think we finally caught a break on this thing."

Chapter 67

THE REST OF my morning consisted of a *Silkwood* shower and a Jerry Lewis telethon's worth of phone calls.

By midafternoon Chloe, Eli, and I were sitting around the kitchen table with our bags packed and ready to go. I guessed our ride was out front when my phone went *bzvvvvt bzvvvvt* on the table and UNKNOWN NUMBER popped up on the screen. I went to the window and looked down.

When the NSA chief, Mike Leahy, said he was sending a car to take us to a secure location, I thought he had meant, well, a car.

On the sidewalk in front of our building was a camo-colored up-armored combat Humvee, with a soldier manning a machine gun in the steel-plated turret. For traveling with a low profile, I guess.

A young kid with orange hair and freckles, straight out of *Archie Comics,* met us in the lobby downstairs. He saluted.

"Lieutenant Durkin, US Army Third Infantry," he said in that military cadence, a forward tumble of barks rising in pitch.

"Jesus, is it getting this bad out there, Lieutenant?" I said, gesturing at the war machine we were apparently about to enter. Durkin hoisted our bags as though he were a valet and led us toward the Humvee.

"Manhattan below Ninety-Sixth Street is in the process of being evacuated," he said. "We're starting with the hospitals and hospice facilities."

"*What?* Why?"

"Rats."

As we rolled north through Manhattan we saw barricades, checkpoints. The city was swarming with men and women in camo. The only vehicles that passed us going in the opposite direction were government evacuation buses and more army Hummers.

Times Square was empty. I glanced at the darkened marquee as we passed the Ed Sullivan Theater, where they tape *Late Show with David*

Letterman. No stupid pet tricks tonight.

When we turned west on Fifty-Seventh Street we heard the whoosh of fire, and looked out the window to see two soldiers in silver suits kneeling in front of an open manhole, aiming flame throwers beneath the street.

We stopped on Fifth Avenue and Eighty-First Street. A chain-link fence braced with sandbags had been strung across the avenue in front of the Metropolitan Museum of Art.

The Upper East Side was occupied now? When had all this happened? And why hadn't I heard about it? The world had flipped from normal to bizarre in what? Hours? Things had seemed fine to me that morning.

"These two blocks are HQ for the time being," Durkin said as a guard waved us through the makeshift fence. "This kinda reminds me of the Green Zone in Baghdad."

"Or Ground Zero after nine-eleven," I said.

We rolled past sandbagged trailers and stacked crates of bottled water and came to a stop in front of a stately granite prewar building directly across from the Met. The building's interior was all gilded ornaments and Corinthian columns, glass, brass, marble, potted ferns. Durkin led us into the grand lobby, where an NYPD sergeant checked our IDs and, for no discernible reason, wanded us with a metal detector—including Eli, just to make sure our three-year-old boy wasn't packing heat.

"Who's in charge?" I asked Durkin.

"Colonel Walters, but he's in the field."

"The field?"

"Well, the city. I think some of the other scientists are here. Let me show you to your quarters first."

They were nice quarters. The apartment we were led into was a multimillion-dollar duplex with massive fireplaces and twelve-foot coffered ceilings. The living room was cluttered with marble sculptures and African masks. There was a Chagall on the dining room wall.

"Fancy digs. How'd the army sublet Xanadu?" I said to Durkin.

He shrugged.

"Ours is not to reason why," he said. "You guys settle in. The meeting's on the first floor at sixteen hundred hours. Enjoy your vacation at the end of the world."

Chapter 68

WE LEFT ELI in a makeshift day-care center that had been set up for the scientists' children on the building's fifth floor and went downstairs to help prepare for the meeting. I was surprised at how quickly Chloe and I adapted to all this doomsday scenario stuff. One day, you drop your kid off at pre-K, the next you take him to a government evacuation center's day-care facility. What else could we do?

In a large alcove off the sweeping marble lobby, we worked with camo-clad army techs to convert a dining room into a conference room, complete with an interactive whiteboard. The table was a sleek, oblong, blood-colored mahogany, its surface so glossy it reflected light as sharply as a mirror. The room was huge, the ceilings fifteen feet high, with marble cornice moldings in the corners and dark oil paintings of robber barons set in the walls. A chandelier dangled like a bunch of crystal grapes above the table.

Over the next hour, Chloe and I greeted the other scientists whom the government had shuttled in via Hummer and helicopter. In addition to my colleague Dr. Quinn, they had recruited most of the rest of the lab staff from Columbia as well as more than a dozen top-drawer entomologists, environmentalists, and other scientists.

"Ah, look who it is," I said to Chloe behind my hand. "Dr. Harvey Blowhard."

Chloe rolled her eyes.

Dr. Harvey Saltonstall, the Henry Wentworth Wallace chair in biology at Harvard, shook my hand and gave me a cold, curt hello. Being proved right before your enemies is a pretty good feeling, and I couldn't help but smirk a little. I did not like this man. Last time I'd seen him he was on the other side of a split screen on MSNBC, with Rachel Maddow moderating. That was more than a year ago. As usual, he'd made me look like a wing-nut bozo with his whole aristocratic persona—this handsome devil in tweed, occasionally swiping back his elegant shock of silver hair.

Harvey Saltonstall's prominent public opposition to HAC had delayed progress for years. Now, why wasn't I surprised that the officious, elitist asswipe was front and center in the government team assembled to solve the problem?

Soon I was standing at the head of a conference table ringed with the country's best and brightest. I hoped all the expertise gathered in this room would be enough. And that we weren't too late.

I started out by quickly going over what I had seen that morning under Bryant Park.

"At first, I thought HAC had a viral origin," I said, looking around the table from face to face. Everyone nodded back at me. "But after seeing the animals up close today, acting in such a bizarre way, I think it's time to take a new approach. I think this has to do with pheromones. The dogs I saw today were displaying textbook pheromonal aggregation behavior. It's my belief that some new kind of morphed pheromone has entered the environment, and it's probably our doing, because we seem to be one of the only mammals whose behavior isn't affected by it."

"We came here for this?" Harvey Saltonstall took a long, fastidious sip from the cup of coffee in front of him while everyone waited for his next words.

"The environment? Please. This theory is infantile. A pheromone is a chemical that's very specific to communication within species. I've never heard of the same pheromone affecting multiple species. Are you suggesting there's some invisible crazy gas affecting all mammals except humans? Why should it not affect us?"

Irritating as he was, I knew Saltonstall had an excellent point. He'd immediately stuck his finger in the biggest hole in my theory. I bit my lip and thought.

Chapter 69

HARVEY SALTONSTALL MADE a prim cage of his fingertips and began to accordion them in and out, readying himself to redouble his attack. And then Chloe jumped in to save me.

"What about pollution?" she blurted.

"Yes, well, what about it?" Saltonstall said.

"Pollution in the environment sometimes causes mutational changes in animals. Take nylonase, for example. In a wastewater pond beside a nylon factory in Japan, they found a species of bacteria that only eats nylon. The presence of the pollution genetically altered the bacteria that were already there."

"This stuff is all well and good when we're talking about pollution," said Saltonstall. "But I thought we were talking about pheromones. What does pollution have to do with pheromones?"

I rapped my knuckles on the table.

"Hydrocarbons," I said. "That's where pheromones and pollution connect. Pheromones are made up of hydrocarbons. So is petroleum."

Around the table, everyone sat up a little straighter. My mind was racing. I couldn't help it—I sprang to my feet and started pacing behind my chair.

"Hydrocarbons are everywhere," I continued. "Over the last two hundred years, from car traffic and industrial activity, there's been a massive increase in volatile hydrocarbons in the atmosphere. Methane, ethylene . . ."

"Not to mention the prevalence of petroleum," Chloe said. "Petroleum is in everything—plastic, house paint, balloons, pillows, shampoo. It leaches into the groundwater."

"Didn't studies in the nineties explore the health hazards of plastics due to their chemical similarity to estrogens?" Dr. Terry Atkinson added. He was a chemical engineer from Cooper Union.

I felt like diving across the table and giving him a high five. I didn't.

"Yes!" I said. "If hydrocarbons can mimic

estrogen, it's entirely conceivable that they can mimic pheromones."

"Or take the plastic compound used in water bottles," said Dr. Quinn, jabbing a pen in the air. "They found that it caused the estrogen levels of fish to skyrocket for some reason. In a lake outside a manufacturing plant in Germany, researchers found that there were no male fish present at all."

"We are flying down the wrong path here, folks," Saltonstall insisted. He cleared his throat and swiped back his silver shock of hair with his hand. "How do chemical hydrocarbons change without some sort of catalyst? Plastic has been around for over fifty years. If it affected the way animals process pheromones, wouldn't we have noticed long before now?"

I let out a breath and tried to come up with an answer. Saltonstall again had raised a good counterargument.

"Excuse me, Mr. Oz," said Betty Orlean, an environmental scientist from the University of Chicago. "Quick question. When did you start noticing this increase in animal aggression?"

"As far as my data show, around 1996," I said. "But it didn't start getting bad until the aughts."

"Nineteen ninety-six is right around when cell phones started becoming more popular," Betty said a bit cryptically. "And cell phone use has exponentially increased since then." The thought was half formed in her head.

"So?" Saltonstall said.

"Well, Dr. Saltonstall," she said, "we know that cell phones use radiofrequency energy, which forms fields of electromagnetic radiation. Some animal functions at the cellular level can be affected by such fields. The fear for years has been that one field could disrupt the other. That's why there have been so many studies about the link between cell phone use and brain cancer. For years, our world has been swimming in an unprecedented sea of radiation."

"Yes," I said, really going now. "Perhaps cell phone radiation is somehow cooking the ambient environmental hydrocarbons in a way we've never seen before—morphing them into a chemical that animals are picking up as a pheromone. And it's changing their cerebral physiology, as we've seen at Columbia. We know that the affected animals have bigger amygdalae."

"Oz, I believe I remember something." Dr. Quinn jumped in. "It was a study about bees in the Netherlands." She spoke slowly and distractedly as she poked at the laptop open in front of her. "Yes, here it is. I'll put it on the SMART board." A moment later, a graph-peppered scientific paper appeared on the screen.

"This was a study done in the Netherlands in the nineties," she said. "It shows the effects of radiation on bees whose nest was relocated beside a cell phone tower. As you can see in table one, when the bees were in the forest, they had no trouble foraging and returning to the nest."

She got up, walked forward, and pointed at the curving lines of a graph on the screen.

"But here in the second graph, it shows that when the nest was placed next to the cell phone tower, the bees took longer and longer to get back, until the hive eventually died off."

"I, for one, am intrigued by Mr. Oz's theory," Dr. Orlean said. "I think we may have our culprits—pollution from hydrocarbons and electromagnetic radiation from cell phones have coupled together, resulting in critical biosphere meltdown."

There were nods all around. Harvey Saltonstall was visibly irritated. You could see the steam escaping from his ears.

"But that still doesn't explain why these alleged hydrocarbon-morphed pheromones don't affect human beings. Can you explain that, Mr. Oz?"

He gave the "Mr." a very slight emphasis to

remind everyone that I didn't have a PhD.

I bit my lip again. But only to create my own dramatic pause. I did have an answer.

"Human beings lack the vomeronasal organ," I said to Saltonstall. "The tissue at the base of the nasal cavity that causes response to airborne pheromones. Almost all mammals have it, but not humans. In fact, there are theories that the human VNO may have diminished as our relationship with dogs evolved. As it got bigger in dogs, it went away in humans. Many of the genes essential for the VNO are completely nonfunctional in humans."

I looked around the room and realized I had won it. Saltonstall sat there looking as though I'd yanked his pants down, so I assumed he knew what I was talking about. Dr. Orlean smiled at me.

"Bravo, Mr. Oz," she said. "I don't think anyone can deny that this is a breakthrough. I think we've finally hit the jackpot. For the first time I feel like we have a good chance of understanding what's causing HAC."

"Yes, but unfortunately that only leads us to the next question," I said. "How do we stop it?"

Chapter 70

A BATTERED POLICE van emits a feeble, oscillating shriek as it weaves through the clogged, dust-choked streets of East Delhi, India.

Behind the van's wheel, newly appointed sub-inspector Pardeep Sekhar nearly clips a fruit vendor as he wipes sweat off his face with the sleeve of his khaki shirt. The fruit vendor erupts into a torrent of curses, and Pardeep answers him with a dismissive wave.

"Clean the dirt out of your ears, bumpkin," he halfheartedly grumbles out the window. "That sound from my van—that's not a demon but a siren. It means, out of the way. Police coming through!"

Pardeep blames the television and Internet for the last decade's influx of rural migrants into the city. All those channels luring illiterate fools into the bright lights and Bollywood lifestyle they will never achieve. When they can't find work, they turn to petty crime—pickpocketing, purse snatching. That's where he comes in.

At the next traffic-glutted intersection, he laughs to himself as he watches a guy trying to maneuver his cherry-red Lamborghini around a donkey cart. An Italian luxury car revving around a jackass is twenty-first-century India in a nutshell. Digital age, meet stone age.

If only I had a camera, he thinks. The men back at the station would love it.

Pardeep's beat is Yamuna Pushta—the largest slum in Delhi, which puts it in the running for the largest slum in the world. In every direction lie blocks of *jhuggis*, makeshift huts made out of wood and cardboard tied together with string. The shantytown has no electricity or sewers. Today, people are flying kites and playing volleyball; naked children sit grinning as they play in the dirt.

Pardeep brings the van to a stop in front of a three-story concrete housing block beside a particularly fetid section of the Yamuna River. The Yamuna is a tributary of the Ganges. Bathing in its sacred water, according to the holy men, is supposed to free one from the torments of death.

Pardeep rolls up the window and through the dusty glass takes a look out across the smooth brown surface of the polluted cesspool. He sighs and shuts off the engine.

It would free one, all right. But not from death. From life.

He looks up at the grim three-story complex: River Meadow Apartments. They make it sound pleasant, don't they? The calls that have been coming in from the building are confusing. People screaming about a break-in, a crazed killer stalking the hallways.

Pardeep shrugs his narrow shoulders. Looks quiet enough from the outside. Probably a prank.

Still, he lifts his newly issued weapon off the floor of the passenger-side footwell just in case. It's one of the Indian-made INSAS submachine guns that have been handed out in the years since the Mumbai terrorist attacks. He casually shoulders the strap and heads for the building.

In the back of his mind, Pardeep idly hopes it isn't a prank but a real-life terrorist. He would love nothing more than to blow some foreign-born radical scum to smithereens, maybe get promoted out of the city's armpit in the bargain.

He's trying to decide which plum district he would like to be assigned to when an old man runs screaming from the building.

"Raksasom! Rana! Atanka!" he warbles as he runs past the van.

Monsters. Horror. Run.

Monsters. Pardeep smiles to himself, amused. This is a prank. Probably kids playing tricks on some superstitious old fools.

"Hello? Police," he says, entering the lobby. It's deserted. "Police!"

The smell is awful. It smells like shit, garbage, death—which is to say, nothing unusual for this neighborhood.

There's no response. He starts up the stairs.

At the top of the first-floor landing he sees something moving in the dimness down at the end of the hallway. It's low to the ground, perhaps about waist level. In the windowless corridor, it looks to Pardeep like a woman with a blanket over her, crawling on all fours. He is confused. He reaches for his flashlight, takes a few steps closer.

Then there is something moving at him very fast down the dark hallway. He clicks on his flashlight and sees bright eyes flash jewel-green in the darkness. Then he is falling backward.

Pardeep doesn't have time to scream as the leopard opens him from belly to chin.

Two more leopards arrive, skulking slyly in the hallway.

The leopard is one of the most dangerous animals in the world. The beautiful turquoise-eyed creature is sometimes called a leaping chain saw due to the fact that it uses both its rear claws and its razor-sharp front claws, as well as its teeth, when it strikes.

Before a dark mist falls over his eyes, one last word floats up from Pardeep's mind.

Raksasom.

Monsters.

Chapter 71

I HAD A dream that night. I dreamed of a circle of ants. They chased each other in a spiral—a squirming black whirlpool. Turning around and around, each one blindly chasing the pheromone trail of the ant just in front of him. A closed circle. A snake biting its tail. A symbol of futility. Locked in their loop, the ants ran around and around in circles—desperate, stupid, doomed.

I didn't know what time it was when I woke in the dark to the sound of what sounded like the world ending.

There was an alarm going *EEHN EEHN EEHN*. It sounded as though I were on a submarine that had just been torpedoed.

I clawed at the sheets and scrambled to sit up.

Smoke detector? I thought. Some kind of military alarm?

Then I saw a light pulsing on the bedside table and realized the sound was coming from my iPhone. I vaguely remembered Eli playing with it the day before. Three-year-old kid knew more about the stupid thing than I did. I snatched it off the table and shut it off. Kid had set it to some crazy DEFCON 3 ringtone. Which was actually funny, in a morbid way, under the present quasi-apocalyptic circumstances. My heart started beating again, and I almost laughed. Then I answered it.

"Mr. Oz, sorry to bother you at this hour," Lieutenant Durkin said. "I have a message for you from Mr. Leahy of the NSA. A high-level meeting is scheduled at the White House this morning. The president will be there, as well as the Joint Chiefs of Staff. Mr. Leahy has requested that you be there in person to present the new theory you and the other scientists have developed."

I wiped sleep gunk out of my eyes. What? Another meeting?

"Oh, okay. I guess," I said, clicking on the bedside lamp. My brain was still woozy.

"Your wife and son are free to come with you, but since travel is becoming dangerous, it might be safer to leave them here in the Secure Zone. We can have you back up here by dinner."

"That's fine, Lieutenant. When am I leaving?" I said.

"Your flight out of Teterboro will be ready to go in about an hour. Can you be ready in, say, twenty minutes?"

Twenty minutes, I thought, inwardly groaning. The meeting last night had gone on until well past midnight. It felt like I'd gotten about twenty minutes of sleep.

"Of course. I'll meet you in the lobby," I said.

After I hung up, I immediately called Leahy.

"Why the face-to-face, Leahy? Why don't we just teleconference?"

"It's complicated, Mr. Oz," Leahy said. "I know it's a pain in the ass, but I really need you here. You're a persuasive speaker."

I blinked. What was Leahy talking about?

"Persuasive?" I said. "What does the president need to be persuaded about?"

"I'll tell you when you get here," Leahy said.

I smelled fish. For some reason the needle on my bullshit detector was jittering. The last thing I wanted to do with the world falling apart was leave my family, but it looked like I didn't have much choice.

"Fine. See you later," I said.

One of Chloe's eyes peeled open as I was coming out of the shower.

"The president and the Joint Chiefs of Staff at the White House are having a meeting," I said. "They want my input. Face-to-face in D.C."

"Back to D.C. again?" Chloe said, opening her other eye and sitting up. "But you can't. It's too dangerous. Can't they, I don't know, use Skype or something?"

"That would make sense. This is the federal government we're talking about. Sounds like they need some convincing on the pheromone angle. Until they're on board, we won't be able to make progress on tackling this insanity. Besides, I'll have a military escort the whole way. They said I'll be back before dinner."

I was heading for the front door of our lavish government-assigned apartment when Eli poked his head out of the room we'd put him in.

"Hey, kiddo," I said, kneeling down next to him. "Did you change my ringtone?"

"Um, maybe?" he said.

I messed his hair and gave him a hug.

"Listen, Monsieur Maybe. I'm going to Washington. I need you to stay here and take care of Mommy for me until I get back tonight."

"No, Daddy," Eli said, his face crumpling. I stood up. He hugged my leg. "I can't take care of Mommy. Don't go. You have to stay here. I don't want you to go."

By the time Chloe helped pry him off me, I felt like crying, too. Shutting that door was the hardest thing I'd done anytime lately.

I met Lieutenant Durkin in the lobby and we proceeded outside. Alongside the sandbagged gate strung up across Fifth Avenue, soldiers and cops were drinking coffee in Anthora cups beside a convoy of up-armored Hummers and police cars. The row of engines idled, quietly panting exhaust into the brisk white beams of the headlights.

"Are any of the other scientists coming with us?" I asked as Lieutenant Durkin and I climbed into one of the Hummers.

"My orders were just you, but if you want to bring some of the others, I can check."

I waved off the idea. I was slightly surprised, but I actually liked it better that I was the only one they'd asked for. We rolled through half a dozen checkpoints on the way out to Teterboro. As we were coming up the ramp for the George Washington Bridge, I noticed a black column of smoke rising in the distance above the South Bronx.

Lieutenant Durkin looked at the smoke and then back at me.

"There have been problems with the evacs," he said, looking away. "Some looting and such. We're trying to keep a lid on it."

Chapter 72

WHEN WE ARRIVED at Teterboro, Lieutenant Durkin drove us through a gate in a chain-link fence right onto the tarmac. Off to the right, beyond the doors of a nearby hangar, a sleek, cream-colored business jet began slowly taxiing toward us, its wing lights blinking.

I couldn't help but notice that it was the top-of-the-line Gulfstream G650, a luxury aircraft that can hop the Atlantic and reach speeds near Mach 1.

If they thought they could impress me by rolling out a G650 to take me down to D.C., they'd succeeded.

Then I had another thought.

All this—for *me*?

What was up with the sudden VIP treatment?

This definitely didn't seem like your standard government travel itinerary. Was I being buttered up for some reason?

What the hell was this meeting about?

Lieutenant Durkin stayed behind on the tarmac. Another military guy waved me toward the airstair, and I boarded the plane with nothing but the suit on my back.

The Gulfstream had flat-screen displays over mirror-polished teak desks and leather executive chairs you could sink into as though they were pudding.

The interior was furnished in the manner of somebody's corner office, I thought as I chose one of its eight empty seats and sat in it. A corner office that flew at fifty-one thousand feet and more than seven hundred miles an hour.

Not that I had much time to enjoy it. The flight attendant handed me a cup of coffee before we took off, and I was still sipping it when the Gulfstream's wheels skidded with two soft shrieks against the tarmac at Reagan National an amazing twenty-five minutes later.

The jet's engines whirred down as we taxied. I looked out the window. There was something strange about the airport. There were jumbo jets parked along the terminals, but they weren't moving. No other planes were on the tarmac. Nothing was taking off or landing. It looked as if the airport were closed. It was eight in the morning on a Tuesday.

When we approached the terminal I saw that there was some activity here after all. Lined in two vast rows were dozens of military aircraft—Harriers, Warthogs. Marines were scampering around, loading and unloading tandem-rotor Chinook helicopters.

I slowly realized the airport had been commandeered by the military.

Chapter 73

I GOT A call from a number I didn't recognize as I felt the plane jerk to a halt. I answered as the flight attendant unclipped a bracket and the door yawned open with a happy hum.

"Mr. Oz, it's Dr. Valery. I have the test results."

Dr. Mark Valery was a biochemist at NYU whom I had asked to do a chemical analysis on the muck on my clothes.

"What did you find?" I said.

"Your pheromone theory seems spot-on," Valery said. "Your clothes were saturated with a chemically unique hydrocarbon similar to dodecyl acetate—a common ant pheromone. I say 'similar' because it's like it, but isn't quite the same. This stuff has properties we've never seen before."

"What do you mean?" I said.

"The carbon chains are strange. Very strange. The substance has an extremely high molecular weight. Unlike dodecyl acetate, this stuff seems to dissolve quite slowly, which might help explain its unusually strong effect on larger animals. But that ain't all, it turns out. The animals aren't the only ones who seem to be secreting a pheromone. So are we."

"What are you talking about?"

"Long story short, a human being's scent is very complex," Dr. Valery said. "We secrete materials from several different types of glands. There's regular sweat, secreted by the eccrine glands, and then there's sweat from the apocrine glands, in the hairier parts of our bodies. Then there's sebum."

"The substance that contains our smell," I said.

"Right. Sebum is the stuff that bloodhounds home in on when tracking an individual person. Our olfactory fingerprint. The fragrance industry has been doing sebum experiments for years. I used to help run some of them. The thing about sebum is, like pheromones, it's chock-full of hydrocarbons. That's why, after hearing about your breakthrough, I decided to test some skin swabs from humans. I used myself and some of the other lab workers as subjects."

"What did you find?" I said.

"It turns out that our sebum is chemically different from some samples I found in a similar study that was done back in 1994. I don't know if it's the air, our diet, seepage from plastics, or what, but initial tests seem to indicate that our sebum has a new compound in it. With pentanol and methyl butanoate. Not only that, but this new compound's chemical structure seems to resemble several insect attack pheromones."

I stared at the floor of the plane, trying to piece together what I was being told.

"So you're saying the animals are attacking because of *our* smell?" I said. "It's not just them. It's us."

"Think about it, Mr. Oz," said Valery. "The olfactory system of most mammals is incredibly strong. A dog's sense of smell is about a hundred thousand times more powerful than a human's. The power of olfaction is primal. And it seems the critters don't like what they're smelling."

Chapter 74

WITH THESE NEW and even more troubling implications playing a polka in my head, I exited the plane and was guided by a couple of soldiers toward a shiny black-and-chrome government motorcade thrumming by the hangar.

If our innate human odor was helping to cause this chaos, how were we supposed to fix that? How could we humans have changed what we smell like on a molecular level? How could it have happened so quickly? And why?

I approached the vehicles: a marked D.C. police car, a black Suburban, and another military Humvee.

A stocky marine in full camo shook my hand. He was Hispanic and his spiky high-and-tight made him look like he was wearing a hedgehog as a yarmulke.

"Mr. Oz?" he said with a slightly cockeyed grin. "You're that animal scientist guy, right? I saw you on *Oprah,* man. Welcome to the war zone formerly known as Washington, D.C. I'm Sergeant Alvarez. But call me Mark. Do you have any bags or some beakers or something I can grab for you?"

"No beakers this time," I said distractedly as he opened the door of the SUV for me.

"So what are you down here for?" he said, getting behind the wheel. "Lemme guess. Tour the cherry trees, a Nats game?"

We were rolling now. I was trying to think. I wished he'd shut up.

"Actually, I'm starting up a brand-new drug testing program for Marine Corps personnel," I said. "In fact, when we get to the White House, I'm going to need a urine sample."

A long silent minute dragged past.

"That was a joke." I said. "Sorry, I have a lot on my mind."

"No problemo, Doc. I talk too much. Ask anyone," Alvarez said. "You sit there and solve the disaster. I'll just button my lip and drive. This is me, shutting up. Zip."

A few minutes later we were near the Pentagon, approaching the I-395 ramp before the bridge, when

I heard what at first I thought were honking geese.

Then a mass of animals burst from the roadside trees. Body after furry body spilled out from between the tree trunks. Dogs. Dutch shepherds, caramel-colored mastiffs, foxhounds, bloodhounds, greyhounds, mutts of every conceivable coat and color and size. The dogs snarled and barked—a din of barking. Fur flew, spit sprayed up from the horde in frothy flecks.

Most of the animals were filthy, crazed-looking. They looked sick, starved, haunted. Many of them had hides that were mottled with that same white fungus stuff I'd seen under Bryant Park. It was horrific. I felt sorry for them.

The mass of dogs didn't so much as hesitate as it approached our motorcade. The charging herd spilled right out into the road like lemmings off a cliff, right under the lead patrol car's front wheels. Sergeant Alvarez came close to rear-ending the police car as it hit its brakes.

"The fuck are you assclowns doing?" Sergeant Alvarez yelled into his hands-free headset at the driver of the cop car. "Now's not the time to be braking for animals, cockwaffle! Go! Go!"

There was a series of yelps and whines, and then sickening thumps under the wheels, as we ran over the dogs. Our car bucked and rocked over them like a rubber dinghy in a storm at sea. We thought it was almost over when an Irish wolfhound that looked like Lon Chaney Jr. in heavy makeup hurled itself onto the hood.

Sergeant Alvarez stomped on the gas, and the monster sailed over the windshield and tumbled over the roof. I turned in time to see it get run over by the Humvee behind us.

"Damn! Thing wanted to eat us for breakfast, huh?" Alvarez said, wiping sweat off his hedgehog. "You can take that urine sample from my pants now, Professor X."

We glanced at each other for a beat, then exchanged a trickle of nervous laughter.

"Now I understand why the politicians are so concerned," I said.

The marine nodded as he took his .45 out of his holster and put it in the beverage holder.

"Typical Washington, right?" he said. "A problem ain't a problem until it happens in D.C."

Chapter 75

D.C. LOOKED DESERTED. We passed an army checkpoint on the other side of the Potomac. There were dead dogs scattered pell-mell across the usually pristine National Mall, floating in the reflecting pool. The water was cloudy and dark.

I saw that there was a newly erected high electric fence surrounding the White House as we approached it. At each corner of the complex I noticed four Humvees kitted out with what looked like satellite dishes attached to their roofs.

"What are those?" I asked.

"ADS," Sergeant Alvarez said. "Active Denial System. It's a kind of microwave transmitter that heats up your skin. Hurts like a motherfucker. Supposed to be effective for crowd control.

Fortunately, it works on man's best frenemy, too."

We got in line behind two other convoys waiting beside the White House complex on East Executive Avenue. Even when it was our turn, we had to wait for twenty minutes while the operation of ID checking and rechecking was conducted by the Orwellian assembly of security agents at the gate.

I spotted Mr. Leahy as a baby-faced army officer was at long last escorting me into the West Wing. At the end of a hallway, Leahy seemed locked in a heated argument with a staffer in front of a set of closed double doors.

A lot of military types kept coming in and out of the boardroom behind them. A lot of metal flashed on jackets. The staffer shook his head at Leahy emphatically and departed as I stepped up.

"Something heavy-duty is going on, Oz," Leahy said, buttonholing me by the secretary's desk.

"What's the problem?" I said.

"They won't listen," the silver-haired NSA officer said, more to himself than to me. "I can't believe this. They won't even listen to me."

"Who won't listen?" I said.

Leahy tilted his head toward a nearby door. "Step outside?"

Zoo

On the White House colonnade, Leahy shook out a pack of Marlboros.

"I haven't smoked in ten years," he said. He popped a match to life and held it to the tip of his cigarette.

I wanted to shake him by the lapels. "You wanted me here. Now I'm here. What's the problem?"

He didn't answer. He took another drag, held the smoke in for a beat, and leisurely exhaled it from his nose in twin gray streamers of smoke.

Back in New York, my family was in jeopardy while this jackass pulled my chain. As Leahy put the cigarette to his lips again I smacked it out of his hand.

"Stop fucking around with me!" I said. "What. Is. The. Problem."

"The military managed to convince the president that this thing can be taken care of with conventional weapons. They have satellite imagery of some animal nesting sites, and they want to use napalm on them. Imagine. They think they can bomb all the critters to kingdom come. They don't want to listen to reason anymore, Oz. They just want to trot out their toys."

He shook out another cigarette. "To a hammer, everything is a nail," he said, and lit the cigarette.

"But that's nuts, Leahy. Isn't President Hardinson

known for being a moderate? A pragmatist? Mrs. Reasonable?"

Leahy looked around the colonnade.

"We're probably bugged. I should know, shouldn't I? But screw it. Who's around to listen? This is top secret, Oz. Mum's the word, understand? The president's daughter is dead."

Huh? I did a double take.

"What?" I said. "Allie?"

Leahy nodded.

"It's being kept out of the press for now. The way I heard it, she told the president that Dodger had run away. But he hadn't. She'd hidden him in a crawl space above the family's quarters. That's where they found her. The dog had . . . well. You can guess the rest."

"Who found her?"

"Secret Service. The president borrowed a gun from an agent and put the dog down herself. She's just not herself right now. She's signing everything the military puts in front of her."

"Shit," I said.

"Shit is right," Leahy said. "A shit is what they don't give about the fact that this is an environmental issue. They don't want to hear from any more scientists. They want blood, and they're going to get it."

Chapter 76

AIR TRAFFIC CONTROL officer Lieutenant Frank White stirs milk into the first coffee of his shift with studied nonchalance as he steps onto the main floor of the control tower. As he crosses the room to his station, the lanky thirty-year-old is thinking ruefully about the fishing trip he was planning on taking this weekend before the airwaves became a network of doomsday theories. He's focusing on trying to keep his eyeballs from rolling out of their sockets.

MacDill is a backwater air refueling base, and his job is usually a cakewalk. The hardest part is trying to keep twenty-three-year-old recruits with thirty hours' flight time behind their wet ears from coming in too hot and turning the tarmac into a pizza oven.

White blinks down at runway 1, where, for some reason, two dozen F16 Falcons are powering up along the taxiway.

He gawks as a black B2 stealth bomber touches down on runway 2.

This is no fucking joke, he mumbles as he stands, still absentmindedly stirring his coffee.

All the fighters are bristling with underwing ordnance. One of the aircraft maintenance engineers in the locker room swore that they are all incendiary in nature—powdered-aluminum thermite bombs, magnesium, white phosphorus. Said he couldn't be certain, but the B2s looked like they were carrying thermobaric daisy cutters.

Shit, White thinks. They could be goddamn nukes for all he goddamn knows.

The encrypted chain-of-command phone by his radar station rings twenty minutes later. He's been drinking the coffee and is almost feeling half conscious now. The orders he receives from the phone are choppy and quick with terse military precision. They seem to have not the slightest whiff of bullshit in them.

"This is NORAD command at Cheyenne. Who am I speaking with?"

"Lieutenant Frank White."

"Listen up, White. I don't have all the coordinates in front of me, but you are to clear all civilian aircraft south of Tampa and north of the Keys. Clear the deck up to a ceiling of eighty-five thousand feet."

White looks at his shadowy reflection in the control-tower glass and squints for a moment, picturing the area in his mind.

"Isn't that Everglades National Park?"

"Didn't hear that last transmission, son. What did you just say?"

Oh, shit, Lieutenant White thought. What is this? What's going on?

"I said of course, sir. South of Tampa and north of the Keys."

In a moment he is at one of the radar stations, working on carrying out the orders. The two-way crackles in his earpiece.

"Tower, this is two-five-three. Our preflight is complete. Are we clear for takeoff?"

White sits up. Two-five-three is the call sign for one of the B2s.

"Yes, two-five-three. You are clear on runway one."

Clear for what, I don't know, Lieutenant White thinks, slurping the dregs of his coffee as the massive aircraft begins to roll onto the airstrip.

Chapter 77

WHEN THE ALL-HANDS-ON-DECK horn sounds throughout the compound that morning at nine in the a.m., it can be heard clearly all the way down the mountain, in the leafy suburbs of Colorado Springs.

The newer residents of the town who notice the braying alarm may idly wonder if the siren is for the volunteer fire department before going back to their newspapers and breakfasts. Those who have family members working at the station immediately leave their jobs and yoga classes and head to the schools to gather their children.

After exactly five minutes, the alarm ceases. Then the two twenty-five-ton steel blast doors that protect the supposedly nuclear weapons–proof military bunker begin to close for the first time since 9/11.

The corridors and rooms of the facility branch off a wide main tunnel, about as big as a train tunnel, that was bored almost through to the center of the granite mountain. The two-story glass-encased main operations center is at the end of the network of rooms nearest the mountain's westernmost slope. In it, air force techs sit at cubicles, calling orders into headsets as they listen to the squawk and crackle of military radio traffic.

As one enters the room, the forward and right-hand walls are taken up with screens as big as the ones at the local multiplex. The forward screen shows computer maps and blinking radar scopes. The one on the right displays a flickering patchwork of multiple real-time feeds, a montage of ground-level images taken by the cameras mounted on unmanned aircraft and warplanes currently aloft.

Leaning against the stair rail outside the door of his fishbowl office, lofted above the operations center floor, NORAD commander Michael McMarshall stands listening to the staff trading codes and coordinates back and forth. He whispers a furtive Hail Mary for his men and dry-swallows the last three Advil out of the plastic bottle in his hand.

McMarshall had been the CO during the first chaotic hours of 9/11, and this ball of wax is looking like it's going to be a mite bit worse.

He returns to his office and stands behind his desk, an architect's drafting table ratcheted up to midriff level. At work, he always stands, due to a training-flight crash that injured his back thirty years ago.

He flips through a stack of photographs. The images are from the military's most advanced Lacrosse satellites and unmanned aerial vehicles. Ground-penetrating radar and thermal infrared sensor systems have picked up some very disturbing data. Shockingly large pockets of animal swarms, as they are now being called, have aggregated in virtually every corner of the country.

The initial wave of bombings has been ordered on the largest nests near densely populated areas. Miami, Chicago, and St. Louis are first on deck. If there's any good news at all, it's that the animal aggregations seem to be situated mostly in parklands: the Everglades, near Miami; Lincoln Park, in Chicago; Forest Park, in St. Louis. They have been working with ground forces for the last two days, pulling evacs out of their target zones to limit collateral damage.

So, then. McMarshall pauses a moment to reflect. The United States has just begun a bombing campaign on itself. This is some *Catch-22*–type shit.

It's not just the United States, he knows. Russia, several European countries, and China are now working in sync, conducting their own campaigns against the animal swarms devastating their countries.

They have to do something. Though people are being kept in the dark, the attacks have become rampant. In affected areas, which is pretty much everywhere now, the hospitals are full. People are holing up in their homes as though there were a plague afoot. Shipping, the airlines, the stock markets have all closed. The entire industrialized world is grinding to a halt. And it isn't going to be starting up anytime soon, if everyone on earth is in fear of being torn apart by dogs 24-7.

McMarshall hears a polite knock on the glass.

"The B2 out of MacDill is about to deliver its payload, sir," the spry young officer says with a gung ho grin that's actually quite irritating under the circumstances. McMarshall's shoes clang on the metal balcony overseeing the operations room.

The entire forward screen is filled with the image by the time the general arrives at the stair rail. Though it's a black-and-white thermal image, the clarity is startling. Why, look—there's Florida. McMarshall can make out palm fronds, a dock, an old car.

"We are changing our heading for our final approach," the B2 weapons officer says over the staticky military channel.

"And we are away," the weapons officer announces.

And the screen goes white. The boom of the daisy cutter through the pilot's open mike a moment later is a jagged roar that starts and then just keeps going on and on. The screen stays white as the Florida swampland burns.

"Get some!" McMarshall's aide shouts. He whistles through his pinkies and starts to clap. Some of the other personnel join in tentatively.

McMarshall pivots on his heel and heads back to his desk. There's an emergency bottle of Advil in the bottom drawer.

Chapter 78

WHILE LEAHY WAS arranging transportation for me back to New York, I spent the rest of the morning in a cramped, crowded, and distinctly unpresidential staff room in the back of the White House's East Wing.

The whole place was in a full-tilt frenzy with the military actions underway. All around me, and even bivouacked out in the hallway, clustered by the electrical outlets, air force officers and politicos were working their smart phones and laptops. Above their frantic murmur was a constant low thrumming—the rotor chop of helicopters landing and taking off in the Jacqueline Kennedy Garden. It was like my head was stuck in a beehive.

A professionally nondescript Secret Service agent

on break began snoring softly on a couch beside me as I watched CNN natter and flash on a TV bolted to an upper corner of the room. There were a lot of stories about the animal attacks, but nothing about the military response that had just been ordered. I wondered if that was because it hadn't happened yet or because there was some kind of government news blackout.

That might be possible now, I thought, glancing at the throng of soldiers and government officials around me.

I tried to call Chloe several times to tell her what was going on, but the phone would only ring twice and go to voice mail, a sign I decidedly did not like. Text messages didn't seem to be working, either. My guess was that it was probably circuit overload due to high call volume. That was my hope, anyway.

Leahy came back for me in the early afternoon and ushered me through the crowd out into the hallway.

"Unfortunately, no Gulfstream jet this time, Oz, but I did manage to get you on a military C-130 cargo plane heading out of Reagan National to New York in about two hours."

"How's the military response going? Any word?"

"Your guess is as good as mine," Leahy said.

He led me down some stairs into a utility corridor. "They're still keeping me in the dark."

We passed stacks of K rations and a chef in crisp whites cussing a blue streak into a cell phone on the way to the door. At the bottom of some steps was a small parking lot crowded with Town Cars and military vehicles. At the edge of the lot, standing beside the black Suburban that had brought me in, Sergeant Alvarez waved at me cheerily, as if the world weren't ending.

"I'll keep plugging away on this end," Leahy said, shaking my hand and giving it a warm paternal squeeze that was meant to be reassuring and wasn't. "In the meantime, when you get back to New York, prepare a presentation to explain the science of this to the president and her staff when they're ready to listen. That would be extremely helpful. I'm going to try to arrange a teleconference for this evening or tomorrow morning at the latest."

A teleconference? Splendid idea. Now, why didn't I think of it? Oh, wait: I had. I wondered how many thousands of tax dollars had been wasted on my useless trip down here. Then I made the decision not to care. Getting home to my family was my priority now.

"Will do, Mr. Leahy," I said, making my escape.

Chapter 79

SERGEANT ALVAREZ WAS sitting in the driver's seat, locking and loading an M16, as I opened the passenger-side door and climbed into the SUV. The VIP treatment was over. He was wearing Kevlar body armor now, and a grenade vest.

He didn't have to explain to me that things were even worse now on the streets of D.C. I thought about Chloe and Eli back in New York, and wished I was already airborne.

We were two blocks south of the White House, about to make the left onto Constitution Avenue, when we heard music.

Ani DiFranco yodeled from the cranked speakers of a car parked at the corner of President's Park. Around it stood thirty or forty young people, many in hoodies bearing their college insignias, drinking beer. Some of them had painted their faces to look like animals. I smelled pot. They had handmade signs that read

MEAT IS MURDER! AIN'T PAYBACK A BITCH!!!?
HI HO! HI HO! IT'S BACK TO NATURE WE GO!

Everything has gone nuts, I thought, shaking my head. Animals, the president, college kids.

When we rolled past the National Mall again, I thought of all the noble historical assemblies the area had been host to. I thought of Martin Luther King Jr. delivering the "I Have a Dream" speech there, the presidential inaugurations. Now there were dead dogs floating in the reflecting pool.

We took the Arlington Bridge back over the Potomac for the airport this time. About a half mile inbound, we came toward an overpass; standing on it were what looked like more deluded young protesters. The college kids we'd seen back by the White House had been mostly harmless, but these guys looked more sinister in their ski masks and black bandannas. They were waving black flags.

Then there was a flash of darting movement in front of the SUV, and the windshield caved in.

Zoo

Glass dust stung my eyes as the joint-compound bucket somebody had dropped from the overpass whipped just past my head into the backseat.

The SUV accelerated and veered to the left. I turned and saw that Alvarez's face was covered with blood. He was slumped over the steering wheel, motionless.

I reached for the wheel, tried to right the vehicle. The car slid into the Jersey barrier at around eighty. Metal shrieked and showered sparks as we lurched up and rode the barrier for fifty feet before the momentum flipped the truck.

Chapter 80

DARK. AT FIRST I thought the rhythmic *thump-thump-thump* was my heartbeat. Then I opened my eyes. I realized the noise was the windshield wipers beating uselessly against the shattered windshield.

The truck's upside-down shattered windshield.

The SUV had come to rest on its roof in the left lane. I was being held in place by my shoulder belt, dangling like a bat. I felt hot blood from my nose dripping into my hair. I sneezed and sprayed a mist of blood onto my one good suit. I blinked, staring out through the hole in the windshield. My thoughts were slow and oozy.

Hmm. So what now?

I turned toward Alvarez. He was upside down,

like me, still unconscious and bleeding steadily from a gash in his temple.

I reached out for his seat belt and was stopped when I looked out the window. In between the steady slap of the wipers pushing glass crumbs into the car, I heard a strange huffing sound. Outside the passenger-side window, something was moving.

I squinted at it. Brown. Brown. Brown.

An enormous muzzle and small beady black eyes appeared in the window.

Oh, okay, I thought. That's a bear.

It gazed through the window at me with an almost quizzical expression. What I was feeling wasn't even quite fear. What I was feeling was the fear equivalent of when you're so sad you laugh. The wheel of fear went around a whole turn, came out the other side. I thought, well, this is it.

How a grizzly bear had gotten here on this strip of road beside our wrecked truck was unclear. What it was doing in Washington, D.C., was unclear. Escaped from the zoo? I had a feeling that it didn't work for AAA.

It made its choppy huffing sound again and pressed its moist black snout against the glass of the car window. It sniffed at the glass and then made a low throaty moan as it scratched at the window with a paw twice the size of a catcher's mitt.

The screech of the bear's claws on the glass snapped me out of my little absence seizure. Fumbling with my seat belt release, I stretched an arm into the backseat, feeling for Sergeant Alvarez's rifle.

I abandoned my search for the rifle as the bear moved from the passenger side to the front. I felt the truck lurch upward as the bear began squeezing himself under the upside-down hood.

So this is how I will die, I thought. Eaten by a grizzly while hanging upside down in a car wreck. Interesting, at least. If, years before, you'd gazed into a crystal ball and told me that was how I'd go, I genuinely would not have believed you.

I turned to Alvarez and tried to shake him awake. For what reason I didn't know. To wake him up for his death? I wasn't sure. I guess I didn't want to die alone. In any case, he was out for the night.

The bear had shimmied its mass under the hood, and was now nosing the hole the compound bucket had made. It sniffed and huffed as it began peeling back the shattered glass. The bear ripped at the glass as though it were a kid tearing into a stubborn candy wrapper.

Then I remembered the grenades that dangled

like avocados from the sergeant's vest. I unclipped the first one I could reach. I bit out its pin and tossed it at the bear as hard as I could as it poked its head in below the upside-down dashboard.

The bear roared and reared back as the hissing canister clanged off the side of its head. Interesting experience, having a bear roar in your face. The bear shook his head as if he'd been slapped.

Instead of exploding, the canister came to a spinning stop on the asphalt under the hood and began pouring out canary-yellow smoke. Roiling, acrid fumes burned my eyes. The smoke stung like a wasp stings. I covered my mouth as I coughed.

I reached over to Alvarez and managed to wrench another grenade free from his vest. But by the time I was ready to throw it I could see I didn't need it. Beyond the window, I saw the bear in retreat, bounding over the grass beyond the shoulder of the road.

When the air cleared, a long minute later, I finally disentangled myself. Alvarez was hacking up a lung by the time I got him out of his seat belt as well. We crawled out of the wreck. The SUV looked like John Belushi had crushed it against his forehead.

"What the hell just happened?" Alvarez said, slouching against the Jersey barrier, touching his face and inspecting the blood on his fingertips.

"It's just like bees," I said to myself, looking at the smoke billowing from beneath the truck.

"What bees?" said Alvarez, rooting around in the wreck for his rifle. "You okay, Professor? You bang your head?"

"When the animals smell us, they want to attack us," I said, crouching with him behind the overturned truck. "Anything that masks our scent makes us invisible. That's why the smoke drove off the bear. It knocked our scent out of the air."

"No shit," Alvarez said absently, shouldering his gun.

"It makes perfect sense," I said. I was thinking out loud. "Beekeepers use smoke in the same way. When the keeper shakes up a nest, the bees produce a pheromone that signals a mass attack. Except nothing happens because the smoke disperses the signal."

"So that's what happened to all the animals, Professor—why they swarm together? They've all, like, bugged out or something?"

"Exactly. They've all bugged out," I said. "Now call one of your marine buddies to get us the hell out of here. We need to tell them how to fight this thing."

Chapter 81

THE FREIGHT ELEVATOR is pretty rank even before Private First Class Donald Rodale starts collecting the garbage from the Fifth Avenue emergency government residence that evening. By the time he's done, at six thirty, the lush, steamy aroma from the chest-high pile of greasy garbage bags is making his eyes tear and his lunch churn dangerously in his gut.

Stopping the old manual elevator in the basement, a particularly slimy Hefty CinchSak slides off the top of the pile and smacks him in the back of both legs with a wet spatter.

Bull's-eye, Rodale thinks.

Rodale opens the gate to the building's rear courtyard and begins carrying out the garbage bags one at a time, tossing them into a plastic rolling bin. When the bin is filled to its brim, he gets behind it and begins rolling it up a steep ramp leading to Eighty-First Street.

Huffing and slick with sweat, Rodale scowls when he makes it to the top of the ramp. The little security booth by the gate is empty. The guard at the booth is supposed to kill the juice on the electric fence and cover him with an M16 while he makes the journey across the street to toss the trash into the shipping container. But he's MIA.

What to do. The guard who's usually at the booth is a cop named Quinlan. Cool dude. He doesn't want to get him in trouble for not being at his post.

Problem is, if he waits around here any longer, he'll be late to help Suskind, a whiny prick if there ever was one, with the Porta-Pottys across the street at the museum. He's damned if he does and damned if he doesn't.

Rodale looks down the long dark corridor of East Eighty-First through the chain-link fence. It's empty. Just a narrow lane of brick and granite town houses, trees, empty sidewalks. No rabid packs of crazed animals. Nothing at all.

Fuck it, Rodale thinks. Only take a second. He leans into the guard booth, hits the cutoff for the electrical gate, and swings it open.

He pushes the garbage bin through. It makes a rattling, rumbling sound on the concrete as he pushes it off the curb toward the green corrugated fiberglass shipping container they're using for a Dumpster.

Rodale notices something funny when he reaches out to pull up the handle on the container door. It has already been pulled up. Had he forgotten to close it yesterday?

The door yawns slightly open with a groan. He pushes it open all the way. The dark container stinks even worse than the freight elevator. Like something rotting, something dead. Rodale holds his breath. He tips the bin over and starts tossing the bags as far back into the container as he can throw them. The heavy ones he grabs two-handed and kind of wheels around with them, like a discus thrower, to get some distance. He's almost—almost—having fun.

When he's chucked about half the garbage bags, he hears a sound. Like something moving. He's not looking in the container. He figures the sound was one of the bags he had just thrown rolling back toward the entrance.

He lays his hands on the next bag. A heavy fucker, this one. Needs both hands. He's about to do his Olympic toss thing with it, and is reeling back, when from out of the shadows of the container's interior there appears a chimpanzee. Rodale stands at the door, still holding the garbage bag.

Yes, it is a chimpanzee. Face like a strange rubber mask, sweet lucid eyes like marbled brown glass. This chimpanzee is wearing a hat. The hat looks battered, threadbare, and filthy, but it looks like it once was red.

It continues to stare right at him. It looks as if it's about to say something.

In the last two weeks since all the crazy shit started, he's seen dogs attacking, and rats—but a chimp? This is unexpected.

"Hey," he calls into the shipping container. His voice bounces off the narrow walls. He doesn't know what else to say. "Are you okay?"

As if in response, the chimpanzee grabs him by the shirt with its huge black hands, lurches forward, and bites off his nose.

Rodale falls to his knees, the air pulling a scream, like a long scarf, from his throat. Blood dribbles over his lips and chin, between the fingers of the palms cupped to his face. The chimp makes a high, piercing call sound. From the town house beside the container, animals begin to emerge.

They come from the windows, they come from the alleyways, from the brass mail slot in the red town-house door. In five breaths the street is crowded with mange-mottled feral dogs, raccoons, hundreds of cats. But by far the largest contingent is rats. Thousands upon thousands of plump, red-eyed rats. They make a living carpet out of the street. A squeaking black tide.

Rodale runs, holding his face. He tries to run back to the fence. When he's in midstride, the animals take him under. He sinks into the ocean of dogs and rats as if he's drowning. Like a drowning man, he flails and thrashes. The rats envelop him. They scurry over the backs of his legs, his arms, up the back of his shirt. He writhes on the ground, slapping and punching at himself. From his groin to his chin, scissoring, needlelike teeth are puncturing his skin, rending his flesh.

In a moment the rats are eating at muscle, at his organs. The thousands of tiny teeth snip through his tendons and then go to work stripping the meat from his bones.

Attila spits out the soldier's nose and is knuckle-running at a loping cant across the street toward the open gate of the building. Behind him, the animal horde follows, snapping and howling.

Chapter 82

THE BAG OF popcorn in the droning microwave has begun to go from a few desultory *pip-pops* to a full-on clamor as Chloe chances upon a large plastic mixing bowl in the sprawling apartment's pantry.

She takes note of a stash of instant soup boxes above the shelf where she just found the bowl. There is no way to tell how long they will be here in this place, so it's good to know where they stand with food. Things will get better eventually, she thinks as she climbs back down the folding step stool. It's just a matter of holding out.

Arriving back into the bright marble kitchen, for a moment she takes small solace in the aroma of butter and salt. A smell that conjures up family, happiness, safety.

It doesn't work. Her resolve, wavering all day, evaporates. She flings away the bowl and covers her face with her hands.

The comforting scent is a mockery now. There will be no more comfort, she knows.

Her family is separated. No one is happy. No one is safe.

Though she has never told Oz about it, she had panic attacks in grad school that had been serious enough for her family to convince her to see a therapist. It took almost a year of hard work, and a brief hospitalization, to finally conquer them. Since Oz left, she has felt them creeping back. The same itching fear, the same paralysis, the same pathological self-condemnation.

Worthless, says an inner voice as she bends over the countertop, shivering. Worthless. As a wife, a mother, a woman, a human being. Only two things will happen now. She will get her son killed, then she will get herself killed.

The bone-drilling shriek of the microwave timer brings her back out of the hole she's fallen into. She squeezes the cold edge of the marble countertop until her knuckles whiten. She wipes her tears with the back of a hand and checks her face in the glass-fronted cabinet above the sink. She dumps the steaming popcorn into the bowl and heads back into the living room.

In the cavernous room, Eli sits cross-legged on the Oriental carpet, gazing up, wide-eyed, at the monolithic flat-screen TV on the wall. A rerun of *The Simpsons* is on. Homer runs away from an out-of-control car. To escape, the cartoon character dives into a manhole, only to do a face-plant on a hot steam pipe.

Under ordinary circumstances, she wouldn't let Eli watch TV that wasn't at least vaguely educational. Under these circumstances, though, Chloe kneels down and hugs her son, inhales his smell, listens to him giggle.

"I like this fat yellow man, Mommy," Eli says.

Chloe kisses her son on the top of his head and remembers something. One of the therapies that she used to keep her panic attacks away was exercise. She had started going to the gym every night after school to swim laps before dinner. It cleared her head. It worked.

She doesn't want to leave Eli at all these days. In fact she feels like attaching him to herself in a papoose, as she did when he was an infant. But her anxiety is buzzing in her skull like a power drill. Her little meltdown in the kitchen proved that. If they are going to survive, she needs to calm down. She needs to be strong.

"Hey, Eli, baby. Listen," Chloe says, setting the popcorn in front of him as though it were an offering for an idol. "Mommy's going to exercise now in the room on the other side of the kitchen, okay?"

"Okay," he says automatically. His eyes are fixed in an absent, dreamland gaze on the TV. His tiny smooth hand digs unthinkingly into the popcorn, then delivers a fistful to his mouth.

She is in the small workout room, about to step onto the treadmill, when she hears a sound. Coming from the window. It is a soft, distant crackling—almost like the microwave popcorn cooking.

She slowly walks to the front of the apartment. She hears more sounds as she opens the door to the hallway. A kind of strange chugging sound starts up, coming from one of the lower floors, followed quickly by a violent knocking, as if a stone fist is banging on a locked door.

Chloe bites her lip hard enough to draw blood. Gunfire, she thinks. Someone is shooting.

She slams the apartment door hard enough to topple a vase from an antique table beside her, her heart chugging in time to the machine guns as her fingers turn the locks.

Chapter 83

WE HAD TO wait around awhile before we were picked up and taken away from the place where our SUV had crashed.

Being out in the open while we waited was a strange feeling—simultaneously boring and terrifying. The whole time, I stood on the highway median, leaning on the smashed truck as I looked up and down the flat, empty highway through the sight of Alvarez's M16, praying we wouldn't see another animal.

A Humvee with a roof rack full of blazing lights finally arrived about fifteen minutes after we'd called. Two marines jumped out. There was a dead Saint Bernard lashed to its hood with bungee cords. They were taking trophies now. This was a war.

I wondered who was winning.

"The fuck took you so long?" said Alvarez.

"Attacks are everywhere now, Sarge," said the driver, a wiry black man with haunted-looking eyes. "We had to shoot our way out here. The Pentagon got hit. Reagan Airport is completely overrun by a swarm of dogs. The hangars, the terminal, everywhere. No planes in or out until the situation gets dealt with."

Terrific. No flights, I thought as we carefully laid Alvarez, bloody as a butcher's apron and spitting curses, across the backseat of the Hummer. Now how the hell was I going to get home? I was stuck.

The driver pounded the gas and floored us back to the Marine Corps base next to the White House. We didn't encounter any more animal hordes directly, but down alleyways, side streets, inside windows, we could see movement, shadows scurrying. The whole city felt infested now.

Relatively safe back inside the base and the packed medical tent, I was getting stitches in my elbow when an attractive petite woman with reddish-brown hair came in. She carried a walkie-talkie and had a White House security badge clipped to the lapel of a pricey blazer.

"Is there a Jackson Oz here?" she called out. "I'm looking for a Mr. Jackson Oz."

I sat there a moment in silence while she trawled the medical tent. What did they have in store for me now? I thought. An IRS audit, perhaps?

I'd come down here in order to help, and all I'd gotten to show for it was being stranded and separated from my family as the world dissolved into chaos. Oh, and a car wreck, twenty stitches, and a bear.

But as the redhead was turning to leave, I called out to her.

"I'm Jackson Oz," I said. "What do you need?"

Her eyebrows danced as she lifted her walkie-talkie.

"I found him," she said into the radio. "I'll bring him straightaway."

"Bring me where?" I said.

"Rianna Morton, deputy cabinet secretary," she said, offering a hand.

"Bring me where?" I repeated.

"A cabinet meeting is adjourning as we speak," Ms. Morton said. "Mr. Leahy said you have a presentation?"

Five minutes later I was back inside the White House compound, hurrying with the staffer past the flower beds and boxwoods of the Jacqueline Kennedy Garden. We went through a basement door and up some stairs and turned to the right down a majestic paneled corridor lined with fireplaces, antique bookcases, bronze busts.

I guess this isn't another runaround after all, I thought as I realized we were walking through the White House's West Wing.

In the Cabinet Room vestibule, a hulking marine in dress blues checked my ID with a white-gloved hand. Among the crowd of suits behind him, I saw the vice president and the secretary of state. They were joking around with each other, something that involved sticking Post-it notes onto the BlackBerrys they weren't allowed to bring into the meeting.

Outside, the nation's capital was melting down, probably the world, too, but the well-protected politicians were sharing a pleasant *bon mot*.

No wonder people liked Washington, D.C., so much, I thought.

Chapter 84

I HEARD A familiar voice behind me call my name.

There was a soft sound of electric buzzing, and the crowd of suits parted as Charles Groh hummed up to me in his wheelchair. I grasped his hand.

"Finally, a friendly face," I said. "What's the word? You hear anything?"

"Are you okay, Oz?"

I remembered that I was filthy and covered in blood. My sleeves were rolled up and my loosened tie dangled absurdly down the front of my blood-speckled button-down.

"I'm fine. Car crash, bear attack. I'll tell you later. Any news from the world?"

"It didn't work, Oz," Dr. Groh said as I followed his wheelchair from the security line to the other side of the hallway. "The bombing campaign was nothing more than a lot of sound and fury, signifying jack shit. Now that they're done with their temper tantrum, they want to hear from us."

"We should take a minute to compare notes," I said, motioning Dr. Groh toward the corner of the room.

"Sounds good, Oz," he said, producing a thin gray MacBook Air from a leather satchel dangling off his chair. "These are thick skulls we're going to have to try to get through."

Aides were sitting like ducks along both walls of the Cabinet Room when we came in some fifteen minutes later. Rianna Morton directed me to a chair at the end of the oblong table farthest from the door. As she tipped a pitcher of ice water into the glass in front of me, I noticed there were several glossy monitors set up on rolling carts. The chancellor of Germany was on one of them, whispering with an aide. On another screen was the British prime minister.

"This meeting will be videoconferenced with several world leaders," Ms. Morton explained. "The paramount leader of China should be online in a moment."

As I tried, unsuccessfully, not to let that

information rattle my chain, President Hardinson arrived. Everyone in the room who had been seated shot to their feet. Except for Dr. Groh.

It was the first time I'd seen President Marlena Hardinson in person. She did have a remarkably arresting presence, this slightly heavyset woman with bags under her dark green owlish eyes, eyes that had an almost intimidating intelligence in them. She was stately in pearls and a midnight-blue blazer.

"Okay, everyone," Hardinson said, waving the people to their seats. Her voice had that familiar husky rasp that I'd heard on TV a thousand times before, but it was an odd feeling to hear it in the flesh. She smiled as she sat down at the center of the table. Her smile had no warmth in it. I reminded myself that her teenage daughter died yesterday, and that I wasn't supposed to know that.

"Mr. Oz, Dr. Groh," she said, nodding to us. "Please. Tell us what you know."

All eyes were on me. I sucked in a deep breath.

"Thank you, Ms. President," I said. "Everyone, my name is Jackson Oz, and for the last ten years I've been researching the aberrant animal behavior now known as HAC. Animal attacks on people have been around as long as people have been around, but over the last fifteen years or so we began noticing a startling, exponential increase of animal-on-human violence.

"Coupled with this increased aggression, animals also began exhibiting behavior uncharacteristic not only of their particular species but also of mammals in general. All over the world—as I'm sure you've noticed by now—animals are aggregating in swarms or hordes and attacking human beings en masse. This is not happening at random. Animals are forming into insect-like swarms."

"Insects?" said the secretary of defense. "Why? And why now?"

Charles Groh cut in. "Inadvertent man-made changes to the environment, sir," he said, clicking his laptop to control the PowerPoint display.

I waited for the hydrocarbon graph to pop up on the screen before continuing.

"Recently, human beings have caused two things to become prevalent in the environment that weren't around before: electromagnetic radiation and the by-products of petroleum. Petroleum is an organic compound made up mostly of hydrocarbons. We believe that in the last fifteen years, the explosion of electromagnetic radiation due to cell phone use has begun 'cooking,' if you will, the hydrocarbons that are all around us, ultimately changing their chemical makeup.

"This new hydrocarbon mimics animal pheromones. But it's stronger. It's this pheromone-like pollutant that's making the animals go haywire. In essence, we believe that because we have changed the way the environment smells, animals have changed the way they behave."

"Pheromones?" the secretary of state asked. "I thought they only worked with insects or something."

Charles Groh shook his head. "Many animals respond to pheromones. Communication, food gathering, mating behavior, aggression—all these things involve scent. That may be one reason why dogs in particular have been so susceptible. Their sense of smell is one hundred thousand times stronger than ours."

"But why are they just attacking us?" said the president. "Why not each other?"

"That's where another factor comes in," I said. "It seems that due to all the petroleum-based products we use, the human scent is actually mimicking an attack pheromone. The animals are being drawn to us with the same automatic ferocity of wasps in a disturbed nest."

"Hmm," said the president. It was almost a harrumph. "Toxic pheromone pollution. How can we combat that?"

Charles Groh and I looked at each other. This was it. We'd finally arrived at the hard part. What had to be done.

"The first step," I said, "would be removing the factors that are causing the environmental disturbance."

"Remove petroleum products?" said the president.

"And cell phones?" said the secretary of state.

I nodded at both of them, then looked out at the faces around the table and on the screens.

"Desperate times, ladies and gentlemen," I said. "Here's what I think we should do."

Chapter 85

STRAINING HER EARS, her eyes glued to the front door she just double-locked, Chloe sits on a creaking Louis Quatorze chair in the entryway of the apartment.

For the last half hour, she has sat listening as gunfire has cracked and rollicked throughout the building, thudding through the walls and echoing in the hallways. The noises keep getting louder, rising floor by floor, like a fire. Soon they will reach their floor, and she and her son will be consumed.

And yet all she can do is sit there. The wild fear is so great that she is almost immobilized now. She can't act, can't think, can't plan her next move. All she can do is sit and stare at the crack of light beneath the door, wondering what will happen next.

The pressure in her tightly clenched jaw seems to double, triple when she hears a sound that is clearly in the hallway outside the apartment. It's a brief creak, followed by a click. Then she hears it again. Creak and click. Something is pushing at the stairwell door in the hallway, she realizes.

Probing.

It's something that isn't human.

Or even really animal anymore, she thinks.

It's true. What they are up against is something that has never been seen before. She has thought of it as devolution. It is as if the nature of every higher animal has been erased and replaced with the alien instinct of the insect world, an instinct older, more terrible, more pitiless than human beings have ever seen.

She thinks about her career as a biologist, all the tireless work, the cataloging of animal species and genera. It has all been made useless now—all animals are joining into one, a roving amalgam of fur and bone and teeth no different from any other wave of destructive energy. What is happening is like a lava flow, a raging inferno of animated protoplasm that seeks the same thing as fire itself. To initiate change. To consume until the thing consumed is gone. To devour.

Why is this happening? Who knows, really?

Life and existence can never be fully understood. Stars are born only to explode. Creatures hunt other creatures, and then they die. The universe is a chaos of irrational forces wrestling with one another in a war without end. The human race is on the receiving end now.

Chloe finally stands. On legs as stiff and unresponsive as stale bread, she returns slowly to the living room. Eli is still planted, glassy-eyed, before the television. On the TV, there's a cartoon movie of friendly animals talking to each other. *Madagascar,* comes a useless thought, like a bird flying through the opaque cloud of her fear. She looks for the remote to turn off the TV, gives up, and clicks it off by pressing the button on the set itself.

"What's wrong, Mommy?" Eli says. Stars in his eyes.

He's an impressively smart kid—obedient, especially perceptive of her feelings, especially when she isn't fooling around.

She lifts him up. She goes to the corner of the living room and switches off the light. She sits on one of the plush white couches, beneath a canvas that screams with garish splashes of color. Here it is. Her grand plan, she thinks.

Soon she hears a skittering by the front door. Or has she imagined it?

I will not let you in! Chloe thinks. Not by the hairs of my chinny chin chin!

Her hands are shaking violently. She clenches her fists to make them stop.

"What's wrong, Mommy?" Eli whispers.

"You have to listen to me, Eli," Chloe whispers back. "We have to be quiet now. Can you do that? Can you be a good boy for Mommy?"

"Yes," Eli says, squeezing her hand. "Don't be sad, Mommy. I can be quiet."

She tries to regulate her breathing. To breathe with steady deliberation. She tries to will down the throbbing in her stomach and her chest and her brain. Tears well up in her eyes. She tries to dam them back. Her vision blurs. Think. Control. The world is receding into focus. Keep it there. Control it. Control it.

She thinks, trying to come up with a rational next step. She thinks about the building. There is a set of front stairs, an elevator, a freight elevator. Wait, she thinks. There's also a set of back stairs, which might be accessible from the kitchen door, in the rear, where she tosses the trash. Maybe that escape route is still open, she thinks. She could carry Eli and get out that way. But then what? Be out in the open? Go to another building? The best thing to do is just sit here and hope they are ignored and —

Another sound makes her heart skip a beat. It is coming from off to her right. There is a set of French doors there. She has forgotten about them.

They lead out to a balcony.

She watches a shadow fall onto the balcony from above, just outside the glass. Then another. Then a third.

Slowly, Chloe pulls Eli to the floor with her. Lying on her belly beside the coffee table with him, clutching him to herself, trying to protect him with her body as best she can, she raises her head very slowly until she can see the French doors and the balcony again.

There are three adult chimpanzees with their faces squished against the glass, blowing hot fog on it, like children pressing their faces to the window of a candy store.

They are huge. Their fur is bristling, erect. Two of them hold something in their hands. Sticks? No, they are pipes. Tool use, the ethologist still left in Chloe thinks.

The sound of tapping comes a moment later.

The chimps are smashing the pipes against the glass doors.

Clink. Clink. Clink.

Then there is a cymbal-crash burst of glass breaking.

Chapter 86

GLASS SHATTERS. JAGGED triangles tumble piecemeal to the wooden floor—clang, clatter, and chime. The chimps clear the glass from the frames with the pipes. The alpha male steps forward, gently shoving the others out of the way. He is wearing a ragged red hat, rakish and totemic on his head, like a barbarian's scavenged crown.

It is Attila—or what used to be Attila. He is a changed ape. There is a tightly wound, guitar-string tautness to his musculature, a ravenous, lean, and hungry look. His hair is rangy in places. His nose is running. It seems his whole physiology has changed. His brain functions are dulled, perverted, his metabolism stuck in fast-forward.

Attila sticks his face into the apartment, sniffs.

All is smell now. Sound, touch—even sight—play second fiddles in the orchestra of sensation. They all know there are humans here. They know there is an adult female. That scent is unmistakable—the sweat, the sweet tiny reek of ovulation. And what smells like a young juvenile. Their mouths tingle with salivation at the proximity of the prey. They want to feed on them the way fire wants oxygen.

The animals communicate almost exclusively by smell now. Emotions and intentions are detectable in body odor, in sweat.

Attila wants it even more than the two others with him. He hasn't had a fresh kill in hours, and the hunger gnawing at his belly is a scissors in his stomach, cutting him in half.

Attila is about to enter the room from the balcony when he catches another scent. There is something, something subtle in the human smell of the other one, the young one, something almost undetectable that pokes thinly through the wall of his rage.

Across the red screen of Attila's mind, a memory plays. A man's face appears—vague, watery, but there. It comes down close to the bars of the tiny cramped cage he is trapped in. The man opens the door of the cage, cradles him, talks to him, soothes him. The first kindness he ever experienced.

Zoo

Rocking his dazed head from side to side at the strange vision, Attila stops in the shattered balcony doorway. He is in there somehow, somehow a part of the boy. And yet Attila is angry, so angry. He stands there, his impulses warring with his memory.

The other two apes, squirming with the blood rage, struggle to squeeze past him.

Attila grabs the first one by the shoulder, and then the other. He draws them away from the doorway, back into the outside. There is other meat.

"*Heeaagh!*" Attila shrieks. It is a violent noise, high-pitched, grinding. "*Heeaagh! Heeaagh! Heeaagh!*"

Chapter 87

"MOMMY! MOMMY! WAKE up! Listen!"

Chloe's eyes flutter open. There is a high, ear-piercing primate-call sound coming from the balcony. The chimps on the balcony seem to be tussling with one another.

She sits up.

Chloe reaches out and wraps her arms firmly around her son. As they watch the animals jostle and shriek, she recognizes the familiar sound the chimp is making. It is a warning call—a kind of siren that chimps emit when a threat is close.

One is warning the others not to enter?

After a moment, the apes break it up. The largest of them—who, bizarrely, seems to be wearing a ragged old red hat—knuckle-walks to the balcony railing and hops onto its edge, beckoning the others to follow. A moment later, all three of them slip over the railing and are gone.

Chloe expels a long, shivery breath. First, the chimps wanted to attack, but then, suddenly, they stopped.

Attila. How could it have been him? How could it *not* have been him—how many chimps are there at large in this town?

Chloe sits on the floor with Eli in the dark. Outside the shattered window, she can hear people yelling, people singing and chanting in Central Park. It is as if human beings are regressing, becoming primitive again. Maybe human beings will start reacting to the pheromones now. Create human zombies to join the four-footed ones. Anything is possible.

Eli struggles in her arms like a giant fish. Struggles to escape her grip.

"No. Stay here," Chloe says in a curt whisper.

"I'll be right back."

She thinks he needs to use the bathroom. But he returns a moment later and hands her something. It is the bowl of popcorn.

"Daddy said I should take care of you while he's gone," he says. "Here."

She kisses him.

There comes a heavy, pounding knock on the door.

"United States Army," a voice shouts. "Is there anyone in there?"

Chloe scoops up Eli and rushes to the door. A young blond soldier with glasses smiles in the glow of his flashlight as she lets him in.

"Thank God you're alive, ma'am," he says, lowering his rifle. "Somebody turned off the electric fence, and they got in through the basement somehow. We think we have it under control now. Are you hurt? Is your son all right?"

"We're fine," Chloe says. "Chimpanzees tried to get in through the balcony, but then they left."

"So that's what they were," the soldier says, shaking his head. "I knew I saw something jump over the perimeter fence from the second-floor balcony."

"Are many people hurt? The other families?"

"I'd be lying if I said no," the soldier said. "Three families on the fourth floor seem to have taken the worst of it. There have been about half a dozen casualties so far. We're still sweeping. In the meantime . . . ," the soldier says, offering her something.

Chloe just stares at it.

It is a flat black pistol.

"We can't be everywhere at once, ma'am. You might need to use it to drive off the next wave."

"What if I can't?"

"Then you might really need it," the soldier says, slapping it into her hand and turning to go.

The gun lies dark, cold, and heavy in her hand. She hates to touch it. She knows all too well what he meant about needing it. He meant that she should use it on Eli and herself rather than be eaten alive.

"Mommy, is that a real gun?" says Eli.

"No."

Chapter 88

THE MESSAGE, AS it has come to be called at the White House, is delivered the next day at 0900, and put on a loop to repeat for the rest of the day.

On all TVs and radios, programming is interrupted. The message is broadcast through megaphones on helicopters and through the speakers on army vehicles roving the streets.

An image of the Oval Office appears on the forty-foot LED screen at One Times Square. The forty-fifth president of the United States of America, Marlena Grace Hardinson, sits behind the desk. Her smoky, dark green eyes look resolutely into the camera, and in a slow, careful voice, she begins.

"My fellow Americans, I would like to say good morning to you," the president says. "But as we all know, this isn't a very good morning for many of us. We are currently experiencing a dark moment in the annals of human history.

"I say this from hard-won personal knowledge. My own daughter, Allison, died yesterday. She was killed by our family pet. This is a tragedy that I and my husband, Richard, may never recover from. But we need to go on. We all do, and we will. That is what the United States of America does.

"Despite the efforts of our military, all across our nation, and indeed all across our planet, animals continue to attack human beings savagely, and without cessation. Fortunately, after much careful research, our scientists believe they have discovered some of the responsible factors underlying these attacks.

"For many years, there has been much heated debate over industrial pollution and its contribution to global warming. As we researched the dangers of industrial activity on climate change, it seems we were simultaneously overlooking another problem that has been developing unnoticed right under our noses for years. This problem amounts to the destabilization of the biosphere.

"It has come to light that the aberrant animal behavior may be directly related to human activity.

The recent buildup of hydrocarbon-rich petroleum products, coupled with radiation from cellular phones, has caused changes in the environment, which these animals are reacting to. It has been explained to me that the hydrocarbons normally found in the human environment have subtly morphed into a substance that many animals' sensory faculties are interpreting as a pheromone, altering these animals' behaviors. These new airborne chemical particulates are causing animals to swarm together and attack human beings.

"In the interest of public safety, we must do everything in our power to reverse this process. That is why I am asking for the people of the United States of America to come together with the rest of the world this morning. Though I know it will be a great hardship, for the next two weeks, we must cease the use of all cellular phones and electricity, and cease the burning of fossil fuels. In essence, we need to clear the air, literally, of both radiation and petroleum by-products if a first step in ending this disaster is to be made.

"I have just signed an emergency executive order stipulating that all cellular communication towers and power plants in the United States of America will be shut down as of midnight tonight. Except for hospitals and designated emergency personnel, the use of portable generators is banned. The driving of vehicles will also be prohibited, and any violators are subject to arrest. The heads of other major industrial nations, among them the United Kingdom, France, Russia, China, and Japan, have agreed to do the same. You will be informed of any and all further instructions. This two-week cessation is essential to allow our scientists to confirm the causes of human-animal conflict, and for us to formulate a coordinated plan for the future. Thank you for your cooperation. God bless America, and God bless us all."

Chapter 89

WHEN THE PRESIDENT'S speech came on, Charles Groh and I were downstairs in the Navy Mess, drinking coffee and trying to brainstorm. It was more of a light brainshower—we were too spent and frazzled to stir up a storm.

Really, we were just waiting and watching until the minute hand oozed into place to form the perfect backward L of nine o'clock, and we followed the scuttling commotion into the adjoining stainless steel kitchen and gathered with the crowd of kitchen staff where they stood, vigilant and hushed, beneath a TV mounted to the wall.

When the broadcast was over, the crowd dissolved into anxious murmurs.

"The power's going out, and the army is going to

lock people up for driving their cars?" said a portly black chef. Somebody switched off the TV. "*That's* the brilliant new plan?"

He seemed skeptical. Everyone did. I was skeptical, too, and I was the primary architect of the brilliant new plan.

"How does it feel?" said Dr. Groh as we arrived back at our table in the nearly empty dining room.

"How does what feel?"

"To finally get what you want," he said. "You've been trying to warn people for how long? A decade, almost? Now they're listening. It's got to be pretty weird to finally get what you want."

"I just hope it's what we need."

I drank the last of my coffee and looked at the sludge in the bottom of the paper cup as though I were a gypsy reading tea leaves. I thought about it. My feelings were definitely of the mixed variety. I was glad the idiotic carpet-bombing campaign had been stopped, but the problem was that my petroleum-radiation-pheromone theory was still just that: a theory.

There was a strong possibility I could be completely wrong, or only half right. It was impossible to rule out other factors contributing to the problem. It was even possible that radiation, electricity, and petroleum had nothing to do with it—that we'd just been barking up the wrong tree. (Ha-ha.) Science is like that. It doesn't have the answers. It guesses, tests, and guesses again. I had my guesses, and now they were going to be tested. Turning off the world's lights was an unprecedented, historic event. What if it didn't work?

"It feels like the weight of the world is on my shoulders, Charles," I said. "I'm pretty much scared shitless."

Dr. Groh shrugged.

When we returned to the Cabinet Room for another round of meetings, everyone seemed dazed, exhausted. But it was the kind of upbeat dazed and exhausted you see in people racing to meet a deadline, the pizza-box-and-black-coffee all-nighter, the burned-out look of dedicated people in the final push of getting something difficult done.

When the president walked in, a spontaneous burst of applause filled the crowded room.

But as the energy secretary whistled through pinched fingers, I kept my hands at my sides. This wasn't the end of something. This was just the very beginning of what I anticipated was going to be a long, hard journey. I couldn't quite join in the self-congratulation just yet.

Because letting the public know was one thing.

Getting them to comply was quite another.

In order for this to work, people had to actually stop using electricity and driving cars.

Would they?

It all depended upon people observing the new emergency ordinances. Realistically, there were nowhere near enough boots on the ground to enforce these contingency laws—so all we could do was to count on people to cooperate. In officer training, one of the first things they tell you is to never give an order unless you're sure it will be obeyed. If a law cannot be enforced, it's easy for it to crumble. As Frederick the Great said, diplomacy without arms is like music without instruments.

As the president found her seat in the middle of the room, I tried to think of other instances in which Americans had been called upon to sacrifice for the good of the country. Or of the world, as the case may be. World War II is a good example. I also remembered all the charity and camaraderie that had abounded in New York after 9/11. It could happen again, right?

I crossed my fingers under the table as President Hardinson cleared her throat. I hoped so. I prayed so.

It was all up to us now.

Chapter 90

BECAUSE OF ELECTRICAL load and supply concerns, large-scale power grids take time to shut down without damaging the equipment. It isn't until twelve hours after the president's stated deadline that the US grid has fully powered down.

The rolling blackout catches some people unawares. Water pumps fail in some areas and people are stuck in elevators as everything grinds to a standstill.

And then there is silence, and darkness.

But most people are ready for it.

By 2100 EDT, every power plant, airline, and factory in the United States and Europe is powered down, as well as every commercial cellular communications site. In the United States, army

438

units are deployed to stop all vehicular traffic. For the first time ever, the US Air Force Space and Missile Systems satellite that monitors nighttime data shows only blackness where those twinkling crystalline spiderwebs of light used to be: New York, London, Paris. Dark.

At the break of rosy-fingered dawn in the Virunga Mountains of Rwanda, Barbara Hatfield wakes inside a shipping container that her zoological research center used for storage. The primatologist locked herself in it almost three weeks ago in order to avoid being ripped asunder by gorillas or the rhinos that appeared out of nowhere.

She is in big trouble. The container is a broiler by day and an icebox at night. Her food has run out. There is only one gallon of water left. She is weak, hungry, dehydrated. Isolated from the goings-on in the rest of the world, she does not understand why no one has come to her rescue. Why has the supply plane not been here in three weeks? Isolation. Hunger. Deprivation. Fear. She is feverish, hallucinatory, the borders between reality, nightmare, and dream blurring and dissolving. She is being punished in some way by God, abandoned in the jungle to suffer and die.

With great effort, she rolls over onto her hands

and knees, crawls to the hole in the container by one of the hinges, and peeks through the slit of vision it offers her.

What she sees amazes her. In the clearing near the edge of the tree line, she can see the gorillas. But the females are present again. When the craziness started, all the females seemed to have disappeared. Now they are back. The gorillas are no longer menacing. They are doing what they usually do: eating, mating, playing with their children, lazing in the grass.

Barbara stands on spindly, weak legs and unlatches the container's door. She steps outside. The gorillas look up at her. Barbara rears back, stumbling. The hollow metal clangs and drums under her staggering feet, and she grasps the edge of the doorway, catching herself from falling.

Should she head back to the safety of the container? Are they going to attack again?

Then she stops and watches as the gorillas slowly lumber back into the jungle, vanishing into the trees and ground fog.

In Delhi, the sun trickles over a sea of flat rooftops, over a dark and quiet city. Strict government enforcement helps ensure compliance with the global energy ban. The two new power plants east of the city have been shut down, along with all the communications towers, the filling stations.

In Yamuna Pushta, the sprawling slum east of the city, the usually traffic-clogged streets are empty of everything but pushcarts and rickshaws. The migrant people who inhabit the slum tentatively peek out from the cracks in their hovels. They have been easy pickings for the roving packs of pariah dogs and jungle cats that have overtaken the city.

As they peer out from their hiding places, they see movement in the streets. Animals—leopards, tigers—are moving northward. A soot-faced child ducks fearfully beneath a window, then his head rises again to look at a passing leopard: patient, lazy, its shoulder blades undulating, its tail a pendulum— it is walking away. The big cats are moving out of the city, returning to the jungles, where they belong.

All around the world, it is happening. In London, in Paris, in Rome, in Beirut, in Iowa City. Animals are leaving the cities. Massive packs of animals are dissipating, going home like a crowd after a ball game.

Chapter 91

CHLOE HAS BEEN up for two hours when the sun rises in New York on the second day of the global power freeze. With the electricity off, she lights a candle, and spends the flat, empty stretch of time going through family photographs. She is glad she included them when she packed her bags for the government evacuation headquarters.

She smiles to herself as she slowly turns the pages of her photo album. She can't decide which is her favorite: the wedding photos or the shot of Oz at the hospital, holding Eli for the first time. Or the one of a two-year-old Eli chasing a seagull at a picnic on Jones Beach.

She settles on the wedding picture of Oz waiting for her at the altar, a neon-blue Hawaiian shirt under his tuxedo jacket. It is the expression on his face, she thinks. His smile, the glimmer in his brown eyes—they are a freeze-frame of joy and life. God, she misses him. God, does it hurt to be apart.

But she cannot go back to the panic and depression. She has to be hopeful. They will be together soon, she knows.

Because it's working.

The plan is working.

The night before, she and some of the other scientists had gone onto the roof of the building. She had held Eli's warm tiny hand in hers, and they looked up into the sky. They could see the stars.

To Chloe, the starscape above was like the night sky in her girlhood home on her grandfather's farm in the French countryside. Eli was a city kid—he had never seen so many stars. She pointed out the constellations to him, and the planets. Mercury, Venus. Jupiter, Saturn—those winking faraway giants. The galaxy unfurled in a fluttering ribbon of star smoke.

They could see the stars, of course, because every light in the city was off. Even the streetlights. There was not a drop of electricity running in the city's veins. Chloe had listened for any remnant of the great vibration that had once been New York City. It was gone. There was only darkness and silence. The city was a coral shell of darkness and silence.

And holding Eli's hand on the roof, Chloe had felt warm tears sliding out of the corners of her eyes and down her cheeks. Her tears had come partly from sadness, and partly from the cold joy of seeing all this terrifying, useless, lonely beauty.

Progress is being made, she thinks now, tracing a picture of her husband's face with a finger. She can feel it in her bones. They are going to make it through this.

After breakfast, Chloe decides to take Eli onto their terrace for some fresh air. Just entering the room where the animals had almost gotten in makes her palms tingle with sweat, but she wills herself through it. Using a broom, she sweeps away the broken glass from the French doors, and then she opens them, and they are outside.

It is a gorgeous September day. Clear blue sky, sunny, slightly breezy.

"Listen, Mommy," Eli says.

She listens. The only sound is the swish of the wind pushing the leaves of the swaying Central Park trees.

"I don't hear anything, Eli."

"Yeah!" he says. "Someone turned New York off!"

Zoo

Chloe smiles. It's true. The streets are still, silent. Down Fifth Avenue, morning light trickles through the side streets to lie warm on the wide avenue in golden stripes.

There is something sad about it, and yet wonderful. Beyond the trees in the distance, the roof of the Plaza Hotel could almost be a Mayan temple. It is as if they have traveled back in time.

Chloe puts her arms around her son. Her small, bright, warm son. For a moment, for the first time in a long while, she feels halfway safe, halfway happy.

She thinks about Oz again. The feel of his back under her fingers, his goofy American laugh.

He is okay. She will see him again soon. She kisses her son, wiping the trembling jewel of a tear from the side of her nose.

The world will not end.

Chapter 92

SPLAYED ON HIS back on a rock outcropping overlooking a softball field near the Central Park carousel, Attila watches a high white cloud sail across the ocean of blue sky above him.

He makes a soft mewling whimper, an almost sigh. His shoulders droop, his muscles slacken. He is serene now.

The massive pack of animals he led into Central Park several nights before has dwindled considerably. First the rats left, and then the cats. There are a few dogs left, but even they are starting to circle in ever-widening loops, wandering aimlessly, like electrons in an unstable atom.

The scent in the air that so strongly compelled Attila to act is weak now, just a tiny trace of what it had been. Wracked, spent, limp with physical exhaustion, he dozes on the sunny rock. The aftertaste of blood in his mouth is strong, metallic, slightly nauseating. All he wants to do now is sleep, sleep, sleep.

He dozes throughout the day, waking occasionally, watching the still and silent city, dozing some more. The soft light on the white buildings. His sweet glassy brown eyes blink languidly. He listens to the quiet. The silence is beautiful. The cool, clean air.

Though he is getting hungry, it is normal hunger. It is not a crazed death hunger. He doesn't want to kill now. The bloodlust has burned away like a fever. He is healing now.

Soon he sits up as another chimp clambers up onto the rock and sits down beside him. She is a large female who escaped from the Central Park Zoo. She has something in her hand. It is an orange. It is like a ball of flame in her hand, a sun. She peels it with her long fingers and offers it to Attila. Attila breaks it in half and hands the other half back.

Together they eat the orange. The cool, sweet, sticky juice feels good in his mouth. The female cuddles next to him and begins grooming his fur. Soon they are lying there together on the warm stone. Feeling her warmth, and the warmth of the earth, Attila is at peace. He closes his eyes and slips back into sleep.

Chapter 93

TWO MORE DAYS of meetings slid by like sludge. It was difficult to see by lantern and candlelight, and hot indoors, so the meetings were held outside, in the Rose Garden. We sat around the tables on springy metal outdoor furniture, using paperweights to keep things from fluttering across the South Lawn in the breeze.

On the third day, going stir-crazy behind the paper-stacked walls of my dark FEMA trailer and the army compound itself, I canceled my afternoon meetings. I'd heard that D.C. had been free of animal hordes for more than two days now, and I wanted to see firsthand if it was true.

I bumped into Sergeant Alvarez coming out of the compound's mess tent and convinced him to come with me. When I met him by the northwest gate a few minutes later, he was in full Kevlar and holding a smooth flat black rifle with a cylinder on it.

"How's the ankle?" I said.

"Getting there. Like my walking stick?" he said, shaking a beast of a weapon. It was an automatic shotgun called an AA-12, he explained, which can fire the thirty-two rounds of double-aught buck in its drum in about an eyeblink at full auto.

"Which is ludicrously destructive when you think about it, but probably just the thing if we run into another tooth-and-claw mob," Alvarez concluded. "They just handed them out. I named mine Justin."

"Justin?"

"My man, Justin Case."

Outside the White House gates, the city appeared peaceful, quiet. The quiet was the most amazing of all. You could hear the wind.

The downtown area was still cordoned off, but they were beginning to allow some residents in to check on their property. We stopped and talked to several people coming in and out of the town houses—a couple of student nurses from Georgetown, an FBI agent, a lobbyist, and her son.

It was as though D.C. had become a village.

For now.

I was encouraged that people seemed to be upbeat and cooperative. But I knew this was only the beginning. This was still the honeymoon. How would people feel after a week of no hot showers or air-conditioning? With the country's dependence on trucking for food delivery, how long would it be before people started getting hungry?

We were on Constitution Avenue when a dog appeared from around the corner. It was a black Lab, and, with knee-jerk immediacy, Alvarez hoisted his new toy to his shoulder, ready to blast the dog to kibbles and bits. But the dog didn't even glance at us. It passed by in the street, pausing just long enough to relieve itself on a fire hydrant.

Alvarez and I looked at each other. Then we burst out laughing.

"Call the *Times*. I have tomorrow's headline," I said. "Dog pisses on hydrant!"

Chapter 94

THAT NIGHT AND almost all the next day, Charles Groh and I attended romantic candlelit policy meetings with the CDC and various branches of the military. After a quick dinner, I was catching a half nap on a couch in a FEMA trailer parked on the South Lawn when I felt an impish tug on my foot.

I sat up, and NSA chief Leahy sat down beside me. Leahy and the NSA had been put in charge of monitoring the effect of the industrial and power shutdown on the animal populations. I'd been waiting to hear back from him. He smiled enigmatically and handed me a cup of coffee.

"Well, the suspense is killing me," I said, yawning and taking the coffee. "What's the story, morning glory?"

Leahy's smile brightened and broadened.

"Come see, boy genius."

We left my trailer and headed into another one near the Rose Garden that had a satellite dish wired to the side of it. There was a rattling hand-cranked generator hooked up to the trailer. It was a comm room. There were a dozen techs and military people barking into phones, staring at monitors, pointing at bright shiny things on screens.

Leahy peeled some sheets off a fax machine and handed them to me.

"Feast your eyes on these, Wizard of Oz," he said. "On the Thursday before the shutdown, we were getting national reports of thousands of attacks every day. Now look at yesterday's tally in the US."

I glanced at the sheet.

"Am I reading this right? Three?" I said.

"Exactly," Leahy said. "Not only that, we're getting in more and more stories about dogs returning to their owners. The industrial and communications freeze really has knocked out the airborne pheromone. Your plan wasn't just a home run, Oz. It was a grand slam. You're going to be very famous. I think you may have just saved the world."

Leahy put his arm around my shoulder.

"That's why we're going to get you out of here,

kiddo. I pulled some strings. I'm going to get you back to your family in Nueva York."

I looked at him. Was that even possible? It felt like weeks since I'd seen Chloe and Eli.

"Surely you're joking."

"No, siree. And don't call me Shirley. They're gassing up your chariot as we speak. You're on the G6 again."

I thought about Chloe, about the actual possibility of touching my wife, holding her, burying my face in her neck. And Eli. I wanted to put that kid up on my shoulders and just walk with him and show him everything that —

I stopped. What the hell was I doing? What was I thinking?

What were they offering? To let me break the rules? And if they "pulled some strings" for me, how many others were they pulling them for?

"Hold it," I said. "Wait a second. I'd love more than anything to see my family, but it's too soon. There can't be any travel now. No combustion engines, no electricity for at least two weeks. That was the plan. You know this."

"One twenty-minute plane trip won't break the camel's back, Oz. You deserve this."

"Deserve?" I said, feeling a bubble of fury

flare up inside me. I grabbed him by the lapels. "That's Washington, isn't it? The rules are for the little people, right? We deserve it. Which part of the continuation of civilization do you morons not understand? You think this shutdown is the end? This is the beginning of the beginning of the beginning!"

"Let go of my jacket," Leahy said.

I shoved him away.

"Do you think this will work without real sacrifice? Without *everyone's* sacrifice? The bans on gas, cell phones, electricity—they have to be for everybody. The NSA, the military, VIPs. Hell, even the president and the holy Congress. This is just stage one. Don't you understand? We have to do this until we come up with a permanent solution.

"If everything goes back to normal, then it's going to be feeding time again at the zoo, Leahy. You tell all the fat cats to cork the Champagne and cancel the tee times. It's time to suck it up like the rest of us."

"Relax," Leahy said. "I get the picture. I understand. You're right."

"Do you? I wonder," I said as I was leaving. "But I hope so. For the sake of the world."

Chapter 95

ON SATURDAY MORNING, I blew off every meeting on my schedule. The Senate Committee on Environment and Public Works wanted a meet and greet, as did a group of clinical pathologists from the CDC.

But after the row with Leahy, I was almost sick to death of policy makers who were looking at this thing as if it were already over. For them, this was just something they could pad their resumes with, tell their grandchildren about. They needed to understand that if they didn't take it seriously, there weren't going to be any grandchildren to tell it to.

Instead, I did something useful, something that needed doing. I signed up to help a contingent of marines clean the streets and collect the bodies of the dead.

There was something turn-of-the-century about it. That is, the turn of the last century. Horses had been brought in from a farm in Rockville, Maryland, to pull U-Haul trailers. By noon, the trailers were laden with body bags.

Having served in Iraq, I thought I could handle the detail. I was wrong. The first child I encountered was a little Asian girl in an alley behind a dry cleaner's shop in Dupont Circle. She looked about eight, nine years old. Guts strewn across the alley like spaghetti. Sergeant Alvarez and I stuffed her in a bag and laid her down in one of the trailers. It broke me up. I snapped off my reeking rubber gloves and sat on the curb between a couple of parked cars for a while, weeping.

So many lives had been lost.

It was early evening when we arrived at Arlington National Cemetery. Near the Tomb of the Unknowns, the contents of the horse-drawn trailers were unloaded into a row of portable morgue units. An army bugler played taps as we were leaving.

It was getting dark by the time Sergeant Alvarez and I made it on foot back across the bridge, heading for the Marine Corps base next to the White House.

Near George Washington University, we were walking down a block lined with trees and bracketed with quaint homes.

And I saw a chrome-and-yellow Hummer parked on the street, idling in front of a town house. When I reached in and shut off the engine, a tall, handsome guy wearing a Yankees cap and a rumpled blue suit ran out. He looked pissed.

"What the hell do you think you're doing?" the guy said.

"I should ask you the same thing. Maybe you've been under a rock, but there's a ban on driving."

"No shit, Sherlock," the guy said, glancing at Sergeant Alvarez and showing me his ID. "I'm Gary Sterling, congressman from New York. This is my apartment. I'm heading back to Long Island to get a few things."

"Says who?" I said.

He fished a document out of the inner pocket of his suit jacket.

"Says the president," he said, making little effort to suppress his smirk.

I looked at the piece of paper. I couldn't believe it. It was a presidential order that authorized the bearer to operate a motor vehicle despite the ban. I looked at the president's seal and signature, dumbfounded.

I guess I shouldn't have been that shocked, but I was. Everyone needs to follow the rules, except for the people who don't. I knew it. This was D.C. I was afraid this would happen.

Representative Sterling snatched the permit out of my hand and promptly restarted his car. But I couldn't take it. Permit or no permit, I reached in and shut it down again. I took the keys out of the ignition.

"Are you blind? I showed you the permit," the congressman said.

I curled my right fist around the keys and raised my left. My fists were shaking. I knew what I was doing was crazy. But I guess I had seen too much that day. I'd seen too many dead bodies. Did this guy care? The answer was no, apparently.

"I don't give a shit!" I said. "You think the rules don't apply to you? You're above it all, right? I don't think so. Fuck your permit. Come and get your keys."

And I put them in my pocket.

Then what did he do? He simply turned on his heels and walked back up the town house steps. When he got to the top, he took out a cell phone, hit a button, and began speaking calmly into it.

"What the hell? This fool's two for two. He's got

a Hummer *and* a working cell phone?" Alvarez said.

A military Hummer roared up a couple of minutes later. Sergeant Alvarez stiffened and came to attention as a marine colonel climbed out from behind the wheel. He spoke to Alvarez, and then Alvarez very reluctantly spoke to me.

"I'm sorry, Oz, but it's true. They are issuing these permits, or whatever they are. It's legit. The asshole wins. You either have to give him back his keys, or I arrest you."

I bit my lip. I shook my head for a little while. Finally, I stopped.

"Fine, okay. You're right, everybody. I'm sorry. Got carried away," I said. The congressman came back down the town-house steps. I walked over to him. I held the keys out to him at the curb. As he reached for them, I flung them aside, into a storm drain.

"Whoops!" I said. "Clumsy me. My arms are kind of tired from carrying the dead all day. Truly, truly: my bad."

Alvarez, even with the glaring colonel present, was having trouble burying his smile. I walked away, and nobody tried to stop me.

Guy Smiley was beside himself, cussing like a sailor with a toothache, frothing with self-righteous indignation. He gave me the finger.

"Hey, that's nothing new, is it, Congressman?" I gave him a little feminine wave. "I'm an American citizen. Telling us to go fuck ourselves is what you guys are best at."

But it was a brief, small victory. As I walked, still seething, in the gloaming, I heard it from all over the city: gasoline generators being started up—air conditioners humming back to life. All the people of the world were back to their old tricks. And I'd thought the bugle was sad.

I realized it then. In the dying purple light as the sun set over Washington, I realized it. I listened to the gathering chatter in the dark, and I knew it.

There would be no recovery. We had lost. It was over.

Chapter 96

BY SUNDOWN OF the third day of the Big Stop, as people have begun to call it, a loud chugging sound breaks the still, death-like silence in midtown Manhattan. Playing Candy Land with Eli in a pale band of streaming sunlight in the apartment's back bedroom, Chloe hears it and goes to the window.

She scans the sky over Central Park. The sound picks up volume, and then she sees it. Half a dozen tandem-rotor Chinook helicopters are throbbing over the city, coming in from the West Side. They pass through the gap between the skyscrapers of the Time Warner Center, which stands like a goalpost at the end of Central Park, near Columbus Circle, and continue northeast across the rolling green of the park toward the government Secure Zone.

"No," Chloe whispers from the terrace. "No, no, *no*."

In the sky above them, now there is another roar. A 747 is shrieking westbound, its lights blinking red and green. It's the first plane she's seen in a week.

"What is it?" Eli says.

"Helicopters and planes," Chloe says. "Why are they breaking the ban? It's been only three days."

She goes to the terrace. It's true. Across Central Park West, lights are beginning to twinkle on in the luxury apartment houses, like tiny pieces of luminous candy. She can hear generators whirring on, an ugly, hammering chatter.

Down in the street, she watches as a truck screams onto Fifth Avenue from a side street. Then a motorcycle. Then a Mercedes SUV.

It isn't just happening in New York, either.

In the absence of animal attacks, people have become emboldened. The air force satellite picks up the imagery as lights start to flicker on in Dallas, in Cincinnati, in Dublin, Milan, Madrid. By the next morning, Beijing smokestacks are throwing up clouds of smoke, fluttering in the air like black satin scarves. The Canadian legislature overturns the cell phone ban. Mexico and the EU follow suit.

All over the world, people go back to work. Coal

plants are turned on, nuclear facilities, cell towers. Clouds of petro-chemicals and hydrocarbons rise back into the air currents, electromagnetic radiation emanates from cell phones and towers, buzzing, shimmering, sweeping across the land like an invisible poison gas. Chemical bonds click back together, re-forming. Energy mixes with matter to create something new.

Change is here to stay. It is the way of life, the way of the world.

The Big Stop is over.

So is human civilization.

Chapter 97

ON HIS SUNNY rock in Central Park, Attila awakens. Tense—so tense now. He can feel the adrenaline bulging his veins, pumping in his heart, sending blood to his brain and muscles. The flash of energy. Dendrites, synapses firing. The feeling surges in his body, warping the molecular structures in his brain, that hypersensitive lump of squishy electric meat. His blood pressure increases. His saliva dries as he begins to sweat. The hair on his back bristles.

He is readying himself for attack. Something has triggered the attack impulse in his brain and left the switch on. His breath comes hard and heavy as his aggravation builds. His respiration comes in ragged huffing sounds, almost a snarl.

The smell in the air is back, calling him, dragging

him to his feet. The female beside him is seething as well, her eyes bright with anxious rage.

The animals are back by the time he climbs down from the rock. They cover the softball field like a living rug. The pack is bigger and more bloodthirsty than before.

Attila leads the swarm east, toward the apartment-building lights. His eye is trained on the terraces of the high-rises. He knows how to climb them, how to get in. He will go alone and open the doors for the others. The smell tells him this. This time, he will not fail.

Any mercy he has shown to man is not even a memory anymore. Because he has no memory. He has the smell. The smell is master, friend, mate. The smell is all.

A man and a woman on a motorcycle are riding crosstown on the Sixty-Fifth Street Transverse. Attila gives his pant-hoot call to herd the others, but it is unnecessary. In the pheromone cloud, sounds are unnecessary. The animals can smell what he wants in his breath and sweat. His orders become scents. The mass moves, anticipating him almost as easily as his own hand.

A roaring cascade of bodies falls from a bridge onto the motorcycle. It is a husband and wife, both in their fifties. The woman is enveloped first. She screams as teeth and claws meet flesh. Attila, at the bottom of the scrum, gnaws chunks out of the woman's leg, blinking against the jet of arterial blood.

The man, a retired cop from Queens, reaches for a sidearm that hasn't been there since 1999. A rat makes off with his left pinkie up to the first knuckle. Then a squirrel attaches itself to his face with a squeak, clawing at his eyes. A rottweiler bites into his crotch, and he sinks to the ground.

The animals lacerate the people, carve them to ribbons as efficiently as the blades in an abattoir. In less than three minutes, all that's left of the two is very dirty laundry.

Stained red with slaughter, Attila moves himself and the swarm toward the smell of humans. All the animals are moving together now with the same rhythm, like cells in the bloodstream.

There is no Attila anymore. He is bigger now. Something else has broken through, taken over. He is only energy now, a soulless organization of bones and blood and meat propelled by electricity and surging chemicals. He moves toward the sounds, toward the lights.

Chapter 98

AH, HOW QUICKLY the tide turned back. The blood-red tide.

With the sounds of generators came screams and roaring gunfire. Were we really this stupid? Yes, apparently.

It was just coming on midnight when the door of my trailer whacked open and Alvarez darkened the doorway behind it.

"Grab your shit, Oz. We're overrun. They're evacuating the White House."

The East Wing had been overtaken. Inside and out, hundreds of thousands of mammals—dogs, raccoons, rats, squirrels, possums—were streaming uphill into the iconic building, swarming like ants. The gunfire was constant now. As I ran alongside

Alvarez I saw a luminous orange glow lighting up the sky to the northeast. I pointed to it.

"What's—"

"The Capitol's on fire" was all he said. We kept running.

Alvarez rushed me into a waiting truck. The marine guard at the east gate was down, blood running over his dress blues, his face chewed off. Alvarez glanced at him, raised his AA-12, and squeezed a lackadaisical stream of firepower in the direction of the handful of mold-spotted dogs still working on the body.

"God help us," Alvarez said, crossing himself.

"Help us?" I said. "God destroyed Sodom and Gomorrah, didn't he? I know I'm just a scientist, but it looks like we've pissed him off again."

An hour later, I was wheels-up in the air on an air force 737 back to New York.

With the White House overrun, a new plan had been hatched. The government was moving north. Extremely north. About as north as you could get, actually. The scientists and government were supposed to pack up and regroup at Thule Air Base in northern Greenland, 750 miles north of the Arctic Circle.

The only good thing to say about it was that

we were coming to New York first to get the other scientists who had come to the meeting.

Great, I thought. That means I get to spend the apocalypse holed up in an igloo with Harvey Saltonstall. Then they told me Harvey had been mauled to death by dogs.

"Oh," I said.

They said family had to stay behind, but I was having none of it.

I found Leahy up near the plane's cockpit.

Reluctant to throw any of my weight around up until this point, I threw it now as hard as I could.

"You either have my wife and kid on the tarmac, Leahy, or you shitheels can go to Greenland and figure it out by yourselves."

When Chloe and Eli came through the airplane's door, I tackled them into a seat. We hugged each other and cried for about ten years. For a short, dark time I thought I might never see them again, but, luckily, for once I was wrong.

The plane kicked its heels and was airborne again. It began to rain when we were zipping over Canada, but the plane ascended to a higher altitude. As we broke above the clouds, a bright, luminous glow came into the cabin. High off to our right, a full moon was rising bright and clear in the cold, and the clouds skirted by beneath us like a river of silver silk.

That's when Eli saw something.

"Daddy! Look!"

He was sitting in my lap, pointing out the window.

Rising from a cloud to the east was some kind of mass. A kind of dark, moving cone, it looked like. A cloud? It was black, dense. Flapping. Alive.

We seemed to be flying toward it—or did it come toward us? At first I thought it was a cloud of birds. More birds in one place than ever imaginable. But then I realized they were bats. They were swarming in an upside-down pyramid, revolving incessantly, mindlessly flying around and around, chasing each other, endlessly moving up and up . . .

Bong!

"Seat belts!" was all I heard on the PA system. Then we flew into them.

I grabbed my wife and my son and held them to me as what sounded like the fist of God pounded on the plane. The bats flapped against the aircraft, spattered on the windows, were sucked into the engines, and shot out like bloody confetti, a vast black cloud of frantic scurrying and flapping. The starboard engine blew out a moment later, and in another moment we were descending. I closed my eyes and pressed my family to my heart as we plummeted, screaming, toward the earth.

Luckily—in a word—our pilot was an Iraq war vet, used to evasive maneuvers. We dropped several thousand feet in only a few seconds.

But after we came out of the bat tornado, the pilot got the engine working again somehow, and he turned the plane around and headed south and west. We were able to make an emergency landing in Syracuse.

Other planes weren't so fortunate, we learned. Three airliners were downed. Hundreds more gone. How many would die in this war before it was over? I thought as I huddled in Hancock International Airport's crowded terminal with my family. I didn't know. No one did.

Epilogue

PART OF ME still believes that it's possible to turn the world around. I don't know how yet, but we will. The greatest known power in the universe is the resilience of man coupled with his intellect. He tinkers and tests and fights through to solutions.

How noble in reason, as Hamlet said. How infinite in faculty. In apprehension how like a god.

I know we will make it. Because from where I write this, I can see my son, Eli. As I look upon his innocent face, so like his mother's, there is only one thing, one feeling that lingers.

The love my mother and father gave me grows

inside of him, day by day, and one day he will pass it on to his wife and child, and it will continue.

We will survive because, although we make a mess of things, we have the hope and faith and will to make things better for ourselves and for those we love.

Making things better is what we do.

Is it?

I don't know.

Maybe.

I am recording this from a bunker. It's November, the cold season, and temperatures here hover around minus ten degrees Fahrenheit.

It is dark outside now. It's almost always dark here in our new, frigid home. The wind makes the walls shudder. I hear its constant, whistling howl even in my dreams now. As if the earth itself is in mourning.

In the nearly twenty-four-hour darkness, sixty-mile-an-hour winds howl off the mountains onto the white desert of the ice cap. Almost no mammals live here, so we are blissfully safe in using our generators and radios. Lucky us.

No matter how bad it is, I put on my arctic suit and go outside once a day, to stare forlornly at the brutal horizon. I consider it a pilgrimage of sorts, a penance for my sins, for all our sins. It doesn't make me feel better, but I do it anyway. I guess I have finally found religion, in a way. I suppose the end of the world will do that.

There have been several suicides, mostly among Washington people—senators and representatives accustomed to soft living. There is no soft living now.

Communication with the continental US is sporadic. Supplies still seem to be coming in, but there are rumors of chaos back in the States. Lawless bands of people roam the streets, fighting animals and one another. For years, some in our country have advocated modern man's return to nature. It seems as though they have finally gotten their wish.

In the hours of isolation and boredom, I think about what has happened. Unlike many of my colleagues, I don't blame technology. Petroleum improved human life. So did cell phones. No one knew that the combination of the two would eventually lead to biological disaster. We screwed up. It happens.

But I dreamed that dream again last night. I dream it often.

The dream of the death spiral. The ants I saw once in Costa Rica. There was a circle in the sand.

Zoo

The squirming black whirlpool. Thousands and thousands of ants, all running together in an endless circle. Blindly, they follow each other, each one locked onto the pheromone trail of the ant in front of him. Running themselves in circles, circles. Running themselves to death. A closed loop. A snake biting its tail. A symbol of futility. Locked in their loop, the ants run around and around in circles—desperate, stupid, doomed.

A holiday you'll never forget…

SECOND HONEYMOON

Coming July 2013

Turn the page for a sneak preview

ONE

THE BOY WOULD be famous around the world one day, but there was no way he could imagine that now. What little kid could predict the future, or begin to understand it? Seven-year-old Ned Sinclair reached out in the darkness, his hand blindly feeling for the wall as he stepped outside his bedroom. He didn't dare turn on a light in the hall. He didn't dare make a sound. *Not even a peep. Not yet.*

Slowly, Ned tiptoed down the long, narrow hallway, the chill of the hardwood floor in the dead of an Albany winter reaching right up through his footed Superman pajamas. He was shaking, ice cold, his teeth on the verge of chattering.

Searching for the railing at the top of the stairs, Ned's arm waved back and forth like a delicate branch caught in the wind. He felt nothing . . . still nothing

. . . then—*yes, there it was*—the smooth curve of the lacquered pine against his fingertips.

He gripped the railing, white-knuckled, all the way down to the first floor, one quiet step at a time.

Earlier that day, Ned almost forgot how terrified he was of the night. His big sister, Nora, had taken him to see the new movie in town, a sequel, *Back to the Future Part II*. He'd been too young to see the original four years earlier.

Sitting in the dark theater with a big bucket of buttered popcorn in his lap and an RC Cola, Ned was completely and wonderfully transfixed by the film, especially that DeLorean car.

If only I could travel through time, he wished afterward. I don't want to be here anymore. *I don't like it here*.

He wouldn't care where he went, just so long as it was away from his house—and the terrible bogeyman who haunted it late at night. He and Nora would make their great escape and live happily ever after. A new town. A new house. And in the garden of the new house? Nothing but yellow lilies, Nora's favorite.

He loved his sister so much. Whenever the other kids on the block made fun of his stutter—*Ne-Ne-Ne-Ned*, they would cruelly tease—Nora always stood up for him. She had even fought for him. Nora was as tough as any boy. Maybe wherever they went it would be okay to marry your sister.

Second Honeymoon

But for now, he was still stuck in his house. A prisoner. Trapped. Lying awake each horrible night waiting for the sound he prayed would never come . . . but always did.

Always, always, always.

The bogeyman.

TWO

NED TURNED RIGHT at the bottom of the stairs, his hands still guiding him in the darkness as he made his way through the dining room and den, covered in beige shag carpeting, before stopping at the door to his father's library, where he wasn't allowed inside, not ever.

He froze as the baseboard heating gurgled and then clanked a few times, as if it were being hit hard and fast with a hammer. The noise was followed by the sound of a river of water rushing through the old, rusty pipes. But nothing more than that. There were no other footsteps, no voices in the house. Just his own heart pounding madly against his chest.

Go back to bed. You can't fight the bogeyman now. Maybe when you're bigger. Please, please, please, go back to bed.

Except Ned no longer wanted to listen to that voice

inside his head. There was another voice talking to him now, a much stronger one. Bolder. Fearless. It told him to keep going. *Don't be afraid! Don't be a scaredy-cat!*

Ned walked into the library. By the window was a mahogany desk. It was lit by the hazy glow of a small electric clock, the kind with those flip-style numbers that turned like those on an old-fashioned scoreboard.

The desk was big, too big for the room. It had three large drawers on the left side of the base.

The only drawer that mattered, though, was the bottom one. It was always kept locked.

Reaching across the desk with both hands, Ned gripped an old coffee mug that was used to hold pencils and pens, erasers and paper clips. After a deep breath, almost as if he were counting to three, he lifted up the mug.

There it was. The key. Just as he'd found it weeks before. Because curious seven-year-old boys can find most anything, especially when they're not supposed to.

Ned took the key in his hand, pinching it between his thumb and forefinger before easing it into the lock on the bottom drawer.

He gave the key a slight twist clockwise until he heard the sound. *Click!*

Then, ever so carefully, slowly, so as not to make a sound, Ned pulled open the drawer.

And took out the gun.

THREE

OLIVIA SINCLAIR SHOT up in bed so fast it made her a little dizzy. Her first thought was that the heat had come on, that god-awful clanking noise from the pipes that would practically shake the house.

But that's why she always wore the wax earplugs when she went to bed, so she could sleep through it all. The earplugs always worked, too. Not once did she remember waking up in the middle of the night.

Until now.

If that noise wasn't the heat and the pipes, what was it? It had to be something.

Olivia turned to her left to see the time. The clock on the nightstand said 12:20 a.m.

She turned to her right to see the empty pillow next to her. She was alone.

Olivia took out her earplugs and swung her legs

off the bed, her bare feet quickly finding her slippers nearby. The second she flipped on the light, she was jolted by another noise. This one she recognized instantly. It was a horrible scream, just awful.

Nora!

Bursting out of the bedroom, Olivia sprinted down the long, narrow hallway toward her daughter's bedroom, where the light was on.

When she turned the corner at the doorway, she felt worse than dizzy. She felt sick to her stomach.

There was blood everywhere. On the floor. On the bed. Splattered on the pink-painted wall between posters of Debbie Gibson and Duran Duran.

Olivia's eyes pinballed around the rest of the room. She took in a breath. The smell of the gunshots was still thick in the air. In one quick and utterly horrifying moment, she realized what had happened.

And what had been happening for more than a year.

Oh, my God! My daughter! My sweet and innocent daughter!

Nora sat curled up in the tiniest ball by the headboard of her bed. Her arms were wrapped tightly around her knees. She was naked. She was crying. She was looking at her brother.

Across the room in the corner, Ned, pale as the winter's snow outside, was standing frozen like a statue in his Superman pajamas. He couldn't even blink.

For a second, Olivia stood frozen, too. The next second, though, it was as if she'd suddenly remembered who she was. These were her children.

She was their mother.

Olivia rushed over to Ned and kneeled down to hug him, her arms squeezing him tight against her chest. He started to mumble something, repeating it over and over and over. "The bogeyman," it sounded like.

"Shh," Olivia whispered in his ear. "Everything's okay. Everything's okay, honey."

Then, very carefully, she took the gun out of his hand.

Slowly, she walked over to the door, looking back one more time at the room. Her daughter. Her son.

And the "bogeyman" lying dead on the floor.

Moments later, she picked up the phone in the hallway. She stood there holding the receiver for a long moment, then she dialed.

"My name is Olivia Sinclair," she told the 911 operator. "I just killed my husband."

Also by James Patterson

ALEX CROSS NOVELS

Along Came a Spider • Kiss the Girls • Jack and Jill •
Cat and Mouse • Pop Goes the Weasel • Roses are Red •
Violets are Blue • Four Blind Mice • The Big Bad Wolf •
London Bridges • Mary, Mary • Cross • Double Cross •
Cross Country • Alex Cross's Trial (*with Richard DiLallo*) •
I, Alex Cross • Cross Fire • Kill Alex Cross •
Merry Christmas, Alex Cross • Alex Cross, Run

THE WOMEN'S MURDER CLUB SERIES

1st to Die •
2nd Chance (*with Andrew Gross*) •
3rd Degree (*with Andrew Gross*) •
4th of July (*with Maxine Paetro*) •
The 5th Horseman (*with Maxine Paetro*) •
The 6th Target (*with Maxine Paetro*) •
7th Heaven (*with Maxine Paetro*) •
8th Confession (*with Maxine Paetro*) •
9th Judgement (*with Maxine Paetro*) •
10th Anniversary (*with Maxine Paetro*) •
11th Hour (*with Maxine Paetro*) •
12th of Never (*with Maxine Paetro*)

DETECTIVE MICHAEL BENNETT SERIES

Step on a Crack (*with Michael Ledwidge*) • Run for Your Life
(*with Michael Ledwidge*) • Worst Case (*with Michael Ledwidge*) •
Tick Tock (*with Michael Ledwidge*) • I, Michael Bennett
(*with Michael Ledwidge*)

PRIVATE NOVELS

Private (*with Maxine Paetro*) • Private London
(*with Mark Pearson*) • Private Games (*with Mark Sullivan*) •
Private: No. 1 Suspect (*with Maxine Paetro*) •
Private Berlin (*with Mark Sullivan*) • Private Down Under
(*with Michael White, to be published May 2013*)

I FUNNY

I Funny (*with Chris Grabenstein*)

CONFESSIONS SERIES

Confessions of a Murder Suspect (*with Maxine Paetro*)

GRAPHIC NOVELS

Daniel X: Alien Hunter (*with Leopoldo Gout*) •
Maximum Ride: Manga Vol. 1–6 (*with NaRae Lee*)

For more information about James Patterson's novels, visit
www.jamespatterson.co.uk

Or become a fan on Facebook

We support

I'm proud to support the National Literacy Trust, an independent charity that changes lives through literacy.

Did you know that millions of people in the UK struggle to read and write? This means children are less likely to succeed at school and less likely to develop into confident and happy teenagers. Literacy difficulties will limit their opportunities throughout adult life.

The National Literacy Trust passionately believes that everyone has a right to the reading, writing, speaking and listening skills they need to fulfil their own and, ultimately, the nation's potential.

My own son didn't use to enjoy reading, which was why I started writing children's books – reading for pleasure is an essential way to encourage children to pick up a book. The National Literacy Trust is dedicated to delivering exciting initiatives to encourage people to read and to help raise literacy levels. To find out more about the great work that they do, visit their website at www.literacytrust.org.uk.

James Patterson